Pineapple
Kisses
in Iqaluit

◆ *a novel* ◆

Essential Prose Series 187

Canada Council **Conseil des Arts**
for the Arts **du Canada**

ONTARIO ARTS COUNCIL
CONSEIL DES ARTS DE L'ONTARIO

an Ontario government agency
un organisme du gouvernement de l'Ontario

Canada

Guernica Editions Inc. acknowledges the support of the Canada
Council for the Arts and the Ontario Arts Council.
The Ontario Arts Council is an agency of the Government of Ontario.

We acknowledge the financial support of the Government of Canada.

Pineapple Kisses in Iqaluit

◆ *a novel* ◆

FELICIA MIHALI

**GUERNICA
EDITIONS**
TORONTO • CHICAGO • BUFFALO • LANCASTER (U.K.)
2021

Michael Mirolla, general editor
Margo LaPierre, editor
David Moratto, interior design
Daniel Ursache, cover design
Guernica Editions Inc.
287 Templemead Drive, Hamilton, ON L8W 2W4
2250 Military Road, Tonawanda, N.Y. 14150-6000 U.S.A.
www.guernicaeditions.com

Distributors:
Independent Publishers Group (IPG)
600 North Pulaski Road, Chicago IL 60624
University of Toronto Press Distribution,
5201 Dufferin Street, Toronto (ON), Canada M3H 5T8
Gazelle Book Services, White Cross Mills
High Town, Lancaster LA1 4XS U.K.

First edition.
Printed in Canada.

Legal Deposit—First Quarter
Library of Congress Catalog Card Number: 2020947920
Library and Archives Canada Cataloguing in Publication
Title: Pineapple kisses in Iqaluit : a novel / Felicia Mihali.
Names: Mihali, Felicia, 1967- author.
Series: Essential prose series ; 187.
Description: First edition. | Series statement: Essential prose series ; 187
Identifiers: Canadiana (print) 20200361988 | Canadiana (ebook)
20200361996 | ISBN 9781771835886 (softcover) |
ISBN 9781771835893 (EPUB) | ISBN 9781771835909 (Kindle)
Classification: LCC PS8576.I295343 P56 2021 | DDC C813/.6—dc23

Contents

Contents

CHAPTER ONE
Places and People

O NE DAY I happened upon a teaching position in Iqaluit, the capital of Nunavut. The job description didn't give much detail about the task except that l'Aurore Boréale was *"l'école francophone la plus nordique au monde."* Was this geographical achievement so important as to merit the emphasis? Was it so extraordinary to imagine oneself working in a place that had no other counterpart beyond the Arctic Circle?

When I analyzed the job description again, the doubts that had bubbled the day before vanished, and the posting now lured me with all the power of a sea song. It had to be an exceptional achievement to be the most northerly francophone outpost in the world! No French *conjugaison* anywhere else in the Arctic! Time for this history teacher to put the Crusaders' mythology and the Middle Ages charm aside and move forward to the Bescherelle.

Moving away is not about looking for new places, but seeking new people. As you set out to travel, family and friends might guess that you are looking for better company. When better is not possible, less boring would be an improvement.

Boredom was killing me in the school where I had been teaching history for the last six years. It was a public high school like many others where the concept of teaching as a vocation was fading away, corroded by the younger generation's cynicism. Withdrawal from the real world is at the core of that generation's woes, but we were no better than them.

The most frustrating thing for me as a teacher was the gloomy mood of my students. Young people are sombre, driven by a secret desire to get adults on the wrong foot and accuse them of something, usually of being mean or ill-intentioned. Theirs is a generation that doesn't take no for an answer, while at thirty-four I felt already too old to say yes very often. This job blew a kind of excitement into my life. The unknown has attracted people to the Arctic for centuries, yet geographical exploration had never been *my* interest. Unlike Martin Frobisher, the first white man to officially set foot on Baffin Island, I knew from the beginning what I would find in Iqaluit. When you are a lonely person, solitude follows you everywhere.

Yet, the first thing that struck me when I arrived was the geographical misunderstanding I had of my own country. The most shocking was the unexpected odour of putrid algae and saltwater that hit me when I got off the plane on September 4. Iqaluit is set on the shore of Baffin Island, in a small inlet of Frobisher Bay. Those names had been linked in my mind with eternally frozen land. How could I associate the smell of the ocean, the drizzle of rain and the sticky fog with the Canadian Arctic Archipelago?

Then, it was the dust, staining the land a dark-brown. The few passers-by I saw on my way from the airport seemed to have never polished or washed their boots. I would soon figure out this was one of the things people rarely do up North, as rarely as putting makeup on one's cold-reddened face or washing one's oily hair, always covered by woollen caps. In only two days, my shoes were to be coated with as many layers of dust as the roads I was to take across the city.

Someone once wrote that brown was the least valued colour in the Western culture. In paintings, brown is used mainly to depict the land, the least striking detail in a landscape. In Iqaluit, brown was by far the most prominent colour at this time of year. It could be found in everything from the hills, shores, houses, roads, and blackberry bushes, to the fishing boats, seal pelts, and ships. Everything here was a mixture of brown and grey, except for when a hunter's gaudy parka disrupted the dull hues of the landscape.

My arrival up North started under bad auspices. Contrary to what I had hoped, there was nobody from the French school board waiting for me at the airport. My six huge pieces of luggage were the only ones remaining on the baggage carousel and they looked as lonely as I was. When the last passenger left, I decided to take a cab to the address emailed by the Nunavut Housing Corporation, my faceless and anonymous landlord. On the way, I realized I didn't have the key to the apartment, on this fine Labour Day when the whole city seemed like an abandoned ship, beset in the ice. In that moment I had a vision of a Kafkaesque housing castle where tenants were nothing but folders. My arrival, that of a French teacher from Montreal named Irina, had just slipped to the bottom of the stack.

The drive to the city took less than ten minutes, long enough for the taxi driver to give me some details about the building we were heading to. He told me that my rooms were certainly on the second floor, since Canada Post and some other offices occupied the ground floor. There were two entrances to the building, and according to his experience, tenants always used the back door. He unloaded my baggage there and abandoned me with a benevolent wish of good luck.

The day was grey. After a second tour around the building, I saw a light at one of the windows on the ground floor. Perched on a wooden box that I found near the garbage container, I knocked on the glass. An old lady peered out and agreed to let me inside. She searched for a phone number and then spoke on my behalf to a long chain of people until she found the one in charge of new tenants. One hour later, a tall grey-haired man came with the key to let me in. He showed me around the apartment, but the full inspection and signing of the contract were postponed to the end of the week. He just made sure I had all the furniture I needed, that the power was on and the toilet would flush.

I found this incident a fair price to pay for my neglect to inquire about the key. More than anywhere else, survival in the Arctic has always come down to good or bad choices. I knew this after all the lessons I had taught about the search for the Northwest Passage to China.

At the end of the day, I found myself a much luckier explorer than Franklin and his crew. Dozing on the comfortable sofa in my new living room, I even let myself think the worst was behind me. I could have ended up sleeping at the airport till the next day, or paying an exorbitant price for a hotel room in what is the most expensive city in Canada. Instead, I was now in the apartment I would call home for the next ten months.

I was relieved to open my bags, one by one, and forage for the essentials: my pyjamas, soap, towels, toothbrush. At a certain point, I decided it would be a good idea to have a bite to eat after such a day. While slowly chewing a bagel spread with cheese, I got to thinking that everything in life is a matter of technicalities. Everything should go smoothly as long as you pay attention to details, like asking about the key when you move up North.

The Inuit's ancestors survived in this place by taking care of the technicalities. They became skillful hunters, kayakers, igloo builders and tailors, using the available re-sources, yet their daily routine was probably as boring as anywhere else in the world. I imagine these people hated waking up in the morning, getting dressed, wolfing down what food they had and keeping on with living. People can count on this routine every day, from sun-up to sundown. While organizing my canned vegetables in the cupboards, and my yogurt, cheese and fruit in the fridge, then my sweaters on the hangers and underwear in the dresser, I felt reassured that this would be my daily routine for the next ten months and nothing unexpected would happen till my return to Montreal.

L'Aurore Boréale School was built on the outskirts of the city. Along with the arena and the funeral home, these three buildings were the last edifices within Iqaluit's borders. The daily six-kilometre round trip added to my exhaustion as I struggled to keep up with lesson planning. As the only French school in Iqaluit, we were required to follow the anglophone programming and schedule. Historically, Nunavut was part of the Northwest Territories along with Yukon until 1999, when it gained its autonomy. Some recent steps had been made by the northern French school board to adopt Quebec's educational system, but there'd been no ground swell of enthusiasm or motivation, as the administration thought it was too fast, too soon. Until the school board caught up, we had to teach the Alberta curriculum.

As a miniature community within a small community, the French school had its particularities. The most enduring headache revolved around the staff vacancy problem. Most of the personnel were senior baby boomers with a meagre retirement income for whom this job was a kind of palliative response to *une vie de debauche* and the conviction that money would always fall from the sky. The younger teachers were more likely to have worked only in small communities. The thought of crowded big-city schools gave them chills. These groups were annually renewed by people like me, lured by advertising to the northernmost French school in the world. For most, this lure lasted one year only. For some, it was even less. The other vacant position the year I was teaching was filled by a young woman who quit after only two weeks.

Our small team now included the principal, five teachers and two class assistants. In addition, there was the woman at the daycare service, and our cultural monitor.

The senior member of the staff, a woman of both age and experience, was named Ana. She was seventy and teaching first grade. Ana had a specific way of talking about the North. In fact, she had a specific way of talking about everything, a kind of rush to release all she knew and saw at once. She was like a grandmother to most of the students who had gone to L'Aurore Boréale. Before moving to Iqaluit, she led a very typical life in Manitoba. In 2004, she heard by chance about the creation of a French school board in Nunavut. This new city and new opportunity piqued her interest. Instead of going into retirement, she sold her house and moved to Iqaluit. Thirteen years had passed since then, but she had still no intention of giving up her work. This was her home. To her, I was just a visitor, yet she treated me kindly.

During our first lunch in the teachers' room, she gave the new arrivals a historical account of Iqaluit with her Manitoban accent and a tiresome way of placing the particle "*là*" at the end of almost every word. She told me that Iqaluit was first called Frobisher Bay, a settlement built during World War II as an American military base. The scarce Inuit population had been displaced over the hill, to a small village called Apex, from where they were forbidden to get any closer under threat of being gunned down. In the fifties, the construction of the DEW Line, the defence system against a possible Soviet invasion, drew in many Inuit from all over the Arctic for work. They gave up their nomadic life to settle in tiny barracks and feed on white-folk food. Soon after, most of them gave up their hunting practice for good mainly because the policemen shot the people's sled dogs in cold blood.

Ana's biggest pleasure was to tell the story of the Iqaluit airport, where sixty flights took off every day. Its taxiway was the longest in Canada, as during the Cold War the

Americans had planned to bring in the huge Hercules military airplanes. In 1987, Frobisher Bay changed its name to Iqaluit, which translates to "place with many fish" in Inuktitut. In 1999, it became the capital of Nunavut, the newest territory of the Canadian Confederation.

By the end of our lunch, Ana's mood swung abruptly. She asked me if I knew that this place would be soon sunk into darkness. In a few weeks, the polar region would tilt away from the sun for the winter, and we wouldn't receive any direct sunlight for the next six months. The sun sets at the polar circle in September and rises again in March, which marks the beginning of the midnight sun, or polar day, which lasts the other six months of the year. She looked at me to see if I had been good enough to find this information on my own. I silently leaned my head toward the bottom of my Tupperware to fish out the last of my boiled potatoes.

Ana's account of the polar night didn't stop there.

"People can go crazy living too long in the dark," she said. "They do foolish things."

This was not a light-hearted chat about an odd phenomenon but a warning about the polar night causing sadness, detachment, lack of energy, excessive sleep and difficulty concentrating. Many people developed full-blown depression after moving here.

Ana was looking at me to see how ready I was to make it through all this. I was usually too shy to contradict people but I replied in a very low voice: "The Inuit have been living here for a long time."

"I wasn't talking about the Inuit."

I said nothing. Ana looked around the table to the other teachers who were listening with placid eyes. They didn't confirm Ana's warning about my future ordeal with the darkness but didn't deny it either. They didn't seem concerned about whether or not I might struggle with the months of darkness. I was surprised to hear one of them say: "If you find yourself sleeping a lot and still feeling tired, there may be something else going on. Polar night doesn't account for everything that goes wrong with us."

Aside from Ana, I felt wary of any female companionship or closeness. Most of them had lived here a long time, within a sort of foster family, stuck with foreign relatives they loathed. Some were waiting for retirement, others for a male relationship, still others for the sky to fall down.

I felt especially disconnected from people my own age, like the cultural agent of our school. Silvia was tall and endowed with a pair of smiling blue eyes. She was kind to everyone, or tried to be. I thought she tried too hard. Silvia was not actually qualified for the job, so she coped by concealing her lack of skills under a friendly veneer.

I didn't have much tolerance for those who worked with kids but were essentially impostors. Children don't know they have been cheated until it is too late. Good teachers are such a rare prize. I learned this at an early age. Despite my parents' pressure to perform, I hated being brilliant, and like any lazy student, I liked teachers who left us alone and gave us undeserved good marks. It had been a way to buy peace with us and with our parents. Looking back though, I was becoming more and more angry with those lousy instructors.

Brigitte, the class assistant, was in a similar situation to Silvia's, as her qualifications remained a big secret. Some ten years before, the school hired her as a music specialist, simply because she could play the piano. When that position disappeared because of a funding shortage, she became class assistant. Since then she was trying to bury her lack of professional training under a tyrannical attitude, shouting and scolding the kids who feared her, freezing in the corridor when they crossed paths with her. I disagreed with her boot camp style, even though her methods worked well to calm the little rascals running all over the place.

Among the ninety registered students at the French school, very few had a francophone background as requested by the school board. The parents were mostly anglophones working for the Nunavut government, at the hospital, in offices or stores, people who knew the value of being proficient in both languages. They were army officers, lawyers, engineers, doctors, managers. With such a select clientele, the school enjoyed the reputation of being an elite institution. The only Inuit students were those from mixed families, or ones fostered by wealthy white couples.

One of these was Eli Ivalu. In my class, I had fourteen kids of two different levels. Ten of them were in Grade Three and the rest in Grade Four. Eli was ten years old and was registered in Grade Three. She was a constant annoyance to me because of her inappropriate clothing. In my messages to the family, I often complained about her see-through blouses and nylon leggings, but none of them were read or signed by her parents as I requested. Very often, she wore a pair of plastic Crocs on her barren feet. What was her mother thinking sending her to school dressed like that? On windy days, I sometimes hesitated to send her outside for recess.

In the morning, she was running in the corridor shoe-less. In her haste to be the first one in class, Eli never obeyed my request that students put their shoes on as soon as they took off their boots and snow pants. She was much more focused on the tiny plastic figurines she hid in her desk to play with while I was teaching the lesson. She'd stop her task to stare at her pencil or the water bottle on her desk. Each time I snapped her out of her daydreams, she glared at me with a frown.

I seated Eli between two boys, one francophone, the other anglophone. The arrangement functioned as planned, as they were a real annoyance, always talking and laughing. Eli acted as a bumper between those different personalities, one chatty, the other mischievous. Eli didn't interact much with either of them.

One Friday afternoon, I got a phone call from her uncle.

He came to see me the following Monday afternoon at the end of the school day. Most of the kids had taken the bus home, while those using the daycare service were still eating their snack in the Grande Salle, which was used as a gymnasium during the day. My classroom was next to it, and from where I sat at my desk, I could hear the daycare assistant trying to quiet the children's yells and locate Henry. That kid had a particular knack of slipping through her fingers and getting lost in the school.

When I went to check on Eli's uncle at the main door,

I saw his RCMP car in the parking lot. I knew he was a police officer, but was our meeting so urgent that it could not wait until he finished his shift? Most surprising, though, was not the holster barely concealed by his uniform, but the fact that he was white.

He was talking with the secretary and a man who was wearing a military uniform. The three of them were laughing while some of the kids waiting for their parents entertained themselves by running between their legs. Since my arrival, I had struggled to make sense of the hierarchy in the school. Everybody was family or friends with everyone else. Most of the kids seemed to regard school as their extended home, where teachers were taken for caring relatives. Students had siblings in almost every age group, and many parents were involved with the French school board council.

Eli's uncle saw me first as I came down the corridor. He stopped talking, then he stepped aside from the group and turned his whole body toward me. The other two looked at me with prying eyes. I was new and they were curious about everything I said and did. Those first weeks it felt like everyone was openly spying on me, which prompted me to remain in the classroom till the corridor was cleared of students and parents.

The policeman took off his woollen cap and reached for my hand. His palm was icy, which gave me an estimation of the temperature outside. His hair was almost grey, yet he didn't look more than forty. He introduced himself as Constable Liam O'Connor. In the few moments before talking to him, I only had time to wonder which one of Eli's parents was white.

I led him to the class and pointed out his niece's desk.

I praised Eli for being orderly, neat and diligent. The constable's eyes followed my hand to a turtle-shaped yellow label where Eli's name was handwritten in red and blue. Her water bottle was filled to the rim, as usual. I remarked she never left it empty, even when it was time to go home.

At the end of our brief tour, I told her uncle that the only problem I had with Eli was her clothing, which was inappropriate for this kind of weather.

Constable O'Connor listened and acknowledged every word with a slight bow of his head. He was staring at me with big eyes which made me very uncomfortable. Were my comments on his niece that unsettling? Every now and then, he would touch his holster, as though to make sure it didn't hit anything and make noise. The chair he was sitting on in front of my desk looked tiny, as did everything else around him. The whole classroom had shrunk since this man came in. There were other parents who worked for the police or the army, and each time they had asked for a meeting, they came to see me while still in uniform. At first, I thought they wanted to intimidate or impress me. That day, while talking to the constable, it occurred to me that at three p.m. most of them were probably taking a break from work to come talk to the new teacher.

"You know," I said while settling into the chair behind my desk, "Eli's family should not be worried about her, she is a very good kid."

It's what every parent wanted to hear from their child's teacher. The constable didn't seem reassured, though. He leaned back on the chair and tried to avoid my eyes. Secretly, I hoped my words would put an end to our meeting as fast as possible. I assumed this visit was no different from the others: The parents just wanted to check up on me. I was a stranger who had entered their house, and they had to make sure I was no threat to their kids. I wondered how many more of them I would still need to show around the class-room, and how many more attributes I would have to invent to describe their children.

The constable tried to regain his composure and find a proper way to address me. His smile didn't help to relieve his inhibition.

"She's always been a good kid," he said. "Makes it very easy for us. Her mum died two years ago and my brother works up in Grise Fiord. He's mostly away. Eli lives with her granny. I'll read out to her what you wrote in the agenda about clothing. She only speaks Inuktitut and a little Eng-lish, y'know."

In a second I knew what Eli's life must look like, with a dead mother and a neglectful father in charge. Not much discipline around with a granny and an uncle as guardians! Yet my main concern was not letting the constable see how taken aback I was by the news. No one had told me about Eli's mother! I was a stranger in this place, and they wanted to keep me this way. No one had thought to show me the students' files and I didn't know how much I should ask and to whom I should direct those questions. Every inquiry I made felt like an intrusion.

The mother may have died naturally. Yet, probably not! Eli had not seemed to me to be a traumatized kid until that moment. Now, as I was rewinding my memory of her daily routine, the strangeness of her habits struck me.

In my messages to her parents, I often complained about my struggle to make Eli follow the rules. Now I was crushed with shame in front of her uncle. How could I have failed to look into a student's situation before writing down such foolish things in her agenda?

"I saw your messages," the constable said, "but nobody reads French at her granny's. Even me I struggle to understand them."

"Oh, yes, I know, I have awful calligraphy," I replied in haste.

"You don't! It's because of my French. I only took a few classes when I was a student. You're asking for her agenda to be signed every day, but I can only do it on weekends when she comes to my place."

"Oh, no need to bother. You know, this was a general request for everyone."

"Well, Eli is like everyone, isn't she?"

I smiled, embarrassed. Had I implied she was not?

Race was a sensitive matter in Iqaluit. The more I tried to avoid saying the wrong thing, the more hurtful my words seemed to become. Why was I so apologetic? And why was the constable taking so long with his visit?

Surely he understood I didn't know about Eli's mother. Only a mean, neglectful teacher would be so harsh on a motherless girl! Maybe this was the reason for his visit, to let me know in a polite way that my French messages would never be signed, but that there was a good explanation why.

A sudden burst of yelling let us know that the kids at the daycare service had finished their snack and were getting dressed to go outside, where they would play till their

parents came to fetch them. The windows of my class were
too high to see the playground in the back. The only thing
I could see at this hour was a ship harboured in the bay
against the backdrop of the sunset's orange light.

I was thankful for this little disruption, and the constable seemed to understand my relief. Yet he didn't show any
sign of leaving. He smiled and asked me if I liked it here.

"It's too soon to say if I like it or not. I am still busy
fixing up my apartment."

"Are you well settled in?" he asked, patting his holster
again.

"Yes, I am."

"You live in a quiet place. We don't have many com-
plaints from tenants living in the post office building."

"How do you know where I live?"

"I saw you entering the building when I went to fetch
my mail."

Suddenly, I remembered him, the policeman whose body
had filled the narrow labyrinth at the post office, where
about three thousand PO boxes adorned the walls like a
columbarium, with letters in place of cinerary urns. This
morbid image came to mind when I first went to check the
key for my own box.

"I think I remember you too," I said, with a smile. "A
police officer is difficult to miss in a place like this."

He glared again, unsettling me. I too was surprised by
my own remark. I figured a police officer would be one of
the most familiar figures in town, always out and about in
the community.

"Where are you from?" he asked me, encouraged by yet
another noisy diversion created by the kids outside.

Despite the easiness of this question, something in his attitude warned me that he too was on his guard. His attempt to sound light and friendly disturbed me. I had inherited this apprehension from my mother; a fear of authority passed on from generation to generation. My mother had grown up under a dictatorial regime and she would never dare tell a police officer to mind his own business. Me neither!

"From Montreal."

I straightened my back and tried to ignore the feeling that I was not a teacher anymore, but someone who had done something wrong, whatever it was. The authorities would always know better than me.

"What were you doing there?" he asked in the same amiable voice that was certainly hiding very serious things.

"I taught history. I took a one-year leave to come up here."

"So, you're here for one year only?"

"I hope so, if everything goes well."

"Why do you say that?"

"Because my other colleague just left. She was in charge of the third-grade class."

"Oh, I didn't know."

"Do the police know everything that happens here at school?"

He laughed.

"This is an awful small place," he said. "We're not supposed to be informed as police officers, but as parents. Why'd she leave?"

"I suppose she didn't like it here."

"Wasn't it too soon for that?"

"Some people just know right off when they are in the wrong place."

He smiled again but that gave me the feeling he was losing his official composure. Maybe he'd picked up on my irritation.

"What brings you here, if I may ask?"

"I suppose the same thing that brings us all here."

"I didn't mean to be rude," he said after a short silence, but there was no regret in his voice.

"It's a common question. I get it all the time from people at the school."

"And what do you answer them?"

"I say I love the North."

"Is it true?"

"I have already taught up North, in Schefferville."

Just as I said this, it occurred to me that his visit today could be related to my experience on that reserve. Mati-mekush-Lac John was an Inuu community of eight hundred people where I'd spent a year teaching in a high school. There had been an incident that involved the police, when we found the body of one of our colleagues. She had hanged herself in the bathroom on a Friday evening, after she got home from school. That way she was sure people wouldn't check on her till Monday. She had no friends and never came to our parties on the weekends. She kept to herself. Booze seemed to be her only pleasure.

"I know where Schefferville is."

For a moment I kept my silence. Last year a scandal broke out about policemen abusing Indigenous women on some Quebec reserves, and Schefferville was one of them. A woman I used to know agreed to talk on camera about the night she spent at the police station. She was drunk when arrested and her guardians took her condition as an opportunity to humiliate and take advantage of her. The men she accused were never found guilty of any wrongdoing.

"One of my students still writes me," I said. "She works now with the mining company."

He was playing with a sharpener he'd taken from my desk. I kept quiet for a moment, then I dared to question him in turn.

"What brings you here? If I may ask."

"I was born in Iqaluit. My family left when I was ten and we came back when I was fifteen."

"This is your home then."

"Aye."

I was suddenly intimidated by his Irish accent, but mostly I was embarrassed by my own. I was too tired to control it. In Montreal I spoke mainly French, but here I relied on English every time I had to ask for services. The effort it took to focus my thoughts and the sight of his holster in my tiny classroom were exhausting me.

I looked at the clock. It was half past four. Constable O'Connor noticed my gaze and stood up. His gun hit the chair. He apologized.

Before moving off, we shook hands again. His palm was still icy. His body's chill was unrelated to the temperature outside, then. He left me at the door of my classroom with no further goodbye. As he turned to leave, he stepped on a little mitten, forgotten in the hallway. He picked it up and put in on the shelf next to the lunch boxes.

His visit kept me at school longer than usual. As the temperature was still bearable, on my way back home I stopped on the shore, as had become my habit, and lay in the sun on the only bench in Iqaluit. It was white, large and comfortable. The tide pushed the waves right up to the bench's feet, and when they retreated, people picked out oysters from under the rocks, stashing their catch in huge pails.

I wondered if this was the place Martin Frobisher called the *Meta Incognita*. At the end of the sixteenth century, he was the first British explorer to have come this far, searching for a passage to China. He entered the small bay carved into the shores of this island, which he took for a passage to the Pacific Ocean. Reality soon confronted him when he realized he was not on route to anywhere tropical. Unwilling to go back to England empty-handed, he loaded some black ore and one native hunter, who would eventually die, onto his boat.

Many of the explorers who tried to cross the Arctic Ocean above the sixtieth parallel found their end here from the cold or starvation. Some of them died because they were not paying attention to what kind of boots and clothes they should wear or what tinned food to bring on board; others, because they did not trust the local people. At this latitude, following rules set by the British Admiralty was a sure trip to a deadly end. Given that the British Empire's guidelines favoured clothes made of rubber ground cloth over fur garments, no wonder it took four hundred years to chart the Canadian Arctic Archipelago.

Many mysteries still lie buried in the ice, but I was not one of those explorers whose goal was to find the Northern Passage. However, like many other individuals coming up North, I too was on a kind of mission. My main goal was to forget.

Before my departure to Iqaluit, my mother helped me clean my house and get rid of my husband's belongings. The move was a good occasion to empty out my drawers, a project I'd been postponing for a while. It was the kind of job my mother loved. Rummaging through my old stuff was to her a passionate voyage full of discoveries. At the end of the day, all the paraphernalia we planned to throw away ended up at my mother's apartment. It took a whole week to empty my house, ridding it of any evidence that a man had once lived there. I was once again the sole proprietor. Happy with the result, my mother proposed we complete our mission by cleaning up the shelves as well.

That was how we fell upon the magazine that launched my career as the Darling of Kandahar. Ten years ago, I was the most beloved woman of the 2nd Battalion of the Royal Canadian Regiment in Kandahar. A picture printed by chance in *Maclear's* made me famous throughout the country. A photographer had taken it while I was still at the university to illustrate a poll about the best schools in Canada. A Canadian soldier posted in Afghanistan sent the magazine an email asking about the pin-up girl who had charmed him with her smile. The magazine took up the soldier's story and started making inquiries about the two of us, the random protagonists of this public affair. We both become the unhappy heroes of a story that never happened. After a brief exchange of correspondence between us, the soldier was killed in a bomb blast during a mission to a garrison in a nearby village. I learned the news on television while I was still waiting for his answer to my last email. He was buried with full honours back home, but I did not attend the ceremony. We had never uttered words of love in our emails, yet people considered me a widow after he died. Since I didn't know how to act like one, I preferred to stay home.

Ten years now since his death, I rarely thought about Yannis Alexandridis, about his blue eyes and square chin. I saved his emails but never reread them. They spoke only of war, while my own messages were even more stripped of feeling.

That old magazine story was not about love but about accidents, about mismatched destiny and parents' errors. When I got his first email, I felt I could not love him because he was Greek and my parents were distrustful of Greeks. Then I decided to disregard the lessons taught in my family. As young Canadians, Yannis and I should have doubled down on a vision for the future. Our duty was to create new meaning and propel ourselves forward. That was how every newspaper in the country concluded their articles about the Canadian mission in Afghanistan. I had felt we both should subscribe to this way of forward-thinking, but the tragic conclusion to our hazardous blind date came too soon. There was not much joy in the story, but no deep suffering either. We were young and had spent too much time trying to prove something to each other, whatever that may have been. We had kept silent about our young bodies' craving because we thought we had a vast future ahead in which to claim our desires. We were a generation that had no reason to rush. We never imagined our lives might be that short. Of the forty Canadian soldiers who died on their mission in Afghanistan, one was the man whom I could have possibly loved or even married. My discord with destiny was so great that I endeavoured to forget about Yannis.

I told my mother to put the magazine back where she'd found it.

~~~~

The basic navigational rule I followed since my first day in Iqaluit was to look for the igloo-shaped roof of St. Jude's Cathedral and take whichever road headed in that direction. This way I was sure I wouldn't get lost. Sometimes I took the paved streets, but more often I just wandered the paths over the rocky slopes among the small houses and wooden garbage boxes. As there were no fences in Iqaluit, I could get as close as I wanted to the houses, their entrances protected against the wind by a piece of cloth.

The post office was located not far from the cathedral. Two of my windows looked out onto Queen Elizabeth Way, where big trucks went relentlessly to and fro on Niaqunngusiariaq Street. The other window overlooked a small lane where ravens and dogs were often fighting around the garbage boxes. Farther on, I could see Koojesse Inlet, still open to the big ships harboured a few hundred metres off the coast. Small boats were busy carrying freight to shore all day long.

I was in a rush to learn as much as I could about the city. Aside from going to the supermarket for groceries, I also needed to access a lot of services that were hidden in various small rooms at the backs of gas stations or corner stores. There were also a few mandatory trips to the government offices, known as the 8 Storey Highrise, which towered over the city from the top of the hill, to sign my insurance forms and have a picture taken for my identity card. As a teacher,

I was officially working for the Government of Nunavut, which, I had to admit, gave me a funny thrill.

Before the winter settled in, I needed to know my way around, as there would be no option to loiter later on. Following Ana's warnings about the polar night's darkness and the six long, sombre months ahead, I took it upon myself to find places where I could spend my free time: the Astro Theatre for movies, the Inuksuk High School for concerts, the arena for craft fairs, the visitor centre for Thursday-evening gatherings and the public library for books.

My colleagues were also in a rush to fill me in about the city's many secrets. I had never heard so many stories in such a short amount of time. History, geography, politics, secrets, they all came to me at once. To each new acquaintance, I was like virgin soil where they could sow the seeds of Arctic knowledge. Except for the first days, when people were still asking about my origins, there was no real interest in who I was, but rather in what I would become.

The first big challenge to me was the weekend, when I was left to my solitude. The polar night had not yet settled in, but my mind was already sunk in a sea of dark thoughts.

Soon I learned that, on Saturday mornings, people usually slept in late after the Friday-night parties. The hallways in the building seemed to have traded the usual smell of marijuana for one that evoked a cellar filled with barrels. The aroma of alcohol was potent enough to smother the background notes of dust and wool. By ten o'clock, the fire alarm would ring almost every hour, as people forgot the bread in the toaster or the bacon on the stove. The first time I heard the sharp sound of the bell, I was the only one to go out into the corridor. The next time it happened, I remained inside with my boots and parka on till I heard the firefighters' bell in the back alley.

I didn't know my neighbours, most of them Inuit, who smiled at me each time we bumped into each other in the corridor. A woman who worked at the hospital was living in the building with her son. One day, while I was smoking on the porch, she came home with a piece of cake on a small plate and asked if I wanted some. I said yes and despite my protests she gave me the whole plate. For days I thought about what to give her in exchange for her generosity. Undecided, I did nothing.

By the end of September, the strong winds were already blowing hard, wafting mounds of dust through the half-open windows. The apartments were overheated and dry, so despite what people from the housing corporation told me when I signed the contract about not leaving the windows open, I regularly aired out the room. Down South, there was an unexpected heat wave, but up here the weather was following the regular course of a short summer-fall season. No one knew how long it might be before the snow would settle in for the next ten months. The temperatures were down to four degrees during the day and slightly below zero during the night.

Every Wednesday after school the staff went to the Royal Canadian Legion, as the wings were only seventy-five cents each. The Legion was quite expensive, so wing night was an outright bonanza—an occasion none of its regulars would miss. This place was meant to serve the Canadian army and people who were somehow related to it, yet members were allowed to bring three guests. I was on Ana's list from the first day. She had a nephew in the army and took advantage of this kinship even though she was no longer in contact with her relatives.

The Legion was nothing more than a canteen. There was no glamour to it, only a dim light and a sweet smell rising from the saucepans on display next to the kitchen window. Here people placed the order after writing their name on it, and the cook would call them on the mic to collect the food. Inuit men and women wandered around the tables offering local crafts: soapstone carvings, ivory jewellery, woollen caps, mittens in sealskin, key holders made from rabbit tails.

I made a habit of accompanying Ana and Brigitte, mostly because this outing came with a free lift from school down to the city. After we ate, they would drive me home. By the end of the month, I found out that the Legion was only a few hundred metres from the post office. I usually ordered five wings, French fries and a beer; they'd have twenty wings, a Greek salad and three beers, which tripled their bill. My mother once told me that old people do not count their money anymore, and she was right.

Ana shared a house with Brigitte, who was a few years younger and had come to Iqaluit only because her husband got a job with the Government of Nunavut. Soon after, he left her for a young woman and settled in one of the remote communities on Baffin Island. As for Brigitte, she decided to stay in Iqaluit and make a living on her own. Ana told me this story during our first meal, and Brigitte didn't seem to care about having her private life revealed. Unlike Ana, she didn't like to tell stories, but as they lived together, she let Ana talk about whatever she liked. From time to time, she just interrupted, saying: "Please, catch your breath. Just catch your breath."

When Ana told me about Brigitte's husband, Brigitte glared at me while munching on her wings. Was she judging me for being young and potentially the kind of woman whom men leave their wives for?

The first weekend, Ana and Brigitte invited me for supper. They seemed to get along well, sharing their tasks like good mates: Brigitte cooking and Ana doing the dishes. In my opinion, Ana wasn't doing her fair share of the chores, but Brigitte didn't seem to care. Ana was so slow that she had been completely ousted from the kitchen and from everything that required any level of manual skill. Brigitte seemed to handle all this in her own way. "*Ana ne va pas mourir de stress, ça c'est sûr et certain,*" he would say from time to time. In return, Ana had to eat everything that Brigitte put on the table, good or bad. Ana confided to me that she missed some of the flavours and aromas of her past, like the sour taste of pickles with her steak.

After supper, they led me to their basement to choose whatever I needed for my apartment. The space looked like a warehouse; every teacher who quit in the summertime left something for the next generation coming in the fall. I took a broom and few glasses. As my packages had not yet arrived in the mail, Brigitte threw in a kitchen towel and some shampoo in a small jar. Ana added a bag of smoked char. Her freezer was full of it from the last shipment. When one of her acquaintances over in Pond Inlet told Ana about bringing in a cargo of fish, she had bought as much as she could, despite the fact that Brigitte couldn't stand it. Looking now to make room in her freezer, Ana was giving away her smoked char to anyone who would take it.

For their belated retirement, the two women had bought a house in Northern Ontario. It was Brigitte's parents' old abode. They showed me pictures of a red-brick house surrounded by high bushes and silver bells. In one photo, an otter was cracking oysters for its breakfast. On the shore in another photo, there were three small oak seedlings that Ana and Brigitte were hoping to see grow into big trees. In the basement, they had piled up all Brigitte's parents' old stuff after they emptied the house. Every summer, they went down South for vacation and tried to find people who needed household items. But who on Earth still wanted those century-old beds, tables, chairs and cupboards, not to mention the mattresses, sheets, gowns, slippers and pillows?

"People only want shiny, new stuff," Ana would say in despair.

It was obvious she didn't share Brigitte's enthusiasm for that red-brick house. She knew everybody in Iqaluit, while in Ontario there would be no one pleased to greet her on the street. Her only sister was in Winnipeg, but their relationship had cooled off over the years after the elder opposed Ana's decision to divorce some forty years ago.

⸺

Three weeks after that dinner with Ana and Brigitte, a retiree substitute named Carole, hired to replace the defecting teacher, joined our small group of after-work friends. She had been living in the community for seven years. After thirty years of teaching physical education in Ottawa, she decided to follow her husband, Grant, who'd gotten a contract with the Government of Nunavut. Now and then, she agreed to come out of her golden retirement to help the French school when they had an emergency, which happened quite often. Schools were often short-staffed as teachers quit regularly, either because their spouses came to the end of their contracts or just because they could not stand the polar night anymore.

Carole offered to pick me up every morning, since Grant drove her to school before going to his office in the 8 Storey Highrise. I took them up on this arrangement, though in the afternoons, I preferred a pleasant solitary walk back to the city. We soon became very close. Carole knew everybody in town and could call on them for any service. In turn, she would do anything for anybody.

The class she was now in charge of was the most challenging in the school, but at lunchtime Carole would be laughing about the students' endless mischief while calmly eating her gluten-free meal. Nothing could make her unhappy or angry. For her, the present was always the best of times. No one could spoil her day, which regularly ended at Steakhouse in front of the fireplace with a glass of wine, surrounded by friends. All she asked for was company, stories and people who needed help.

Carole and Grant were the most glamorous couple in Iqaluit. They lived in a luxurious building where apartments rented for three thousand per month. In the North, where there were so many reminders of life's precariousness, one still experienced this extreme contrast between deprivation and plenty. Carole and Grant hosted parties every weekend, inviting everyone they knew. They were both born rich and lived richly, but Carole had a specific talent for being popular and careful in cultivating her social status.

On windy days, I spent a lot of time at the living room window watching the pedestrians on Queen Elizabeth Way. The window of the bedroom looked out onto the other side of the building to a lane lined with small houses, white water tanks and wooden garbage boxes. Now and then, a rough cough echoed from within the house where, on the outside stair, a duvet had lain on the railing since my arrival. Tuberculosis was rampant and regular health checks had to be done everywhere, especially in the remote communities. Two weeks later, the duvet was still there. A raven would land on it from time to time and make weird sounds, different from its usual cries.

Dogs ran free and dirtied the lane. Almost every day, the Facebook page of Iqaluit Public Service Announcements posted a message about a runaway dog and the promise of a small reward for the finder. I tried to pay more attention to the dogs wandering around the entrance, but none of them matched the descriptions. Some owners desperately toured the city searching for them. On my way back from school, I was often asked if I had seen a terrier or a collie.

The city was small, yet too big to walk from one end to the other in a single go. The neighbourhoods were scattered over the area, separated by rocky hills and small valleys. They were called the Plateau, Legoland, Happy Valley. The streets were more often curved than straight, making the drive easier during the winter blizzards when tires could not bite into the ice on the sharp slopes. The NorthMart store was a five-minute walk from the post office, but Ana directed me to the secret places where many items were a dollar cheaper, such as DJ Specialties or Baffin Island Canners, close to the airport. In the poorer neighbourhoods, big dogs were attached by a chain outside the house. Sometimes, they barked at passersby. They were jealous of the ravens scavenging through the wooden trash boxes, ripping the plastic bags with their beaks.

When I got home from school, I would stop on the porch to smoke. The terms and conditions of my lease stated I could do it inside the apartment, but I didn't want to let this habit form. I'm sure I would have ended up smoking more cigarettes than I could tolerate. More than four a day nauseated me. Mother said that, when you get nausea, it means you're done with cigarettes; you have to quit, which she did. I was not yet ready to give up the habit.

People from the building often gathered outside to smoke and chatter. I never joined them, and they did not attempt to draw me into their discussions. The most fervent smoker was an old woman, tall and slim. Sometimes, she looked so dizzy that she had to walk leaning against the wall. There was also an Inuk man, who always wore a pair of rubber boots and an open parka, no matter the weather. Once, he asked me what kind of cigarettes I was smoking. I told him and he said they looked tempting. I offered him one, but he declined with a broad smile. He sat down on the stairs to smoke. Sometimes he lingered long after he finished, perhaps sunbathing, or waiting for someone.

Soon after, I saw him with an Inuk girl much younger than him. She was a single mother living with her boy at the other end of the corridor. They started coming home together, carrying their grocery bags, but the relationship didn't last long. One night, the woman ran out into the corridor, yelling and crying. I peered out, half concealing my body inside my apartment as I was wearing just pyjamas. The only other person who went out to see what happened was another woman who worked at the hospital. Both women stared at me for a few seconds, then reverted to talking in Inuktitut. Soon after, the guy moved out and I never saw him again.

In my last few smoking sessions, I began to notice a strange coincidence. Every time I was on the porch, one of my white neighbours came out with his cigarette. He lived in the apartment next to the laundry room, so we bumped into each other in the corridor every now and then. He would look my way, casually, but long enough for me to understand the sense of his gaze. We never engaged in any conversation outside of a hello. He too wore a uniform but, unlike Constable O'Connor, a severe grimace was etched into his face. I took for granted that he worked in a tough place.

One evening, I went out for my last cigarette of the evening, and he followed me. I was now sure he was listening for my steps in the corridor. He nodded at me and lit up his cigarette. It was not much, that nod, but it gave me enough to know what he was looking for. Men like him made this kind of thing seem easy and, somehow, natural. Despite the cold, a sexual feeling permeated the air. I knew if I were to get close, I'd feel his body tension pulsing. My neighbour's eyes were famished and filled with sexual desire.

CHAPTER TWO:

Explorers and Legends

S INCE OUR MEETING in September, I had not seen
Constable O'Connor. His visit left me in a state of fear.
I became paranoid that I might unknowingly com-
mit misdeeds against parents or the authorities. This was a
tight-knit community where one friend brought you ten
others while the reverse was equally true. By the end of the
month, I had lost that sense of anonymity from my early
days. For a few weeks, I had felt free to go anywhere and to
look everywhere. I never asked for directions when I got lost,
and never hesitated to go back twice to the same place. The
fact that I was going in circles didn't seem bad or suspect to
me. I was a solitary creature on Earth, faceless and nameless.

Little by little, there were some friendly hints in the
teachers' room and a meeting with the principal who, under
the guise of innocuous questions about my accommoda-
tion, warned me that anonymity was an illusion in this city.
They all knew about my wanderings through the streets.
What were to me just evening strolls seemed a little weird to
the parents. They reported to the principal when and where
I had been seen. He was not a figure of authority to them,

but a big brother, someone who had known their kids since they were toddlers. Each time they came to pick them up from school, they stopped by his office for a brief chat. As for the locals, they watched me from behind their windows and dug around for information about me. A single woman in a community was easy to identify. I soon became the New French Teacher. One woman asked me to confirm the news while I was waiting to pay for my groceries at the North-Mart. Here, even the friendliest attitude required a straight answer.

Soon I was to cut back on my meandering walks anyway. The cold and the wind made the outings even more unpleasant after I lost my anonymity. I was now a government employee, well remunerated according to any Canadian standards, living in sponsored housing that reduced the rent to half of what others paid. Not to mention that I had a home while housing was critically limited in Nunavut. I was a privileged white woman, staring at people's doors, chained dogs, ravens and garbage boxes. I now made my trips short, with no detours or delays.

This new routine helped me get back home earlier after the school day. I was growing tired after a month on the job. The tyranny of the schedule was like nothing I could have imagined. The lack of specialists in arts, music and physical education required teachers to be in their classes all day long, from the first to the last bell. No time was allocated for planning or checking over the students' progress. After one month, I felt overwhelmed. The principal's friendly advice to curtail my wandering came just in time to give me some rest.

I soon noticed though that, during my short walks to

buy food or see a movie at the Astro, a police car would pass
by me a few times. At first I didn't try to see into the car
windows. Why should I? Nothing could be less personal
than a police car making its tour of duty. Policemen were
the faceless shadow of authority in this place, and many
had a long history of resentment against them.

But then, it was not only policemen I avoided peering
at. Since my arrival, I had been experiencing a state of embarrassment, unable to look people straight in the eye. I was
shy not only in front of local population, but anyone, man
or woman, living here, mostly intimidated by the arctic gear
that gave them a second identity. Those parkas, boots, fur
caps and sealskin gloves! Then there were the women carrying their babies in amautiit.

The constable was right to ask me that question: *Why
did people come here?*

For most of the new adventurers, coming up North
meant gain; for others, it meant that there was no better
alternative for them down South. They wanted either to
escape someone or to find something in the Arctic. In some
ways, the modern world was still searching for the Northwest Passage.

Many of us were driven into the small bay of Baffin
Island in the same way Martin Frobisher was lured during
his voyages. Sailing with his two ships, *Michael* and *Gabriel*,
no bigger than nutshells, with no reliable charts or com-
passes, the captain was convinced he was on his way to the
Pacific Ocean. He was not. As he often mistook one land
for another, his voyages created a jumble of cartographical
confusion that lasted for two centuries.

According to some accounts, the Admiralty Council in

London chose Frobisher not because he was a good navigator but because of his unwillingness to play by the rules.
With the heart and soul of a pirate, he was the kind of man
English merchants wanted to lead the search for a passage
to China. When the black ore he brought back to London
proved to be of little value, he lost all his fortune, recouping
it only by returning to piracy. Still, he was knighted for his
part in defeating the Armada. A few years later, he died a
hero's death, fighting the Spaniards at Brest.

For the many explorers who followed in his footsteps,
the North remained a tragic land. Most came hoping to
uncover great secrets but found only sad ends to their lives.
This was a lesson to be learned by all of us: No one dies a
banal death after crossing the Arctic ice pack.

Such was the case of John Davis, whose name was given
to the strait that now separates Canada from Greenland. In
addition to charting the perilous coasts and giving a new
name to each cape and sound he came across, John Davis
was known for bringing musicians ashore and establishing
communication with the local people through music. Sailing with *Sunshine* and *Moonshine* in 1585, he took the first
ethnographical notes on the Indigenous population. He too
faced a tragic death later on, killed by a Japanese pirate in
the East Indies.

The most expensive tribute to the Arctic was paid in
1610 by Henry Hudson, one of the noted navigators and
geographers of his time. Yet Hudson was something of a
dreamer and most certainly a man of infinite stubbornness.
In all his great plans, he failed to consider the crew. While
people followed Frobisher out of fear and Davis out of love,
Hudson's men accused him of holding back food. Fearing

starvation, the crew mutinied. They put Hudson into a boat and set them adrift. No sign of him was ever found. The alleged ringleaders of the mutiny sailed the *Discovery* home in pitiful condition, reduced to eating candles, grass and shreds of bird skin. When the scandal broke, the English entrepreneurs chose to finance a new voyage to the Arctic rather than put the mutinous crew on trial for Hudson's death.

The two voyages that William Baffin made, starting in 1615, took him still farther north than his predecessors. After an initial search around the area where Hudson was set adrift, Baffin determined there was no passage to the Pacific via this route. He guessed that the open water to the west lay through Davis Strait, so the next year he headed in that direction. Unfortunately, his discoveries had a most unlucky fate. When his journals were published in England, they were severely censored. His charts were removed from contemporary maps by his investors, who did not want the competition to learn about this channel. Baffin died at thirty-two, killed in the Portuguese fortress of Ormuz.

After so many expeditions failed to find the Northern Passage via the Atlantic, the British Admiralty proposed to start the search from the other end, tracking backward. The council decided to trust Captain James Cook with the mission of reaching the Pacific coast first, then following whatever route it took to get to the Atlantic coast, where Frobisher, Davis, Hudson and Baffin had tried to identify a navigable way among the ice floes. Cook was an obvious choice for the council; he had already discovered more islands and charted more waters than any white man before. Aboard the *Resolution* and the *Discovery,* he sailed in June 1776, reaching the Bering Strait two years later than planned by the Admiralty. On his way to the top of the continent, he discovered the Hawaiian Islands where he returned to spend the winter. While waiting for the next summer to resume his voyage, Cook was killed by locals.

This long series of hunts through the Arctic ended in the most tragic and spectacular way, with the deaths of John Franklin and his crew of 129 men. Franklin was the finest Victorian "armchair traveller," the sort who would prefer to die of hunger rather than help the cook. He set out from England in September 1845 aboard *Erebus* and *Terror*, two big ships in which the Admiralty put their finest hopes, along with silver cutlery and a library of fifteen hundred books. Despite all previous experience showing that small ships and fewer men were more efficient in the Arctic, Franklin had to keep up with English pride and his wife's ambition. It was said that one evening, while Franklin was taking a nap on the couch, his wife covered him in the British flag she was sewing for his mast. When he woke up, Franklin startled at the image of his own corpse wrapped in the imperial flag.

While the rest of the world considered Franklin to be a great explorer, the Inuit believed he was a lousy navigator. How could the British Admiralty entrust such responsibility to an old, worn-out man? He had lost the enthusiasm needed for the job. Some stories hinted that he had been quite reluctant to embark on this mission. This expedition was to be the last attempt to find the passage, and there was a sense of doom hanging over it from the very beginning.

The wrecks of *Erebus* and *Terror* were found in 2014 and 2016, near the coast of King William Land. Pressured by the Inuit government in Nunavut, England agreed to sign the two ships over to Canada. The Inuit were not fond of Franklin, who had ignored the locals. Their claim on the wrecked ships was a reclamation of their own past.

Writing about those endeavours in the Arctic, the famous Norwegian explorer Fridtjof Nansen noted there was always a high price to pay and little economic value to gain. Yet, despite the harsh cost of trespassing into the realm of the northern lights, those drawn to the adventurous search never ceased, lured by the *hillangar*, the name Icelandic people gave to Arctic mirages.

Like many white people, I came north knowing much about the geography but very little about its people. At first sight, people did not seem to be discriminated against for their skin colour as much as they would have been in big cities down South. Nevertheless, this didn't prevent whites from taking charge of almost everything, especially when it came to things that could bring them a lot of money.

It took me all of one week to understand that, in the city of Iqaluit, the taxi drivers were mostly Middle Eastern, the security guards Black, the construction workers generally from Quebec, the managers from Alberta and the government staff from Ontario. Nothing had really changed since the first explorers.

The mystery of the police car was revealed one cold morning. Despite the heavy snowfall over recent days, the weather had remained bearable. Yet, just before dawn, I watched from my window as the gusts suddenly struck. I didn't understand their power until I reached the end of Happy Valley. Crossing the quiet part of the city, tucked in along the shore and protected from the open tundra by a hill, I wasn't sweating as much as usual. So I knew the outside temperature must be different than on other days when, after a few hundred metres, I usually had to unzip my parka. As soon as I reached the top of the hill, my face was hit by an icy blast. My breath turned into ice crystals. The wind blew hard from the north and there was no shelter against its force.

In front of the Quick Stop, I halted for a few seconds to catch my breath. Every morning, a big white van was stationed in the tiny parking lot that could only accommodate three cars. The convenience store was also the gas station for this part of the city, so drivers often sipped coffee while filling their tanks. The man with the van had precisely the same schedule as mine. At seven sharp, he stopped by for his coffee and gas. That morning was no exception: He came out of the shop with his brown paper bag, nodded at me and got in his truck. I remained on the sidewalk until he turned around in the lot and headed out on the street down to the city.

It took me a while to understand that his company, which provided plumbing and sewage services, used the name of the toothed whale with a tusk coming out of one of its canine: Narwhal. What could have possibly inspired him to use the name of such an uncommon mammal to symbolize his tools stirring the city's dirt? It was not only the anatomy of this endangered species that puzzled me, but its legend too. Bewildered by the twisted tusk, generations of locals had invented a mind-blowing story.

There are many versions of this legend, but it seems that the authentic one originated in Greenlandic mythology. It is said that a grandmother was living in a village with her two orphaned grandchildren, a girl and a boy. The boy was born blind, but he learned how to hunt under the old woman's guidance. Every time the boy killed an animal, however, the grandmother would say that his arrow went astray. She fed him dried meat while she saved the fresh supplies for herself and the girl. The boy knew what was happening but would not challenge an adult. Luckily, his little sister fed him good meat while the old woman was asleep.

One day, they saw a big white whale surfacing to breathe. The grandmother told the boy to harpoon it. This was such rare game and she asked him to attach her foot to the end of the rope which, according to an old tradition, made her the equal beneficiary of the catch. Except this was a huge female whale that didn't give up easily. When the mammal felt the harpoon biting its flesh, it started swirling in the water and dragged the old woman down. Each time the whale came up for breath, the grandmother shouted at her grandchildren to throw her the ulu to cut the rope. The kids remained quiet on the shore, waiting as she was hauled out to sea. Sinking to the bottom, the old woman turned into a dark whale, and her swirling hair, into a twisted tusk.

Bent against the gusts roaring up the road, I thought back to a story the principal told us over lunch in the teachers' room. A few years before, a sudden frost trapped a dozen narwhals in the bay. A police unit had to shoot them all to prevent slow death by starvation. Until the next summer, the ice remained a domino of blood-red patches.

At the crossroads, a car stopped next to me. I didn't halt. My fur-lined hood prevented me from seeing anything but the road ahead. I kept on walking till I heard a voice call my name. A man stepped out of the car, carefully securing the door with both hands to avoid the wind slamming it. I hardly recognized Constable O'Connor bundled up in his parka, his face partially hidden by the hood.

"Get in the car, will ya," he shouted over the howling wind. "I'm taking you to school."

In his car, the smell of the coffee from two Tim Hortons cups pleasantly scented the air. I never brought along my coffee mug in the mornings to avoid weighing down my backpack. Once I got to school, I'd rush first thing to the teachers' room to plug in the coffee machine.

"You should take a cab on days like this," the constable said, pulling back his hood.

I smiled and let him drive.

The road ahead was whipped by strong gusts that removed the snow and piled it up around the garbage boxes, cars and houses. Some of the entrances were completely clear while others were blocked by snowdrifts shaped by the wind like frozen waves.

The drive took us only few minutes, and we didn't exchange many words. My tongue was frozen along with my fingers. Once we pulled into the parking lot, he invited me to linger in the car. At this early hour, no one was at school yet. I was usually the first one to turn off the alarm at the entrance, careful to do so after the few times I forgot, which triggered it and sent the firefighters to the school.

The constable took a cup of coffee from the holder and handed it to me.

In that moment, I understood that he had planned this rescue all along. The police car that had followed me all over the city, in the most unexpected places, was his. I had seen him a few times at the Legion, when I was with Ana and

Brigitte, and once at Steakhouse while I was having a beer with Carole. Iqaluit is a small place and people bumped into each other frequently. At the NorthMart or on the street, I often saw people stopping to talk for a while despite the cold weather. The cup of coffee I foolishly accepted was evidence of a more diabolical scenario. He'd followed me across Happy Valley in this crazy weather while taking the main street over the hill, bought the coffee, then waited to rescue me at the windiest spot on the hill.

"You shouldn't ever go out in this weather," the constable said again in his paternal voice. "It's minus thirty now, but it'll get worse soon."

I didn't look at him. I kept on glaring at the windshield, wondering how the bullying and harassment of women got started in this place. I should have never accepted his coffee. The cup was burning my fingers, but I had not yet drunk any. Maybe there was still time to get out of his car. One mouthful of the sweet liquid would subject me to his power and influence.

"Next time I'll take a cab," I said and put the cup back in the holder.

Then I shifted, as if to get out.

"D'you need a ride in the morning?"

I turned my head and looked at him very carefully for the first time since we met. His face was unshaven, with red eyes. His haggard appearance stunned me beyond words. He understood my surprise and said: "I'm just getting back from Cape Dorset. I spent the night over there."

"Are you coming from the airport?"

"Aye. I'm heading home. My house is on the Plateau, just left of the crossroads."

What had hit me most when I got into his car was not the coffee aroma but a dense whiff of smoke, spirits and motor oil. Those northern scents were all over his parka, carried in the greasy smears above the pockets, underneath the cuffs, at the collar. It hit me like something sweet and sharp, like peppermint.

"You want to come and pick me up with the police car?" I asked without trying to conceal my astonishment.

He laughed and said: "I'll come by with my own car. I don't work till the afternoon tomorrow."

"Why would you do such a thing?"

He said nothing, but I was sure he knew I was just pretending not to understand his aim. He took the cup from the holder and held it out to me. I refused it, still staring at him in disbelief.

"Are you running an inquiry on me?" I asked.

"What? Why would you think such a thing?"

"I don't know, maybe because you are a policeman. People get crazy ideas when addressed by someone in uniform."

"I'm not much of an authority around here, you know, and I would never abuse my role, if that's what you're afraid of."

"People in uniforms scare me."

The constable kept on looking at me in silence. Then he sipped his coffee and turned his head to the window. He appeared reassured that I was not going to leap out of his car.

"People help each other around here."

"And how am I supposed to help in turn?"

"I don't know," he said, turning his face to me.

"Is this related to Eli? Are you waiting for me to do

something for her?" I tried to return his gaze, which was difficult for me.

"Would you?" he said with a smile.

"What do you expect me to do?" I asked, embarrassed, as his stare was too probing.

"Maybe not be so harsh on her because she wears those clothes."

"I'm not harsh on her because of that. I'm not harsh at all."

"But you did nothing when that boy made such nasty jokes about her amautik."

Oh, so it was all about that incident! I knew what he was talking about. My body was suddenly shaking. My stomach churned and a sudden flow of blood heated my face.

He was right. I did nothing the day class pictures were taken and Eli was wearing a traditional-style white parka with a cute little hood. One of the boys said that the kids were going to poop in her amautik. He teased her about the tiny dots her granny had drawn on her cheeks, saying they were rotten pimples. Eli came and told me about it. I said I would fix it, but at recess I went to see the principal and let him deal with the issue. At the end of the day, I read the email he had sent to the boy's parents. I was copied on all their correspondence, but I didn't answer any of their messages.

My voice was trembling when I said: "I didn't know what to do. I'm sorry, but I really didn't know what to do."

"It seems you never know what to do when it's about her. That boy calls her a crybaby because she tells you everything he says, but you never punish him."

"Yes, I know. It's not easy to punish kids, for any reason.

I'm sorry. Everything is so new to me here. I don't know how conflicts are settled in this place. You have to know the students really well before taking action. I don't know what people think here so I prefer to proceed carefully."

The constable looked at me with an amused glance.

"I've never imagined you being on the battlefield with these kids."

"Well, we are, because they are stronger than us, and tireless. They are always getting what they want."

He looked at me incredulous. I realized that my voice was begging for mercy. I was so powerless in the face of his accusations that I had let down my guard. Why was I telling him all this? He was a parent and not really on my side. This wasn't the moment to confess my survival tricks.

"You might be right, but conflicts can't be settled by just one side, you know? There's something else Eli didn't tell you. She was too ashamed. That little bastard asked her if she had kids with her father. If he ever says anything like that again—"

He grasped the wheel with both hands. I couldn't bear to hear his crushing anger and I opened the door, but the wind pushed it back and shut it on me. He grabbed my left arm with a firm hold.

"Stay, will ya! I'm not accusing you of anything. I suppose that was the right thing to do, bringing it to the principal. We can't protect her from being bullied. She has to learn to defend herself."

He released my arm.

"Her granny isn't aware of this conflict. Those messages don't get to her. They're in French anyway. She's not on the principal's list. I am, along with my brother, but he's away

for a while, so I try to help as much as I can. I'm still struggling to convince Eli to put a sweater on."

"You are not doing me a favour," I said, as my own anger rose. "The heating system doesn't work well in our class
and Eli always has blue lips. I know you don't agree with
me, but I believe it's best when kids are warm. They grow
up better and faster when they do not waste their calories
warming up their body. They even sleep better when they
are warm."

The constable seemed intrigued by my outburst. He
had the decency not to ask how many kids I had. I'm sure
Eli had told him I had none. I had told my students I was a
single, very single, woman.

"Grand so, you've convinced me," he said with a broad
smile, "but, you know, it's not that easy. Eli has always decided what to wear, since she was a toddler. Granny's not
used to confronting her. Parents never do it here. They have
a different understanding about how to best raise children.
Maybe they're not good parents by our standards, but it
doesn't mean they're bad either. They're different. Eli has
never left Iqaluit and she wants so badly to be like those
girls she sees on TV. You can't blame her for wanting that
colourful stuff."

I kept quiet for a while, pondering my words. I imagined
him shopping online for clothes that would give Eli the illusion of being on a sunny beach.

Then I suddenly remembered the last message I wrote
in her agenda that got no answer whatsoever.

"I also wanted to tell Granny that Eli should not miss
school so often. Because of her last hunting trip, she now
has a lot to make up and she is not very cooperative. She is

angry with me, saying I give her too much homework. But it's not homework, it's what she missed in class."

"She told me. That science exam is driving her crazy. We tried to remember all those Latin terms for the plants. How important is it, really, to know all those Latin names?"

"I cannot decide what is important for a student to know. It's on our science curriculum. Such plants don't grow here, but they do grow elsewhere."

"You see? You're harsh on these kids."

"I really don't understand what you mean by being harsh. This is school. Aren't you worried about her marks?"

"Rank something else higher than marks, why don't you? This isn't Montreal."

"School is the same everywhere," I said. "One day, she will leave the North."

"And what makes you say that?"

"Do you want her to live in this place forever?"

"Why not? People have settled here for a long time. Eli likes it here. This is her home."

In the side mirror I saw one of the teachers making her way on the slippery road. She would certainly spot me getting out of the police car. Would she believe this was just a chance encounter? I looked at the constable. He knew what I was thinking. He let me out of the car in silence.

I ran to the door, but the wind blew my hood off with a single blast. My hair swirled across my face while I was rummaging for my keys at the bottom of my backpack. My fingers were almost frozen when I found them. The constable's car was still there when I closed the door behind me.

The next day at school we had a fire alarm drill. Fires were a frequent tragedy in the North, and we had to regard them as an ongoing threat. Houses were easily burned down, mostly during the night when smoke went undetected by the sleeping inhabitants.

Teachers had prepared for the drill the day before. They had been told to gather their students as they were, get them out of the school and lead them to the arena a few hundred metres away. We were forbidden to let them put on their parkas or boots. If a real alarm ever got triggered, there would be no time to get dressed.

In the morning, I pretended to survey my students next to the lockers, while actually checking to see what they were wearing. Eli had a see-through blouse over a lace top and pink leggings. I told her to put a sweater on as the heating system was off, but she replied that she had nothing except her Inuit parka.

Many weeks of daily scolding had passed and I had not succeeded in correcting their habits. Once they took off their boots and snow pants, they'd cross the hall with their shoes in hand then dump them next to their desks. That day I took care that they put their shoes on. When the alarm started ringing, I grabbed my own sweater and threw it on Eli's shoulders. She glanced at me but said nothing. In the rush to get out of the building quickly, she refused to button it up.

Back from the arena, the principal gathered everybody in the Grande Salle to meet the firefighters and listen to their brief presentation about what went wrong during our drill. Eli came to me and handed back the sweater. I told her to keep it, but she refused. In class, I gave them another lecture about their inappropriate clothing. Eli was listening to me while staring at the floor.

At the end of the day, I wrote a message in English telling her granny about the fire alarm and the fact that Eli had had to go outside in minus-thirty-degree weather dressed in just a light blouse. The next day, the agenda was signed by the constable. His niece was wearing a white sweater that she kept unbuttoned over a blue top.

In truth, clothing was the least of my concerns about Eli. What I declined from sharing with her granny or uncle was her taste for violent stories. For her art projects, she always chose troubling characters. While other kids were drawing nice whales, polar bears, girl hunters or smiling grannies, Eli drew Amautalik, an ugly beast that fed on lost kids.

There were many versions of this old legend, but she picked the most unsettling one, where the creature comes across two boys harassing a little girl named Kunaju. As Kunaju's mother was very ill and her father away looking for an *angakog*, a healing shaman, everybody in the village considered her an orphan and treated her badly, especially the children. One day, Kunaju was playing outside when the two mischievous boys came to pester her. They mocked her for being alone, with no one to take care of her, and made fun of the amulet given to her by her mother. The girl tried her best to defend its magic power, yet the boys retorted that it was nothing but useless feathers.

They were so busy laughing and poking the girl, they did not see the old Amautalik crawl from behind a rock. With her huge hands, Amautalik grabbed them and threw them in her basket full of putrid weeds and worms. She ran to her cave to look for her ulu to cut the children into pieces. While she was rummaging inside for her knife, Kunaju's amulet turned into a small bird that helped them escape. When the ogress came out of the cave, the little bird distracted Amautalik long enough for the kids to reach their camp.

Eli liked the story and drew the ogress in minute detail: her wrinkled face, her ragged clothes, her huge basket made of sealskin, perched on her back, loaded up with oozing rot. Eli was amused by the ogress's broken language. The kids in the story seemed smart and witty, while the old woman was stupid and inarticulate. Amautalik walked with a back-breaking stoop and her hair was mired with soil and grass. She lived in a cave as she knew no better.

The detail that Eli could not understand was why those two boys were so cruel toward Kunaju. Why did they have to pester a poor girl struggling to cope with her mother's illness and her father's absence?

When she asked me that question, the only explanation that crossed my mind was that maybe she was a stranger and the boys felt threatened. Legends thrived on old apprehensions, a sense of danger, a longing for security. When food was scarce, everybody had a role to play in maintaining the chain of fragile life.

The next day, I came up with a better idea. I told her that the old stories had to be scary enough to keep children close to home and prevent them from going far out on the tundra where polar bears could tear them apart. Nothing better than a monstrous creature to help the parents guard their young. Small kids could not understand the perils of living in such a harsh environment. To them, animals were just helpless creatures, eager to be petted and cuddled. It took something like an ugly creature to keep them away from polar bears.

She looked at me and said nothing, as usual.

From school, I went to the public library to renew my books. In the entrance hall, there was a poster with an exhibition about Dorset crafts, set in the small room adjacent to the shop. The exhibit consisted of a modest collection of reproductions of the few objects remaining from that period, buried in the ice. The texts that accompanied them, though, were quite rich. On the last wall, there was a genealogical tree that traced the genes of the modern Inuit back to the Dorsets. Eli was one of their heirs and perhaps her scribblings were vestiges of her ancestors' memories.

It's possible the old Amautalik Eli drew for her art project was the living legacy of the clash of two cultures that challenged each other in the Arctic for thousands of years. Amautalik was an old Dorset creature facing off against her younger Thule foes. Violence and death were omnipresent in the local legends as a legacy of an ancient mythology where blood, starvation and cruelty were inescapable. Nature and animals were but predators, a deadly coalition against humans who stubbornly resisted. Under the never-ending threat of the elements, people sometimes turned against each other, men against women, grandmothers against grandchildren, kids against orphans. The Inuit myths offered no judgment and no punishment. People were bad, they did awful things to each other, but that did not prevent them from living out their lives. The only moral lesson to be drawn was to survive at any cost.

Eli's ancestors arrived in North America in waves, starting some fourteen thousand years ago. They crossed the Bering Strait from the Asian continent in skin boats, then settled in the most barren region ever inhabited by man.

About four thousand years ago, what ethnologists called the Dorset culture settled around Foxe Basin in the Canadian Arctic Archipelago. As this group came into ascendance during a new period of Artic cooling, their survival techniques improved. They learned better methods for building skin boats, sleds and sea-hunting equipment. Their best innovation was the igloo, the most efficient way of creating shelter in the snow.

The Dorset people left little behind in terms of craft, yet the few objects that survived over time established Dorset art as the most developed in Inuit prehistory. The primal quality of their art was brutal and unsettling. Carvings were used almost exclusively for shamanistic practices, and decorated very few utilitarian objects. Incisions on caribou antlers and walrus ivory revealed images of singed animal and human faces. They depicted chaotic scenes in which humans seemed tortured and psychotic.

About a thousand years ago, the Dorset people disappeared under pressure of another race, the Thule people. These newcomers were vigorous and very skilled in killing big mammals, including whales. Fierce hunters, they developed specialized harpoon techniques and the dog-drawn sled. The Thules spread across the Arctic in fragmented groups and are considered the ancestors of the modern Inuit, though the Dorset culture lives on through their traditions.

Perhaps this was the reason Eli's drawings were so disturbing to me, and why I avoided looking people in the eye on the street. I felt I was no match for them.

One Sunday evening, I went to see Tanya Tagak's concert at Inuksuk High School, which was a big blue windowless building that towered over the city from a hilltop. The concert had been postponed from the night before because of the blizzard that had stalled all the flights to and from Iqaluit. The event was in the main entrance hall. Among the almost exclusively white audience, I recognized the principal and his wife.

Before the concert, Tanya gave a little speech. She spoke about the extent of Inuit women's oppression and the violence they have endured, mainly at the hands of white men. She made it clear that she was not performing the traditional throat-singing music, but a contemporary take.

At the end of her preamble, she added: "If there is anybody who doesn't like it, the exit is right over there."

Her singing was theatrically accompanied by a local artist, Laakkuluk Williamson Bathory, an Inuk woman from Greenland, established in Iqaluit with her husband and three kids. She was known mainly for her Inuit mask dancing. The two small balls that stuffed her cheeks comically distorted her lovely face, painted in stark black and red. Tanya was throat singing onstage, a music that was rather like yelling, mauling and screaming, while Laakkuluk moved around the audience, performing an erotic dance close to people's faces. Laakkuluk got back on the stage to sing with Tanya and to slip the two balls directly into the singer's mouth. At the end, they both performed a throat song together, very close to each other's faces, almost mouth to mouth.

I was very uncomfortable looking at them, mostly because the constable was in the audience. When I arrived, I took a seat in the last row, where I could see the entrance door. This is how I spotted him peering inside from behind the glass windows.

I knew he was looking for me. Maybe he was not certain he would find me there, but he knew it was a place I might be. He bought a ticket at the entrance and went to hang his parka. He came down the steps into the hallway and said hello. I answered with a small nod. He headed to an open seat in the first row.

I watched him during the performance, but whenever he would turn his head to follow Laakkuluk's movements, I avoided his eyes. Members of the audience were shy about being caught in the spotlight and were trying to avoid becoming her next target. The constable was not so lucky. I think the artist had spotted him from the beginning. Maybe she knew him, or maybe it was because of his tall stature that towered over the others. She stopped in front of him, opened her legs, leant forward almost touching his chest with her breasts, got close to his face and smelled him all over. Then she got on her knees, simulating a touch on his crotch and legs. People around the constable were smiling, but not him. He turned his head away, trying to avoid her painted face.

I left my chair before the performance ended. In the small lobby of the main entrance, I stopped to put on my coat. Just as I was getting my mittens and scarf on, the constable appeared behind me.

"Where are you off to running like that?" he asked, trying to sound light.

"I am not running. I just wanted to avoid the crowd after the show."

"May I invite you for a drink? Caribrew is still open."

"I don't drink this late. I have work tomorrow."

"Everybody does."

"I know you want to talk about the show, but I don't want to."

"You're wrong, I don't. You understand this kind of stuff better than me. We don't have to share the same opinion about everything."

Obviously, he didn't like the show. His tone irked me.

"I think it was a very strong manifesto," I said.

He smiled with a hint of embarrassment.

"I don't know about that."

He put on his mittens and cap.

It was the first time I had seen him in a civilian outfit and he looked quite different. He was wearing a beige woollen sweater and black jeans that gave him a youngish look. Or maybe it was because of his new haircut, which showed more of his ears and forehead. He looked tired and downcast.

"C'mon, join me for a drink," he said again.

" I need to get home."

"Then let me give you a lift. It's cold outside."

"I know, but it's only a ten-minute walk."

I turned my back to him and opened the heavy door with some effort. He followed me and took my arm.

"Please, don't leave like this."

"Every time we are together, we get into a fight about Eli. I know this week I did something inappropriate again. I don't want to hear about it. I do learn, you know? I try hard to not hurt anybody."

The constable said nothing, but gently led me to his car. I followed him without resistance.

He opened the door on the passenger side and helped me get in. Then he drove us to Frobisher Inn, just behind Inuksuk High School.

The bar was still crowded. It was not even nine p.m. but with the polar night settling in, days were ending at four in the afternoon. At this time of year, we still had light for a few hours. Almost all the tables were taken; the constable led me to the four armchairs in front of the fireplace. Two were already occupied by some men who greeted him. He responded with a discreet bow. A few minutes later, they quietly left.

The constable asked me what I wanted, and I said a glass of white wine. While he was at the bar, I looked around for people who might know me.

He came back with the wine for both of us, set the glasses on the table and sat in the armchair next to me. It was difficult to find something to say. We both stared at the electric fireplace.

"You didn't like the show," I said without looking at him.

I knew it was an uncomfortable subject, but the silence was worse. Since the start of the evening, I felt I was being forced into something, and now I was looking for an escape. My only defence was talking. Perhaps he felt the same way.

"Every time there's a show in town, they start by announcing something like what you called a manifesto," he said. "Everything's a manifesto around here. Everybody tries to make me feel guilty about something."

"We are all guilty of something."

The constable looked at me with sad eyes. Despite his distress, once again I had that feeling that this was not an ordinary encounter, and I grew all the more determined not to let him intimidate me. He had no right to bring me here, to make me drink wine and talk about things we disagreed about.

"My father was a soldier and my mother a nurse. If anybody did wrong toward these people, it wasn't them."

His voice showed the same determination as mine.

"This is not about personal guilt," I said and was immediately astonished by my lecturing tone.

"Well, I can't be held responsible for everything the fishermen and the whalers did."

"It all started with English explorers."

"I'm Irish."

I said nothing. I took a sip while he was turning the wine in his glass. It was obviously not his favourite drink.

"Tell me what you thought about the show," he said.

He understood maybe he was not going to get off easily and shifted to attack me head on.

I remained silent for a while. Many things were running through my mind but not anything I could share with this man. I was not yet sure if all this was entirely about me or about his niece.

During the show I realized that throat singing could be about something different than what people might imagine elsewhere. For a long time, I thought it was a call to hunters who were approaching home with the game. In stormy weather, the hunters risked passing by their families who had been buried by snowdrifts during the men's absence. In the darkness and fury of a blizzard, the women's voices would be a signal of human presence in the whiteout.

On the stage, Tanya and Laakkuluk gave a different interpretation of throat singing. Throughout their lascivious and intimate performance, this song seemed like an erotic play between women, something to help pass the time so they could forget their hunger while the cold seeped into their core. And perhaps this struggle to hold each other tight and breathe into each other's faces served to awake in them an erotic shiver. Maybe they were trying to make the wait in the cold and darkness less excruciating, or they were awakening their senses for when their men would be back.

The constable watched me as I stared into the fire.

"I liked the purpose they gave to the throat song," I said after a while. "It was different."

He felt the softness in my voice. Was my irritability over?

"Granny was a good singer once. In her youth she sang a lot but her lungs were eaten by tuberculosis."

"What does she think about Tanya Tagak?"

"She thinks she's a witch."

I laughed, incredulous, but he was not joking.

"Really? How come?"

"People are sensitive about the way their past is used."

"But Tanya? What purpose does she have other than speaking about her people?"

"It's about how she does it."

"What about it?"

"It's all so violent. It turns the women into prey. It makes them weak. This isn't how women see themselves here. The North could not have endured without them."

"I don't think she means that."

"Me neither. But when she speaks for those other women, she makes them all victims. It's true that Inuit women suffered a lot, but they made choices too. Women were sometimes stronger than men. They often made decisions for everyone's sake. There's a story called 'Women without Husbands Become Dangerous.' Granny told it to me. By dangerous she meant strong. Women who could hunt and kill. Equals. They're not all victims, you know?"

"Is this what Granny thinks?"

"Not only her. Many women here feel diminished by the way people represent them everywhere, artists and government people alike. It doesn't mean Tanya doesn't speak for a lot of women. But not everyone likes to see themselves depicted that way. Granny's old man lives in Grise Fiord, a faraway community north of here, but she stays here for Eli, in a place where she doesn't know many people. It was her choice, for the future of her grandchild. And the old man had no say in her decision."

The story about his family caught me off guard. Was I ready to take it in?

"Is Eli taking throat-singing lessons?" I asked, turning my head away.

"She can't, she's too weak. She was born with frail lungs. I wasn't here when she was born, but my brother said she stayed in the hospital for quite a while. Her mother wasn't well either. She got depressed and Granny had to come from Grise Fiord to take care of them. She would carry Eli in her amautik and sing to her all day long. That's the real meaning of throat singing. It helped Inuit women keep their babies warm. The resonance of their lungs is like a drum beat to calm them down. I don't like seeing other kinds of ideas going through people's minds when I'm reminded of Eli in her granny's amautik."

"This is a good argument to give her warmer clothes."

The constable looked at me gratefully. He understood we had crossed a dangerous line, but we had backed off without leaving too much blood behind. He changed his tone and the subject, but without giving up the sadness in his voice.

"You're getting obsessed with this issue. Not every illness here is related to the cold, you know," he said, smiling.

"Well, warm is better than cold, my mother said." I laughed.

"How is your mother?"

"My mother? Do you know her?"

The constable laughed.

"Was I supposed to?"

"I don't know, but the way you put the question made me wonder."

"Just asking, no need to know her personally."

I looked at him, puzzled. The feeling that he was questioning me was taking hold again. He was coming on to me strong, but for a man who wanted to sleep with me, he showed a lot of hesitancy. I could see there was some vulnerability to him.

I finished off my wine and put the glass on the table. He understood that the evening was over and didn't push the issue. He gulped down his last mouthful and stood up.

The drive to my house took only a few minutes. The most annoying thing in Iqaluit was the fact that a walk of any distance seemed an eternity because of the cold and the wind, but the journey by car was ridiculously brief. Such a fuss for a few minutes!

He stopped at the entrance behind the building, where the taxi driver had brought me the day I arrived in Iqaluit. I turned my head toward him and I saw that his face was completely changed.

"I don't know what I'm doing wrong or what you expect from a man. Or from a relationship. Maybe I took this all wrong from the beginning. But I like you very much and I would really love to be together."

His voice betrayed a kind of harshness, despite his pleading. He kept his body as far from me as possible, where he could scrutinize me carefully. I did the same, bracing myself against the door as though preparing to escape his reach. The claustrophobic narrowness of the space between our seats and the distinct smell of the car made me struggle to find the right words. When I finally spoke, I kept my anger and frustration to myself and stuck to logic.

"I am not staying here, you know? This is a one-year contract. And you are my pupil's relative. This will affect my relationships with everybody around me."

"In what way? This isn't exactly a small village. People come from all over and they mind their own business."

"I don't think so. I absolutely doubt they mind their own business when it comes to single women. We could never jump on the first sexual occasion and get away with it. There would always be consequences for us. There is the school staff and there are the kids."

"What do the kids have to do with your private life?"

"They are judgmental."

"They're not. They like to see the adults happy."

"I'm happy as it is. I don't want to take risks with anyone."

The only light in the car was from the lamp above the entrance door, but I could see the genuine surprise on his face.

"I think Tanya would be quite ashamed of a fan like you," he said. "If I understood anything from her show it's that she doesn't care about making a bad impression. She does what she believes in."

I smiled. And so did he.

He grabbed the wheel with both hands, a pretext to move his body and get closer to me. Then he took my hand and kissed it.

"Maybe you think I'm looking for a hook-up, just some non-committal relationship that would end and fade away quick like a one-night stand. Maybe that's what's bothering you. You think I'd brag to my colleagues about you, about what goes on behind closed doors. But it's not true. I wouldn't make you a one-night stand."

"What's the point when you know I'm leaving in a few months? My colleagues already warned me people will do anything to survive the polar night. But I do not feel like engaging in a relationship just because of the darkness. It won't help us."

He kept hold of my hand but his grasp was weakening. I tried to pull it back, and he let me.

"It seems everything I do only makes you imagine the worst about me. Like I don't fit into what you'd imagined about the North. What were your plans in coming here?"

"I had no plans."

"Well, you did. And now you're stuck with them. At least you don't wear an Inuit parka. Every woman coming up from the South is wearing one. I bet you came here hoping to see people living in igloos and travelling by dogsled, eating raw meat and throat singing on every corner. And you got stuck with a boring police officer." .

He was watching me again with a keen eye, from which all tenderness had disappeared. I turned away and looked through the windshield as two men exited the building, rushing to their vehicles at the end of the parking lot. The light in our car was off but one of the men bowed his head. The constable didn't respond in kind.

The silence that followed again filled me with anger.

"You don't know me. And the fact that you only want a relationship without knowing me makes me angry. It makes no difference to you if it was me or someone else."

"It's not true. That is not true," he said in haste, but then he suddenly stopped.

I could not stay any longer in his car.

"I would like to go, please."

The constable grabbed my hand and put his face close to mine.

"I can't argue anymore about what kind of relationship you or I want. But I'm asking for more than one night. I could love you very much if you only let me."

His eyes were now in shadow and I could not see them, but his voice expressed his distress. I could not say anything.

I only wanted to step away and run the few metres that separated me from the door. The constable remained silent but his hand held onto mine.

"It would be disastrous for both of us," I said. "I'm really leaving in June. This relationship would only break our hearts. Mine, at least."

Tears started filling my eyes, but the constable didn't notice.

"Let's not think that far," he said.

I turned to get out of the car, even though my hand was still captive in his solid grip. But he wouldn't let me.

"Please think about it and let me know," he said. "There aren't many chances to cross paths with you in this city. I have to leave quite often, and then it takes me a while to track you down again. Could you make things a little easier for me?"

"You won't quit, will you?" I asked, without looking at him.

"Not until I understand what you have against me. And not until we have a proper talk."

I remained silent. He kissed my hand again and watched as I got out.

❧

One evening in mid-October, I went outside on the patio for a smoke. A few minutes later, my white neighbour followed with cigarette package in hand. It was the first time we were alone, and I was sure he had heard my boots while crossing the hall. He looked exhausted but tried to seem upbeat.

He took out a cigarette and lit it. He drew for a while,

watching the post office door, where people were coming to collect their parcels.

He turned to me and thrust out his hand.

"I think this is a proper time to introduce ourselves. My name is Fraser."

He smiled, but it didn't fit him very well. Obviously, he didn't smile very often.

I introduced myself and let his big hand take mine.

He was a short but very robust guy. It was the first time I'd seen him without his cap and he looked rather old. Yet, there was a beauty to his features that overcame his down-cast presentation.

I was waiting for the inevitable question about what I was doing in Iqaluit, but he stopped talking. He withdrew a step toward the balustrade while I leaned against the op-posite wall. He took a few drags while watching two ravens scavenging in the garbage box across the street. The lid had been pried open by the wind and a mess of plastic bags was now scattered around. As I finished my cigarette, I wished him a good night and made to enter the building. He moved a little farther to give me room and said goodnight.

Despite his apparent indifference, there was no doubt he was interested in me. I had a sharp sense of him nosing around in my business, learning what he could about me and imagining the rest. But men like him were in no rush. They were adroit hunters and knew how to lure their prey into their nets. The last thing they wanted was to scare it off. Like a hunter who stayed motionless next to a hole in the ice, waiting for a seal to come up to breathe, he was patient, playing out the game. Fraser's apparent disinterest didn't fool me. I caught his look once and I knew what he was after.

Over the next few days I wore my soft slippers to go downstairs. Fraser wasn't home or he didn't hear me crossing the hall, and I was able to enjoy my cigarettes alone. I took up the habit of leaning over the balustrade to watch the ravens circling in the sky.

Two days later I found him outside already, smoking in the company of two Inuit women. I greeted them and turned my back to them to finish my cigarette. Fraser didn't seem to have noticed my presence and continued his conversation even while I re-entered the building.

The next Sunday I got confirmation that my instinct had been right. When I went out, I found Fraser talking with that middle-aged woman. She too was an old smoking acquaintance of mine, but we had never exchanged a word except for a casual greeting. There were some folks in this area that radiated the deepest solitude and sadness; she was one of them. She never chatted as people usually did about the weather and the crows. Her eyes were big and always red, as if she had just stopped crying. On the weekends I could see, underneath her long parka, the pyjamas she kept on all day long. She was alone, despite the fact she wore a wedding ring.

This time, she was laughing with Fraser. I greeted them, then turned my back to them. Smoking was not a social activity for me, quite the opposite. As my mom once observed, it was the fullest expression of my solitude.

I smoked half my cigarette then deliberately chose the moment when Fraser was in the middle of a sentence to throw the butt away. Before I could close the inner door, I heard him say goodbye to the woman. By the time I'd reached the middle of the corridor, he'd caught up to me.

"Are you staying home today?" he asked me as he got close.

"Yes," I said, only half turned.

"Then, I'll come over to have a little chat."

My mind froze.

"Okay."

He disappeared into his apartment and I continued on my way.

Why did I agree so quickly? I knew on the spot this was a terrible mistake, one that could put me in danger. Fraser was not the type you fool around with. Despite his friendly look, I didn't doubt he was a predator.

I made my mind to not open the door. I covered the peephole with a Band-Aid, switched off the TV and lay on the couch.

Half an hour later, he knocked. I was on the sofa, waiting. A few seconds later, he rapped once again before giving up. Maybe he was still confident that I wanted to let him in. That I was probably taking a shower, getting ready for him.

I remained on the sofa, motionless. Somehow, I guessed he would be back.

Five minutes later, he was knocking on my door again, stronger and harder. I thought he would call my name or ask me if I was inside. I was more worried about the fact the noise would alert my neighbours. Every so often, there were harsh knockings on some doors, mostly at night. Once, the police had to intervene and arrest a drunken man. I thought that I should maybe go ahead and alert the police before Fraser alarmed any of my neighbours. But he decided to make no fuss. He left after one last knock, so harsh it startled me.

CHAPTER THREE:

Wind and Snow

NOVEMBER STARTED WITH a terrible blizzard. Despite early-morning warnings, the school decided to keep its doors open till the bad weather was actually upon us. The bus drivers had the power to shut down schools, because of the slippery roads and bad visibility. That morning both were good, so the drivers followed their regular schedule. The six buses came one after the other and unloaded the kids. Before the bell rang, the youngest ones were on top of the mound of snow that had been piled up when the parking was cleared, while the older ones were sliding on their backpacks down the slope facing the bay.

That day I was in charge of supervising the north gate where parents usually dropped off the kids. I was talking to a girl from another teacher's class when I saw the constable's police car stop across the parking lot on the other side of the road. He was scanning around to see Eli, but she was already in the yard behind the school. Through the open window of his car he saw me turn around like a weathervane against the wind that changed direction every minute. He waved at me the same way parents did when they left their kids.

Shortly after, Ana joined me, decked out in the fluores-
cent vest over her parka. I was often forgetting mine inside,
despite the fact that it was mandatory to wear it during our
surveillance period outside, but no one made a fuss. She
greeted the constable and then looked at me. Everyone at
the school was aware he was chasing me, but no one had
asked me about it. Their daily hints and hunger for gossip
made me even more reluctant to speak about it. What
should I tell them? I was surrounded by women waiting for
a man, and me, I was running away from one deemed eli-
gible and suitable. I turned my whole body against the wind
and when I looked back, the car was gone.

The early morning was rather quiet. The snowfall was
a gentle forecast of Christmastime. By ten o'clock, though,
the gale got up like a hungry dragon out of its cave. The
morning's gentle snowflakes suddenly turned into fluffy
feathers. The sky became a big swollen pillow. The blasts of
wind were swirling and throwing the snow against the
windowpanes, splashing like pebbles. In the classroom, the
kids left their desks to cluster around the windowsills and
peer outside. The small island in the middle of the bay was
lost in the fog. The swings in the playground were swaying
so hard the chains were getting tangled around the iron
poles. Eli said that ghosts were rocking there.

I was the only one to stare at her in surprise, since her
classmates no longer reacted to her gloomy ideas. Why was
this girl so morose? Her bad moods made me nervous. The
air became unsteady around her, filled with danger. Nothing seemed light around Eli except her see-through blouses.
I supposed this was why the constable wanted me to be
more comfortable and easy-going around her. But when

parents intervene to make a teacher befriend their child, the effect is usually disastrous. I couldn't even feel pity for her loss. I figured motherless daughters would act more softly, but Eli was a feisty fighter. She was merciless to her peers and made imposing demands on me to punish them for each tiny mischief.

She started focusing her entire soul on one classmate, chubby Isabelle, who was getting uncomfortable with all that love. When Isabelle chose to pair with someone else for teamwork, Eli looked bewildered. She stared at her friend, dumb with sorrow and pain. Afterward, it took Isabelle a long time to restore their friendship.

It was not easy for me to defend Eli after listening to what the other girls had to say about her mood swings or hurtful remarks. Sometimes, I even had to intervene and ask Eli to at least listen to their explanations. Her classmates would discuss this in my presence, which irked Eli even more as she was convinced I always took their side.

A few days before, during recess, one of her classmates gave everybody candy except for one girl. Eli told her she should be nicer to people. The girl who gave the candy started to cry and came to tell me she was always nice to people. I asked Eli to come and apologize, which she did, saying it was only a joke. If everybody knew that girl was kind to people, then why would she get angry? Why would she care what Eli said? The conflict didn't stop there, though, because now it was Eli's turn to hold a grudge against someone who had no sense of humour. Which surprised me, coming from some-one whose gloomy mood was a constant.

Everything Eli did was dark, ominous. She drew igloos with bolded lines as if the snow tiles were cut in charcoal.

While the others were playing, enjoying the rare free time on their schedule, she opted to search the Internet for pictures, then copy them by tracing overtop of the outline. Now and then, she came to show me her attempts.

Weeks earlier, I had started a competition to choose the best drawing of an Inuk grandma for an art project. She kept on attempting to create the best image even after the contest was over. She won the competition not because her sketches were the best, but because she did dozens of them. She drew not only the characters I asked for, but a whole story, replete with blue whale, dwarfs and many, many igloos in all shapes and sizes. The snow tiles and the tunnel-like entrances were drawn with extraordinary precision, each igloo true to a single perspective.

The zipper of her parka had recently broken, so at recess she would go outside with the two flaps of her coat swaying over her sleeveless top. I had sent a message in English to her granny, but the parka was still not fixed. Every time I was around to watch them getting dressed for recess, she came to ask for help. At one point I almost fixed the zipper, but she did an awkward twist and the two sides of her parka hung wide open again. When I hurried her outside despite not having solved the problem, she said to me in a harsh voice: "You told us we should be properly dressed when we go outside."

I looked at her, struggling to repress my anger.

"Then why don't you put a sweater on?"

"But my problem is with the zipper."

"If you are too hot for a sweater, you don't need to fix the zipper. So, please go outside."

I hated seeing how cleverly she exploited her situation.

The other kids could be oblivious to her being a motherless daughter, but she knew that adults should not be that insensitive. She had been through something tragic, and those who did not care about it were cruel and heartless. I was cruel and heartless. And I was sure Eli understood that this mortified me.

That day, the principal decided to send the students out for recess despite the raging gale. I monitored their dressing in the corridor, with one eye on Eli and her half-open parka. Five minutes after they were sent into the cold, the principal called them back inside. The strong winds were toppling them over and snatching their hats. The principal announced over the radio that we were closing the school, following the usual procedure. No adult could leave till the last student had left the building. Kids were paired with their older siblings and kept in the classroom till their parents could pick them up. Some of my students went to join their older siblings in other classes, but I had to shelter the little ones in my classroom.

They came in small groups, dragging their winter gear down the corridors. Soon, their snow pants, parkas, mittens and mufflers were lying all over my floor. After staring at me for a few seconds, some rushed to write on the blackboard. Those who had already put on their snow pants and parkas decided to wait for their parents lying on the floor.

When a blizzard warning was in effect, the whole city closed down, including the government offices, shops and public services. Everybody had to stay indoors. Walking and driving were both highly restricted in bad weather. Slippery roads and poor visibility were the worst nemeses during blizzards. When I was ready to go home, Carole and Grant offered me a ride. The roads were already very dangerous and street signs were invisible more than few metres ahead.

Grant stopped at the Quick Stop to fill the tank. While he was paying inside, Carole turned to me from her front seat.

"Sunday evening, that handsome man came to the Legion. I think he was looking for you."

There was no point pretending to be surprised by her remark. Carole knew everything in the community. After so many years living in Iqaluit, she could easily detect a broken heart. And hearts seemed to break often at this latitude. Everybody was aware of the constable's pursuit, but the mystery she couldn't yet solve was why I would turn him down.

I remained silent, watching the passers-by through the car window. They were struggling against the wind, their faces hidden inside their hoods.

Carole looked at me with curiosity in her eyes and a flicker at the corner of her mouth. Was I going to tell the truth?

I said nothing.

"Why are you rejecting him?" she asked with a benevolent attitude.

"Because he is my pupil's uncle."

I knew she would never accept this excuse.

"I don't see your point," she said without blinking.

"I don't feel comfortable having a relationship with a pupil's guardian. Everybody would know, especially the girl. I have enough problems with her already. She is so headstrong."

"You're in the Arctic! Forget about what people would think or say down South. We aren't just parents or teachers. We're human beings."

This sounded like such an incitement to indecent behaviour that I smiled.

"I'll find another way to make it through the year," I said. "An Arctic fling won't make it shorter or warmer."

"That guy is unhappy, and so are you," Carole said, unconvinced by my reasoning.

She was a tough teacher, but I could also be a pretty disobedient pupil. I won't kowtow to a summons without a strong argument against me.

"I'm not unhappy. *Au contraire*. I am quite satisfied with my life," I said, trying to hide my growing impatience with her.

"When you're that young and that satisfied, you are unhappy. Young people should never be satisfied."

Carole's idea about me being unhappy seemed silly and dramatic. I was not buying into her philosophy that divided human feelings in two categories—happy or unhappy. We were all relentlessly looking for happiness through love, or just sex.

And how well did Carole know the constable? Was she playing cat and mouse with me?

"Why would he be unhappy?" I asked in a bland tone.

"He seems so," she answered. "I mean, what man runs after someone who keeps rejecting him?"

"He knows I am leaving in the summer and he wants no commitment. Everything is so easy for people like him! They believe they can run this place on their terms and they are not used to being rejected, especially by women. I'd be nothing more than a commodity to him. Something like a one night-stand.

"My guess is that he wants you for more than one night."

"I don't know about that. But you have to admit that even a six-month relationship is technically a one-night stand around here."

"Many good romances don't last that long."

I saw Grant come out of the Quick Stop fighting to catch his breath, one hand holding a coffee mug and the other, his cap. I made a small signal, and Carole turned back in her seat. I was sure that Grant was aware of my personal life, but he had the decency to show some discretion.

Carole let me off the hook and I started wondering why Grant would buy coffee on his way home. Maybe it was just for the aroma. This place was so odourless that people would do anything to enjoy some familiar scents.

In the car, Grant pointed to the sky and we looked up. Three ravens were circling above us, floating in the air, carried by the gusts, joyfully swirling with the changing winds.

"They adore this weather," he said. "Look how they enjoy flying in the storm."

Grant had a different vision of the Arctic than his wife. Carole was interested in people's stories, while Grant focused on the broad history from an imperial perspective. His ancestors had fought in the battle for Montreal in 1812. They had built ships in the harbour of Quebec City and made some money in the lumber industry after the fur trade was over. From the Arctic Circle, he was able to look back on the past with a peaceful mind.

He drove the car toward Happy Valley to avoid the traffic on Niaqunngusiariaq Street. Half turned to the back seat, Carole started talking to me again, in French. Despite her marriage to an anglophone, she was still more comfortable in her mother tongue. They both came from Gaspésie.

Carole had been born into a wealthy francophone family and Grant into an old-stock Loyalist one. His ancestors came to Canada after the American Revolution, which is how Grant inherited his unconditional faith in the British Empire. Carole said the reason they got along so well was because they were both country folk, "*des gens de region.*" I supposed they were right. In Montreal they would have probably never become acquainted even if living two blocks away in the same neighbourhood.

At the second turn in the road toward Happy Valley, Carole pointed to a red two-storey building. The previous day, a woman had hanged herself from the window using her bed sheets. Grant didn't look in the direction of her hand.

Close to the post office, she asked me if I cared for a drink before going home. She said they had too much alcohol at home and wanted to get rid of it before leaving in December. I said no, so they let me off at the back door of my building. They waited till I entered before driving on.

I was smoking on the patio when I saw Fraser buffeted by the gusts blowing down the back alley. He saw me too, despite the snow. It was too late to run away. Maybe this was a good opportunity to put an end to our misunderstanding. Since that incident, I rarely went down for a smoke in the evening. I made do with a last smoke the moment I got back from the school. My vigilance in avoiding Fraser had reduced my cigarette intake to only two a day, and I was slowly getting used to it.

He went up to the porch in what seemed like slow

motion. His reddened face contrasted with his white beard, heavy with icicles. He greeted me and fetched his pack of smokes, but then pretended to look for his lighter.

I took off my glove and gave him mine. Our fingers touched, though I'd tried to prevent it. It took him a long time to light his cigarette because of the wind. He drew repeatedly to keep it burning, then he handed back my lighter. I thrust it into my pocket and put my glove on as fast as I could.

After another puff, he asked me the question I'd heard so often, while looking straight into my eyes. "So, what are you doing in Iqaluit?"

This time, he made no effort to put a chatty smile on his face.

"I teach French."

"Where? The government offices?" He turned his back against a new gale.

"No, the French school."

He made a move with his head, but he didn't comment. A gust of wind rattled the whole shelter, hitting us with snow. We turned to the wall simultaneously.

"Do you know what I do for a living?"

"No," I said.

"I'm a correctional officer."

"Oh." I drew on my cigarette.

He added nothing, looking at the ravens circling in the sky.

"I heard there was an incident at the prison last month," I said. "I saw it on the local news."

"Oh, yes! Those guys really wrecked their cell," he said, then went silent.

We both smoked quietly.

"How long have you been in this city?" I asked after a while.

"Twelve years," he said without looking at me.

Twelve years of smoking on this patio, blown by the wind, looking at the ravens!

"This is practically your home."

He laughed and shook his head.

"I don't think so. No one is quite home in this place."

"It is a tough city."

"I'm tougher," he replied with a smirk.

I felt my cigarette almost burning my glove and threw it away. I rummaged for the keys in my pocket, but Fraser opened the door for me.

"Stay warm," he said when I was half inside.

"You too," I said with a smile as I turned to him.

The next day, the school remained open despite the announcement that the weather was not getting any better. The ploughs had passed through the whole city, and the bus drivers succeeded in picking up students from all its remote corners. The rule was that, if there was a single kid who could not attend classes because of the weather, all schools had to close. In some neighbourhoods, the wind had caused a lot of damage, tearing off the roofs and uprooting the hydro poles. By morning, the gales had diminished in strength to under ninety km/h, which was the threshold for blizzard warnings.

The principal decided to send the kids out for recess.

As usual, they tried to stall, lingering over their snow pants, parkas and boots. Then, they complained about their lost mittens or toques to gain more time inside.

Except for the time spent fiddling with her broken zipper, Eli never stalled when recess began, no matter the weather. It was like she was in a ferocious competition to be the first one in front of the gates to the schoolyard. Outside, she would drag Isabelle to a remote corner so they could whisper their secrets in English, which was against the rules of this French-only school.

Isabelle had three siblings and she took good care of them. When she came across them in the corridor, she kissed and hugged them. She was a chubby, soft-spoken girl with a broad smile, the sort of person whom everybody wanted to befriend. Most of the time, she seemed to prefer Eli, yet her allegiance could switch quite fast. When they were on good terms, they held hands and hugged now and then. Isabelle's mother was of Egyptian origin, but the girl got her features from her father, a blond, blue-eyed lawyer from Nova Scotia.

Like many of the kids at the French school, Isabelle had not been born and raised in the territory. The kids were nomadic like their parents—RCMP officers, soldiers, doctors, nurses, federal agents. They stayed in one place for three or four years, then moved onward to yet another location: New Brunswick, Nova Scotia, Alberta, Manitoba, Quebec. Since birth, they grew up in rented apartments, following local traditions, changing Halloween costumes according to each new environment and celebrating Christmas around a meal cooked with local flavour. Such rootlessness instilled a harsh and unsentimental attitude.

Yet, those who were born and raised in the North were much the same. From my perspective, there was little overall unity in my class. Ties were limited to very small groups. Contrary to my teaching philosophy, after a month I allowed the students to follow their allegiances and move their desks next to their friends. It was noisier than usual, but it reassured me to let them spend the day next to their soul mate.

At the recent parents' meeting, I learned that one of my students, Thomas, was to leave Iqaluit in three weeks as his father had been dispatched to Halifax. He was sad but not overly so. Lately his appetite for learning had dropped a notch while his insolence mounted exponentially. He had been a mischievous kid from the beginning, full of intrigue, but subtly so, and he succeeded in never getting caught. He was always plotting, but other children invariably paid for his schemes. He grew quiet and sweet as soon as he sensed retribution coming. The others never accused him of any wrongdoing. Except for Eli, no one understood they were being manipulated. She was the only one to complain about him. Yet, her criticism made me angry. I knew Thomas was cheating, but who didn't?

One day, Eli came to tell me that Thomas had left the classroom without permission. It was the end of the day. Sometimes I allowed them to fetch their clothes before the bell. Getting all that winter gear on was frustrating at the best of times. When the bell rang, they were all in a panic not to miss the buses. What they felt was not the excitement of going home, but rather the fear of being left behind.

That day I was busy sorting things on my desk, so Thomas took the chance to sneak out. There were two more minutes till the final bell, so he thought I wouldn't notice. He would have been right, if it hadn't been for Eli.

I put aside my papers and looked at her sternly.

"Je n'aime pas les porte-panniers," I said.

She didn't understand the word, but my frown gave her a good hint that she was the one in trouble, not Thomas. Her French was still quite bad. She could only guess at the meaning of many words, and she was unable to form full and complex sentences. Her lack of fluency was not a surprise given that outside of school she only spoke English. She stared at me, waiting for an explanation she could make sense of. I said nothing.

"Thomas left," she said again. "Before the bell."

"Why do you bother with what others do?"

Now she understood that I was not going to punish Thomas for stretching the rules. Worse still, I was angry with her, not with the culprit.

She took her place in line, looking at me with astonishment, unsure what it was she did wrong.

I was angry because she was always asking me to be vigilant and mete out justice. I was waiting for them to sort out things themselves. I didn't want to be the judge of their petty crimes.

What was my mission anyway? To teach them the encyclopaedia? To make them mathematicians, physicians, astronauts?

I was tired of the curriculum. Children didn't trust us the way pupils of long ago trusted their mentors. Technology was replacing us. Kids were now caught in algorithms that decided for them.

I wanted to tell Eli it was not for me to decide the

consequences of their wrongdoings. They knew better than me what was right and wrong. I was just another inadequate teacher of modern times, out-dated and old-fashioned at only thirty-four. Why did she ask so much from me? Thomas would know what to do because he himself knew better than me.

Why wasn't she doing the same, instead of appointing me as judge?

The police car had stopped following me. Eli wore the same summer clothing and my messages in the agenda were never signed. I guessed the constable was on his usual tour in remote communities investigating gory crimes. The latest news reported on a man in Kimmirut, at the south end of the Baffin Island, barricaded in his house, firing at everything in sight. One woman was shot dead and two others wounded. People were warned not to get any closer to house number 435 for their own sake.

On Monday, Eli got a poor mark on her science test. Apparently, she didn't study, because no one saw my message where I had asked parents to help review the material. The next morning I found a message in her agenda from her uncle saying that she didn't know about the slip of paper with printed information about the exam. The message also asked for a meeting after school. I should have known he was around after seeing the cotton sweater Eli was wearing over her T-shirt. I decided to make an excuse and invented a meeting with the principal.

At noon, I got an email from the constable. Parents

knew our Government of Nunavut email address and could message us anytime. The constable was asking for confirmation of our meeting. I replied that I would probably be busy with a staff meeting. He quickly wrote back saying he could wait. My defence was useless. Eli had been in this school from kindergarten, so he probably knew there were no meetings on Tuesdays.

Usually, after school, I left as soon as possible. Regardless of the weather, I liked to walk back home, to clear my mind and stretch my legs. I usually hurried to catch the last glow of light. Since the clocks had changed, daylight was ebbing at three p.m. Close to the bay, the sun was like an electrical bulb screwed into the clouds. The light seemed like a huge ray projected over the surface of the water. I stopped every day to savour it at the last turn of the road before entering Happy Valley.

I was angry about being deprived of those moments of pure delight. That solitary beam would fade away long before I reached the bay. No matter what I said to him, I was sure the constable would keep me late at the school.

I did my last tour of the corridor to see my students to their buses and spotted the constable in front of the office window, talking with an army guy, the father of an autistic boy. The dad was at the school often to watch over his son. When tired, the kid ran around the desks and threw things. The situation would get to the point that the parents had to pick him up, since the school offered no services for students with such specialized needs.

The constable saw me and nodded while still talking to the officer. There was no way to avoid him. Eli was on the bench with the other kids, waiting for the school bus. A red ribbon cordoned them off from the entrance hall, where some parents were waiting for the kids who were not registered with the bus service. Eli smiled at her uncle when their eyes met. She sat next to Isabelle, waiting for the moment when the secretary would tell them to go outside. The six buses had not yet arrived. The French school was the last stop on their route.

Eli didn't look at me. She had never been the most cheerful of children, unlike her peers who usually rushed to greet me every time we passed each other in the corridor. Her uncle was now the focus of all her attention. When she saw me stopping next to the benches, she realized the reason for his presence here and her smile froze instantly.

I said hello to both men and asked the constable to follow me. He took off his boots and tossed them in a corner. When he stooped under the red ribbon, he touched Eli with his gloves. The girl giggled and pulled back her head.

In my class, there was a little stench from the bean seedlings. We were growing them for our science project on germination, but many experiments had gone wrong, leaving a rotten odour from the cotton soaking in the water for too long. The small pots were lined up on the windowsill. Every morning, Kaniq, the other Inuk boy in my class, asked permission to turn them around to prevent the plants growing one-sided. He was the only one who remembered that tiny detail about the impact of light on seedlings. After completing his task, he'd stand there and stare at them for minutes. A few seconds of exposure to the cold outside meant a cruel death for them. He sometimes asked me what would happen if we opened the window. I would make a scary face, like someone seeing a ghost, and he'd laugh, hard.

The students had put their chairs up on their desks, but pieces of paper, crayons and crumbs were scattered all over the floor. After two months, I had not yet succeeded in curbing their messiness. Eli was right: I was too loose on discipline. Maybe she knew better than me that one day they would get completely out of my control.

The constable followed me to my desk, then waited for a signal from me to grab a seat. At that moment, Eli popped inside the classroom, boots in hand. She said she forgot something. She headed to her place to search for her notebook, but I knew that she never usually bothered to bring it home. Was she checking on me and her uncle?

I asked her to stay and clarify the misunderstanding about the last exam. The constable was not happy about raising the issue, but Eli hastily agreed.

She brought a chair to my desk and sat next to her uncle. I was enjoying my authority: I had finally trapped them both. My desk was as clean and neat as my intentions. On one side, there was a tidy pile of binders, on the other, a box full of colouring pencils and crayons. I have never been fond of excess. For the most part, a student can make do with a crayon and an eraser. Yet that box of goodies was a real lifesaver for those who often misplaced their school supplies.

The constable was not prepared to face me in Eli's company. I wondered if he felt unable to protect the girl against my ire. For the moment, he seemed to be preparing to hear a rundown of her misdeeds.

Eli, on the other hand, was happy to see her uncle facing me. His police uniform must have given her the idea that he would finally teach me a lesson. I was waging a war against everything she did and believed in, and now it was time for her revenge.

The constable kept his parka on to hide his gun from Eli. Sweat was beading all over his forehead. He was quiet but his eyes were fuming with anger. I was jubilant. He was finally trapped.

"So, if I understand correctly, this is all about the science exam."

I moved my eyes from one to the other. Eli was not preoccupied with this issue. She'd received a bad mark, but this was not the first one. At my remark, she realized, though, that this could be a problem for her uncle.

"Eli said she didn't know about the exam," he said while looking at his niece.

"But the message to parents was there, at the bottom of the page, in their agenda. I understand her granny doesn't speak French, but Eli can translate. Not to mention that the message was a reminder to her and not to Granny."

"She said she also forgot to bring home her science notes."

I threw a suspicious look at Eli.

"That's very surprising, Eli," I said, "because *I* put the homework in the agenda, not you. And I do this *every day*, with *every kid*. How did I skip yours?"

Eli stared at me in silence. She knew this was not like a typical day when I could scold her, and she had to swallow it because her limited French made it hard to argue back. Sometimes she would try to reply with a mumbling "*Mais, mais*," but usually she was quick to abandon the fight.

This time Eli figured she had a strong ally against me. Moreover, she could catch every word of our English exchange.

Powerless in front of his niece's growing anger, the constable tried a last diversion. "Granny can't help with homework, though."

"I told Eli many times, homework is not for the parents, it's for the kids. If they don't understand, it's okay. Next day at school we will correct the errors. It has always been like this. I have told them many times that parents shouldn't get involved too much."

The constable was running out of arguments and Eli sensed his weakness. Her eyes were bubbling with anger, waiting for a solution. He gave up.

"Grand so, that's a relief," he said, trying to seem light and watching her tenderly. "You see? Homework doesn't have to be perfect. You do what you can, then you complete it in class."

"Homework is not an exam," I said. "It doesn't count for marks. I only have to see evidence that you made some effort at home."

The constable was looking kindly at Eli, begging her for mercy. They both felt he had let her down.

"You heard, Eli?" he said. "It's okay if you don't finish your homework. You just have to try."

He was addressing her in English, but she was no more talkative than in French. She was in shock that all this fuss had not been to her advantage as she expected.

The secretary peered in from behind the open door and addressed Eli in French. The bus had arrived. She looked at her uncle hoping for a ride, but he said: "It's better you go home on the bus. Granny will be worried."

"But you could drive me home," Eli said in a plaintive voice.

"Still, Granny will think something has happened at school."

Eli stood up in haste. The constable tried to grab her arm, but she left without saying goodbye to either of us.

He looked at me. There was no anger, no interrogation, just a blank void in his eyes.

I was playing with a pencil, looking out the window. Darkness had fallen over the bay. There was nothing I could see except for our own reflections.

"I should be going," I said, but I didn't move from my chair.

"I could give you a lift."

"I prefer to walk. It clears my mind."

"It's pretty fierce cold outside."

"I know. I have my snow pants."

He stood up and went to the door. I didn't follow him into the corridor.

Before leaving the room, I watered the seedlings and put the two chairs back on the desk.

At the end of the month, the school closed again for two days in a row because of the strong winds. The gales were coming in warm from the Atlantic Ocean, full of sea water. The rain melted the snow around the houses and over the hills. A few roofs and many lids from the garbage boxes were snatched by the wind and tossed away. Hydro poles were uprooted and toppled across the roads.

I was happy to stay home. On Monday, we went to school for only a few hours before the announcement that we had to close. Staff went through the usual routine with the kids, then went home by taxi. At NorthMart I stopped to do some errands. As usual, people were buying all they could grab. The checkout lines were too long, so I left and cut through the empty field in front of the Nakasuk School to get home. I had enough bread and milk in my fridge and I doubted the storm would last more than a day. I was eager to nestle down on my sofa with my new book from the library.

I was becoming more and more like my mother. For many years she had taken the liberty of spending the day on the sofa, oblivious to the outside world. But even my mother had changed lately. Ever since my stepfather died, leaving her a widow with a secure income, she didn't enjoy staying home anymore. The pleasure of doing nothing had been more satisfying when everybody else was bustling like ants, expecting her to do the same. Now that she had no one making demands on her, my mother found staying home quite boring.

She started volunteering at the community centre, and soon after the director asked her to teach the kids art classes. With her talent for knitting and sewing, she proposed adding some workshops for those interested in crafts. Now she was out three days a week, the longest work hours she had ever put in. During our last phone call, she told me about an art exhibit they were setting up at the public library in Côte-des-Neiges.

In one of her emails, my mother suggested I should teach my students knitting. I laughed at first. I just couldn't imagine my pupils bent over their needles, careful with those tricky loops. In our conversation over the phone, my mother persisted. She said that adults were guilty for kids gradually withdrawing from the real world. That it was inevitable that people's creative skills become dormant, repressed by the convenience of manufactured products, but that the ability to survive is just waiting to be brought to life. That my students' ancestral skills were simply repressed by decades of ready-mades, that their manual abilities were just waiting to be unearthed. She even said that, in her craft group, some boys had better knitting skills than the girls. In the end, I decided to give it a try. Mother volunteered to send me yarn and needles.

I lingered on the sofa the whole afternoon, listening to the strong gusts. I ate and took naps whenever I felt like it. Sometimes, I got up to peer through the window onto Queen Elizabeth Way. For some time, there were still cars and passers-by venturing to pick up their mail as the Canada Post remained opened a few more hours. As time went on, the blasts strengthened and the rain started drumming against the windowpanes.

Darkness had settled in by two o'clock. I turned on the light and decided to cook something. I had taken up the local habit of making a stew with chunks of meat like isolated icebergs on a sea of vegetable floes. People made use of anything that was fading in the back of the fridge: celery leaves, crushed tomatoes, withered carrots. Everything made it into the stew, a veritable jigsaw that reflected the scarcity of food in the North and the inflated prices at the shops. This meal was eaten with a spoon, fishing first for the best pieces and lingering over the sometimes unrecognizable chunks left at the bottom of the bowl. Food was not always a joy, it was survival. Even the rich experienced this sense of poverty.

In the teachers' room at noon, we snuck glances at each

other's lunches. Who was eating grapes, watermelon, strawberries? And how many of us resorted to spaghetti with no parmesan on top?

I fried the meat with the onions then added a full plate of carrots, rutabaga and potatoes. I let it simmer for a while. The smell filled every corner of the apartment. The strong odours throughout the building indicated everybody had taken the day off. The potent scent of seal meat from my Inuit neighbours was sweet and heavy.

I heard a knock on the door and ignored it. After a few more knocks, I knew it was someone who wouldn't go away.

When I answered it, I saw the constable standing one step outside of the doorframe, with dishevelled hair and his wet parka. Now that I was in slippers and he in his winter boots, he towered over me at the threshold.

I let him inside without a word. He stopped at the door and took his boots off. Suddenly I realized how dirty my apartment was. I had not swept the floor in days, and the sand brought in off my boots was crunching under my slippers. It didn't bother me anymore, but the constable was going to get it all on his socks. The bathroom was the worst, the sink marked with toothpaste that I never bothered to clean out. Why was I worried about it, though? Would he really need to use my bathroom? From the entrance, he would have been able to peek through to my bedroom and see my pyjamas tossed over the unmade duvet.

I led him to the living room. On the sofa, there was a pair of socks from the morning and on the armchair, my outdoor gear. It had been a few weeks since I stopped going to the trouble of hanging them in the closet. The big table in the living room was an even bigger mess. Stuff had been piling up for a long time: the envelope with my last pay, my wallet, my keys, a cup of tea, a nail clipper, a burlap carrier bag for grocery shopping, a plate with orange peels, a bowl of dried fruit, a bottle of Tylenol and a pile of books. I never ate at the table, so it had turned into a shelf. On top of all that mess, there was the odour of my cooking, the whiff of onions and potatoes, testimonies of a poorhouse kitchen. It made me feel puny and meek.

I made no excuse for the untidiness. He had no reason to be here, to breach the intimacy of my home and breathe the stench of my fried onions. I got rid of my clothes on the armchair, and the constable sat down without a word. Then I gathered the socks, took them into the bathroom and came back to sit down on the sofa as silently as before. We were like two armies finally brought to the negotiating table. There was no reason for niceties; the bargaining would be tough. We both stood to lose something.

The constable stared for a while at the coffee table that separated us and analyzed the cover of the three books I was reading concurrently. This gave him another few minutes to settle himself calmly in the room. My empty cup, where the dregs had dried on the bottom, likely gave him another minute of deep reflection, while I was busy wondering about my own lassitude.

The constable passed his hand over his face wet with rain. A box of tissues was on the table, but he didn't reach for one. I wondered if he'd come in the police car, but either way, he would have had to leave it in the parking lot behind the post office. As there were not enough places, all visitors had to park at the other end of the lot. When Iqaluit was built, there were only a few cars, so parking lots were low on the list of the city planners. Now the number of cars was growing every year, and getting a spot in front of shops, offices and churches had become a challenge.

The constable was discreetly peering around, but I was not at all embarrassed by my dwelling's emptiness. After spending a childhood in a house full of knick-knacks, I liked the simplicity. The furniture was provided by the Nunavut Housing Corporation, and I felt no compunction to add a personal touch. The constable must have been used to this kind of desolation, which likely marked so many of the rooms where he led his investigations. Folks like me, coming for a season or a year at most, did not invest much in home decor.

One of the windows was ajar to let the fresh air clear out the odour of fried onions. The vertical strips of the blinds clattered, hitting the walls as they were blown by the wind. I went to close the window. When I came back, I saw his eyes looking down to the floor. I was wearing baggy gym pants and a beige T-shirt, both a little frumpy. My hair was unkempt, twisted around a pencil on the top of my head. Not only was the apartment a mess, but my own appearance exuded sloppiness and indifference.

The constable had put on a new shirt for this meeting. He was freshly shaven and wore a spotless cotton sweater. Still, I could sense his body's distinct odour, the same as I picked up on in his car. His specific signature was a mix of fuel and smoke. As a parka could not be replaced or cleaned too often in the North, it carried in its folds and seams small particles of the owner's skin and hair. Lingering human scent followed people everywhere, testifying to their passage long after they moved on.

He was staring at the empty cup, but I didn't offer to make any tea. We could not pretend anymore that this was just a teacher-parent relationship. I found this so difficult. The constable must too, I thought.

"I wonder if you gave any thought to what I said. About us." His voice almost choked.

I said nothing. My eyes were wandering from one place to another, pondering my reaction.

"I am not really ready for this."

"Are you married?" he asked, raising his eyebrows.

"No. Not anymore."

The answer surprised him, but he quickly passed over it.

"Did you get a divorce?"

"Yes," I said without looking at him.

"D'you have any kids?"

"No, no kids."

"Was that an issue for your marriage?"

I looked at him, gave a faint shrug. How could he be so stupid to assume that not having kids would end a marriage?

"No, it wasn't."

My voice made him squirm a bit with embarrassment.

"Is there anyone in Montreal?".

"No!"

This interrogation drained me. I looked at him. His mouth, nose and eyes gave him that ripe beauty of a man at the age when youth and maturity are well balanced. There was kindness and knowledge in his face. The constable was a likeable man, and I knew I could easily fall in love with him. Maybe too easily.

Right from our first encounter, I felt that he was way too cautious for a man seeking a fling. He didn't laugh much and didn't tell jokes. Being funny can be helpful when you want to entice a woman to bed. That's why I wondered if he even liked me.

"I think it's rather a matter of convenience for you," I said at last. "And I am not interested in a convenient relationship."

He gave me a sad look.

"Love doesn't come all at once. We'd get to know each other first."

"I've never been with a man without being in love with him, or imagining I was in love with him."

He kept on looking at me.

"We should stop acting like we're twenty," he said.

He was growing slightly impatient and I became worried.

"A sexual relationship is not what life is all about."

I was surprised to hear myself saying this. He felt lectured, and this saddened him even more.

"Relationships are important. It doesn't have to be sexual."

"So, you are asking me just to be your friend. In which way?"

"In any way. Just to meet up, see a movie, eat together. You could even come to my place."

"I do not want to be involved in Eli's life."

"I understand that. She won't be there, if that's the problem."

"I don't want to make you stay away from your niece. She needs you. You are the only other adult who cares for her properly. There are many things I really do not understand.

What I do know is that I want to stay out of this ... this family situation."

"I understand that. But it only means we won't be able to meet on Sundays and Saturdays. During the week she doesn't come to my place."

I kept silent for a while.

"There are a few things you should know about me," he said, "but first we'd have to meet more often. That way we could speak our minds. Maybe this would help us make up our minds about what to do in the future."

Again this talk about *us!* I think he became aware of my quiet rage.

He got up to leave. I followed him from behind to close the door. As he reached the entrance hall, he looked at me with hesitation, then said: "Do you have a thing for your neighbour, Fraser?"

His eyes showed a cold detachment, the first time I'd seen this in him.

"What do you mean?"

He looked at the floor, then at me again.

"I saw you smoking on the patio with that guy. Not just smoking, but talking."

When had he seen me and Fraser? I had no recollection of seeing a police car around any of the times I was smoking outside. I knew all the angles of the street and all the possible venues from where he could pop up. I too was gifted with the intuition of a detective. Yet nothing came to mind.

The constable pondered awhile. Then he decided to tell me the truth.

"I saw you on the camera."

"What camera?"

"From the post office. There's a surveillance camera above the back door, next to your building. They're connected to our office to avoid break-ins."

"You mean you're following me on your surveillance camera?"

"Not you precisely. The whole building."

I didn't believe him. This had to be a lie. No policeman would just amuse himself by rewinding video surveillance footage unless it was necessary.

He let me calm down for a while, then he said again: "I have to warn you about that man. He's dangerous. Don't trust him."

I tried to keep my voice down, but I knew I was shouting when I turned back to him. "That man never followed me against my will. I turned him down and he accepted it."

The constable's eyes were downcast. I still encountered Fraser now and then in the hallway. Sometimes I was on the porch smoking when he was arriving home, but he never stopped to light a cigarette. His demeanour remained sombre; he never gave even a glimmer of a smile. Smiling was not in his repertoire. Frowning at people was his profession.

How many surveillance cameras was the constable monitoring to keep an eye on me?

"That guy has been the most civil person I have met since I got here," I said.

The constable looked at me coldly.

"That guy wouldn't be all that civil if I hadn't told him to be," he said, then opened the door.

CHAPTER FOUR:

Fathers and Children

I N DECEMBER, FROBISHER Bay got its final frozen coat. First, the sea became like a thick grey soup. Then it coalesced to form pancakes of ice that thickened into rafts. The layers gradually piled on top of each other, moved and pressured by enormous force, to the point that the ice formed ridges and hummocks. The air became alive with darting crystals and ice smoke.

Two weeks before the Christmas holiday, I finally met Eli's father.

When the principal called to tell me that one of the parents wanted to see me, I was cleaning the classroom, in a hurry to leave. Getting home was a kind of emergency even if there was nothing to do once I got there. I think that the urgency of getting home is nourished by the fundamental need to be in a secure place for the night, to sink deep in sleep as a sanctuary against the elements and, especially, against oneself.

It was past one o'clock and the dark and the cold were rapidly settling over our surroundings. In the blink of an eye, the sun slipped below the horizon and the polar night closed like a curtain. For the past weeks, the sky seemed to be a fluid ribbon between the white hills and the dark lid above. The movie of the short four-hour day played briefly in this hollow space. By ten o'clock, the hazy light of the dawn was highlighted with an orange tinge that timidly glowed till noon. Then, it rapidly darkened to the brief one-hour twilight. The sun was going to sleep without even touching the horizon, vanishing between the frozen bay and the shadowy layers above that seemed to comprise the whole universe.

Every day I made a resolution to follow that mysterious trajectory, but in vain. At the apex of the glowing light, just before sunset, something always seemed to be happening in my class that forced me away from the window. At two, I would suddenly realize that the neon tubes of our classroom were the only source of light around.

After the buses left, silence gradually prevailed over the daycare service next door. The daycare teacher was having problems with some of my students. To my surprise, once they left the classroom, they completely transformed. Seated behind their little desks, stirring on their plastic chairs, they were a flock of disciplined pupils. Beyond the door of my classroom, their repressed energy blasted like a solar eruption. Snack time was a good occasion for some to ask permission to go to the bathroom or get a drink of water and never to return until she began calling their names through the intercom. Furthermore, past that door, their English fluency instantly vanquished their broken French. In small groups, they scampered under the tables, barricaded behind walls built out of plastic boxes, trying to dodge the adults' vigilance over their oral skills. They became fierce commandoes defending the right of their dolls and soldiers to speak and play in English. Any adult who tried to command them otherwise got a mouthful of back-talk rife with discourtesy. What they acquiesced to do inside the classroom as a duty imposed by an unfair destiny and heartless parents became outside a questionable task they felt entitled to defy.

I put the rest of the chairs on top of the desks and gathered the last books, crayons, erasers and bottles. My revenge was to place them higgledy-piggledy on the table in the back of the class. In the morning, the pupils would have to spend some time finding their own tools and putting them back on their desks.

The secretary phoned to notify me that Eli's father was waiting for me in the hallway. I took a few minutes to compose my attitude and release the stress that had cramped my stomach. I was finally to meet the neglectful father! Where was he when I sent all those messages? Yet, my curiosity overshadowed my irritation. How much did he look like the constable? Why had he taken four months to inquire about his own daughter?

Maybe, the trauma he had experienced two years before was still so vivid that he needed to avoid anything that might resurface a memory of his wife! Meeting a new teacher could be a trial for people who had lived here for a long time. To him, I was just another visitor who'd come north with no awareness about this place, casting judgment on what I could not grasp. He was likely to predict that I might question his biracial marriage or, even worse, hold him responsible for his Inuk wife's suicide.

Maybe Eli had already given him a thorough description about me: intolerant, harsh, demanding, obsessed with values that did not belong in Iqaluit. I was as inadequate as any visitor who came here to experience something new and failed to appreciate it. The constable might have given him a rundown of my story: a single woman who took on the world on her own but was afraid to set herself free or to love. That I had come this far only to withdraw into a little cage, victim to my own limitations.

The class was now tidy, and I couldn't find any other excuse to postpone the encounter.

I went to the entrance, but the only person I saw was an Inuk man sitting on the bench. I bowed my head in his direction and continued to the secretary's little window.

"Where is he?" I asked.

She didn't answer, but she tilted her head in the Inuk man's direction. Her eyes expressed her shock at my blunder.

The man could not see her, but he heard my question and looked at me. He understood I was the teacher and stood up with a broad smile on his face.

"Hi Miss, my name is Victor Ivalu."

I was so taken aback by the fact that he was not white that I could only smile back, forgetting to introduce myself. We shook hands, regarding each other with interest.

He seemed to be a man with a frail constitution. His appearance hinted at a tumultuous existence. His complexion was mottled with dark patches, a testimony of his life on the open tundra. Frequent frostbite, likely endured since an early age, had left its impact. He didn't seem old, yet only his smile still maintained the spark of youthfulness. His left cheek down to his jaw carried the marks of a recent fight. Old and new bruises suggested eager fists had landed there.

He looked happy to see me.

"Eli speaks so highly about you," he said while still shaking my hand. "She said you are so kind."

I knew very well that this was not the truth, but there was no malice in his voice. Eli would not have passed on such praise. Her father was surely lying to me as an excuse for this belated visit.

I asked him to follow me into the class, and he did so submissively. When we entered the room, his excitement was sincere. "So, they moved in here! This is a nice classroom. Last year, they were in the other wing of the building. Do they see the bay from the window?"

"Yes, exactly, we look out on the bay from here."

"That's why she likes it so much," he said with childish enthusiasm. "Last year, their windows looked out on the parking lot."

I was in no position to agree with him on Eli's love of the landscape. She never looked outside. Even during the parhelion phenomenon, when three suns aligned at the horizon, she rarely paused her activities to peer out. She dismissed her colleagues' excitement with an elusive, "Those suns are just mock dogs!" During our reading period, when I allowed them to move around and choose whatever place they liked, Eli would ensconce herself under the table by the windowsill. She preferred the dim light of this cave-like hideout to the orange glow of the sky at its glorious zenith.

Her father continued inspecting the classroom. I showed him Eli's space with her binders perfectly lined up. He seemed very pleased to see it.

"She is a very tidy person," he said.

"Yes, indeed, she is."

On the wall opposite the door, we had pinned up the children's drawings about an Inuit legend. The father stopped to admire the artwork. He asked me which ones were Eli's. I pointed to hers, and he turned to me with that same enthusiastic expression.

"What do you think about them? I think she is very talented."

I glanced at him again, but there was no irony in his voice.

Despite his enthusiasm, Eli's drawings were not the best on the walls. She had worked too many details into them, suffocating the story. Eli didn't like empty spaces. When she was uncomfortable with a subject, she cushioned her discomfort by tracing lines, spirals and dots of different colours. More than shapes, she liked smells. After taking off the top of her Sharpies, she smelled them at length. Her favourite was the coconut aroma that emanated from the brown markers.

Her father took a chair and placed it at a modest distance from my desk.

"I really wanted to meet you before leaving for Pond Inlet tomorrow. I'll be missing for some weeks again. I must apologize I didn't come to see you sooner. I was very busy with my job. I know my brother takes good care of Eli."

To my surprise, he didn't have that soft-spoken Inuit rhythm. There was often a lot of wariness and care in every word the Inuit said, but this man had the same inflections as the constable. The way he pronounced some sounds, with that Irish emphasis on the last syllable, proved that they really did grow up together. Did this make them real brothers, though?

"I am very happy to meet you," I said.

"I must apologize that I don't speak French. When I was young, there was no French school in Iqaluit. My brother and I were educated in English, but he took French classes at university. And he worked with French people. I am sure you have nice talks '*dans la langue de Molière.*'"

He laughed at his accent, uttering that most ancient cliché about the French language. Why was French more Molière's language than any other writer's?

I smiled too, amused not by his pronunciation but because I imagined having a nice talk in French with the constable. Everything Victor said could be taken as sharp irony, but there was no meanness whatsoever in his tone. He was openly good, and he seemed to believe every word he said.

"To be honest, we speak in English."

"Really?" he said with genuine surprise. "I always thought his French was good."

"Maybe it is, but we prefer to speak English."

He laughed again with an open heart. He had an easy laugh, and I wondered how someone with such good manners got all those bruises.

I was struggling to focus on our conversation, overtaken by my own thoughts. The man was a shock to me. His presence upended everything I'd imagined about Eli and her family. I tried to identify a resemblance to his daughter, but there was none. The man's face was rather broad with rounded, slightly upturned eyes. His eyebrows were bushy and his lips thick. Eli's long face was organized more on a vertical plane, with a thin mouth and thin eyes.

His soft voice drew me once again from my thoughts.

"I am away from Iqaluit most of the time, but you should know I'm very much concerned with Eli's future. Education is important for our kids. You have my full support in every-thing."

His kindness was not enough to erase my old resent-ment. No wonder Eli was wearing those summer clothes, having such a credulous father. He saw talent where there was little, and a fervent pupil instead of a quarrelsome one.

As my silence grew longer than before, her father seemed to lose his confidence.

"Is she doing all right? Does she still love math? Last year she loved math." His tone was pleading. All he wanted was a positive report.

"Yes, she still likes math."

This was only partially true, as Eli loved only what she understood well. Every new lesson was a challenge to her, and she listened to my explanations with a frown. Once she got the meaning of it, though, everything went smoothly. She always tried to finish her work before the others and her hand would shoot up so that she might show it to me. I found her continuous efforts to please me tiresome.

"What else does she like this year?"

It was obvious her father was taking a yearly pulse of his daughter's progress, and I wondered if this was the first and last time I was to see him. He probably wouldn't show up again till next December to ask the new teacher about his daughter's whereabouts.

"She likes drawing and reading, more in English than French, though. I often catch her with English books hid-den in French ones."

He laughed and I smiled, even though Eli's little tricks were getting on my nerves.

"Aye! She reads a lot. I know."

I wasn't that enthusiastic about her choice of books either. She exaggerated her annoyance about every title I proposed as mandatory reading, complaining that they were "*pour les bébés*," as she didn't know the word for "boring" in French.

"Does she like her class now?"

"I hope so," I said, wondering if we would resume our discussion from the beginning.

"Last year she didn't get along with her teacher. I was really worried about it. Now, everything has changed, because you are so kind."

Who had given him such an inaccurate portrait of me? Granny? With all those French lectures about Eli's clothes and hunting trips?

I was now certain he hadn't spoken to Eli's guardians since September. Was he on a short leave in Iqaluit and suddenly decided to meet me, before talking to the constable or Granny? They would have given him a much different account of me.

Maybe a visit to the school was a way for him to glean news about his daughter, without facing those who were really taking care of her. How did the constable deal with this man? And what kind of brothers were they?

After Victor Ivalu left, I rushed to see Carole. As usual, she was making photocopies, cutting out words and sticking them on her walls.

"Did you know that Eli's father is Inuk?" I asked her from the door.

What I wanted to come across as surprise sounded more like anger.

Carole was perched on a ladder, stapling the words to the wall. She stopped and looked at me with astonishment. She stepped down, but the bewilderment remained on her face. Then, she realized the reason for my fury.

"You mean you didn't know?"

"Who was supposed to tell me?"

"People just learn things without asking too much. Or they pay more attention."

Her attitude changed fast. Now that she knew about my negligence, she regained her teacher's composure. If I'd missed such important things about my students, it was not her fault. She was not going to apologize for failing to clear up my confusion.

But then, she saw my miserable face and tried to sweeten her voice.

"I thought you knew."

"How was I supposed to?"

"By looking in your student's file."

"But the files are in the secretary's office."

"The scanner is also in her office. And she leaves at four. No one would accuse you of sneaking around if you just took a quick peek into the cabinet drawers."

"I am not used to this way of doing things."

"It would have saved you some commotion, though." Carole looked at me with pity, but she found nothing to soothe my confusion.

"So, I suppose Eli's mother was the constable's sister," I said.

Carole smiled for the first time. Now, she was really sorry about my candour.

"Not at all, dear. She was Inuk."

"How did she die?" I asked in a hurry, before she could catch my complete surprise. I didn't want my ignorance to give her any more satisfaction.

"She committed suicide, two winters ago. She swallowed a handful of sleeping pills then went to lie down in the snow in her nightgown. They found her the next morning, covered in ice."

"Did she leave a note?"

Carole took a breath to hold her spite.

"A note? People don't leave many notes in this place. They just act."

"How old was she?"

"I don't remember exactly. About thirty-five, I suppose. Not very young, but not old either. I knew her. A very quiet lady. She would tiptoe in the hallway when she came to pick up Eli after school. Never spoke much with us."

I didn't say anything, hoping for more details. Carole understood my growing appetite for this story, but had nothing to add. She fiddled with the stapler, staring at her wall. Stickers with French words written in capital letters covered the whole surface up to the ceiling. I followed her eyes and, despite my other concerns, I wondered how the kids would read them at that angle.

"Were you here when it happened?"

"Yes, but I wasn't teaching. Eli missed school for a while. They took her away up North. To her grandparents, I imagine."

"How come they put Eli in a French school?"

"It was the grandmother's idea."

"Granny? The one Eli calls Anak?"

"Not that one! The other one, the white grandmother. She was already sick with dementia, but she still had moments of lucidity. She insisted on putting Eli in this school."

"Because it's French?"

Carole glanced at me with what resembled a wink at the corner of her mouth: "Because it's white."

She was playing with the stapler again, glaring at me. She seemed to have no intention of offering more information. For some unknown reason, she was torturing me.

"Who is this brother, then?" I dared to ask, embarrassed.

"He was adopted by Liam's parents. The father was a ranking officer in the army and the mother a nurse. The boys grew up together."

I was surprised to hear her call the constable by his first name. I'd never realized she had known the trio for such a long time, and that they'd been in contact since Eli was first enrolled in this school. I suddenly realized they must have spent many Christmas seasons together, outings on dogsleds, appointments in the principal's office. Carole had definitely met the mother who, one day, decided to sleep in the snow, without saying a word about her pain.

"Are they really brothers?" I asked, trying to avoid sinking even deeper into my resentment against everyone, not only Carole.

She scrunched her eyebrows and smiled. "You never know with those army guys. White men have a reputation in this place, especially ones in uniform. The father died when the boys where quite young. This is their secret. No one knows if Victor is Liam's real brother."

Carole was too smart not to see my bewilderment. For the first time, I hated dealing with someone holding so many secrets. Worse, she was doling them out, drop by drop.

"Their mother was a nurse at the hospital. She died just before Oona took her life. She was living at the elder centre, which is very rare. White people aren't usually admitted, but I think Victor did everything in his power to get her there. He's well connected."

I stared at her again. The man I just said goodbye to was full of bruises. Roughed up.

I turned my back to leave. She did nothing to stop me.

The next day, I told Eli I had met her father. She said nothing, but a tiny blink of her eyes disclosed that she hadn't been aware he was in town.

Over the next few days, I tried to find out more through Ana, but she didn't know much about Eli's Inuit family. Unlike most of the kids at the school, this girl had never been her pupil. Ana knew about the constable and his Inuk brother. This was all she could reveal.

She was at school when Eli's mother died, but the incident was no different from many others. The school moved on quickly from those deaths. They were statistics.

When I asked Brigitte about the constable and his Inuk brother, she was surprised at my curiosity. She was faithful to the official version of history told by white people. In her narratives, Indigenous peoples were always tragic and naive victims. Her pity deprived them of personal identity. Her answer was quick and sarcastic, revealing to me that she had never questioned those commonly held beliefs.

"Yeah, he was adopted. White people living here do this frequently."

Brigitte had worked for a few years at the hospital and her image of the locals was limited to drunkards and beaten women, coming to Emergency Services on stretchers.

In her view, white people had always helped local people.

People like Brigitte had zero interest in mingling with local people. In this way she resembled the British explorers who, during their Arctic wintering, preferred to remain in the belly of their ships, keeping busy by running newspapers or taking reading classes from their officers.

Only a few explorers took notes about Inuit customs. The most detailed were those kept by Captains William Parry and John Ross at the beginning of the nineteenth century. They wrote of a disciplined and orderly people raising quiet and resilient children, and were especially interested in the Inuit's developed taste and soul for music. British explorers often brought musicians with them to the Arctic as a source of entertainment to make the long polar nights more enjoyable. Sometimes, they would invite the Inuit aboard to their concerts. One entry in Parry's journals marked his amazement at the Inuit women's skills in drawing the outlines of shores, islands and sounds, but the British viewed those maps as unusable, as the commanders did not trust the local people's knowledge.

The only other person who could tell me more about Victor was the principal, but he was eternally stuck in his office writing long messages to parents. Every one of his letters was a thorough dissertation on our struggle to keep their children on the right path of *la francisation*. I always wondered what they got out of these letters, as most of the parents did not understand French at all.

⸺ ❧ ⸺

During my first week in Iqaluit, I had come upon a book at the public library called *North Pole Legacy*, written by S. Allen Counter, a Harvard professor. I'd overlooked it at first, but after meeting Victor Ivalu, I remembered the picture on the cover and suddenly realized that the book was not really about finding the North Pole. It was about fathers and children.

I went to look for the book, and it was still there, on the shelf the librarian identified for me as "northern topics."

Over the course of the weekend, I read the story of two estranged fathers and the children they left behind in Greenland. The legacy mentioned in the title was not referring to the great deeds accomplished by the two Americans who first reached the North Pole, but focused rather on their human nature and sins.

History has long afforded the American commander, Robert E. Peary, the honour of being the first to have discovered the North Pole. The story of his voyage noted, in small print, the fact that five other people were present during that discovery—his Black "manservant," Matthew Henson, as well as four Inuit from Greenland: Egingwah, Ootah, Ooqueah and Seegloo.

Later geographical measurements tended to contradict

this story as, unlike the South Pole, which is set on hard land, the North Pole is on ice that shifts yearly. Although Peary and his team didn't quite get there, in 1909 they were the ones who'd gotten closest.

What remained incontestable about their expeditions were their two offspring, Kali and Anaukaq, whom Peary and Henson left behind and never returned to see again. They may have been outstanding explorers, but they were very bad fathers.

In 1986, the author of the book learned about a Polar Inuk whose curly hair was clear proof of his Black heritage. He decided to travel to Greenland to the American military base established in the Arctic during the height of the Cold War. After filing a pile of security paperwork, one day a helicopter brought him to the remote village where the eighty-year-old Anaukaq was living with his four children. The old man, known in that area for his hunting skills and good nature, told Counter something even more astonishing. Anaukaq's so-called "Cousin Kali" was none other than Commander Peary's son. They had both grown up like brothers till they were fifteen, when their parents moved to different hunting settlements. They had not seen each other since then.

Both children were born in 1906, aboard the *Roosevelt,* where their Inuit mothers worked as servants for Peary and Henson. Most certainly, both women were teenagers. At that time Henson was divorced from his first wife, while Peary was happily married to Josephine, a stoic woman who often followed her husband to the Arctic. A few years before Peary fathered Kali, Josephine even gave birth to their daughter, Marie, in Northern Greenland. Called Ahnighito, "the Snowbaby," by the locals, she was the first white baby born at that latitude. When years later Josephine made an unexpected visit to the Thule area, she found a small baby with Inuit traits aboard the ship. There was no doubt that he was Peary's son, but she chose to forgive her husband.

Counter brought Kali and Anaukaq together and listened to their stories. He was most surprised by their lack of resentment or bad feelings toward their real fathers. Kali's mother was already married when she met Peary. In exchange for a menial job, her husband let her go aboard and work as a white man's servant. At that time, everybody knew that such a job was about more than cleaning, cooking and doing laundry. White men took advantage of the common Inuit practice of exchanging partners for pleasure or fertility.

Anaukaq and Kali both had good memories about their parents. After the *Roosevelt* returned south, their Inuit stepfathers took care of the young boys, teaching them to hunt and provide for their families. The boys knew from a young age who their real fathers were, but they never considered themselves to be anything other than people of the ice. Kali would tease his cousin Anaukaq, saying he was born in the ship's coal room, hence the colour of his skin. But everybody knew he was Matthew Henson's, the Black man's, son.

Counter felt this was too big a discovery to let it fade away. He decided to establish a commission for reuniting Anaukaq and Kali with their American families. Back home, he reached out to both Henson's and Peary's heirs to coordinate with them in this project. He learned that Henson had had no children by his second wife. Long forgotten and neglected for his contribution to the North Pole expedition because of the colour of his skin, Henson had lived a very modest life till he died in 1955. Peary, on the contrary, was hailed as a national hero and his grave in the famous Arlington National Cemetery was adorned with a marble terrestrial globe with a gold star marking the North Pole on top of it.

Henson's descendants were excited about the idea of reuniting with their relatives from Greenland, but the official representative of Peary's family refused to acknowledge any kinship with Kali.

After I finished the book, I kept it on my coffee table for a few more days before returning it to the library. I'd flip through the pages to look at the pictures, mostly ones of the two teenaged mothers carrying their newborn boys tucked into their *amautiit*.

⚭

I was now hoping to cross paths with the constable, but he never showed up at school. After our meeting at my place, he stopped following me or instigating meetings with me through Eli's agenda. My French messages remained unsigned and likely unread.

I checked out every person passing through the door at the Legion on Wednesday, when we had our usual ribs and beer. On Thursday evening, on my way to the visitor centre to see a documentary, there was no police car tracking me from Federal Road. I knew I had been decisive in my demand to be left alone. But after talking to Victor, my apprehension of the constable was surpassed by my curiosity. What kind of family had Victor grown up in and why was it so difficult for the constable to acknowledge their kinship? He had certainly known all this time that I didn't know Eli's father. Maybe he didn't want to disrupt the sweet innocence of those coming up North with rubber boots and thin gloves.

Whatever his reason for avoiding me now, I grew impatient to see him again. I knew things now that gave me an advantage over him. Why was he so protective toward Eli, but couldn't bring himself to say anything about her real father?

Where was he anyway? Had he been dispatched to Arctic Bay, where a body had been found shot in the head next to a hole in the ice? The first police investigation as to the cause of death proved to be wrong. The man was found not far from the hole, yet no seal had been caught, which proved the killer must have gotten close while the man was still waiting for the animal to come up for air. But who could get that close to a hunter without being noticed? The shot was at close range which proved that the killer was almost at the victim's side.

The police thought it could have been anybody in the community, so they were ready to close the case. However, the autopsy revealed that the shot was meant to cover up the real killer, vitamin A. The coroner was diligent in discerning the yellow coloration of the victim's eyes, evidence of hypervitaminosis A, which people develop from eating the liver of polar bears. The inquiry then evolved into a different scenario. Who could possibly feed a hunter that dangerous piece of meat without him noticing? Was it a close relative who mingled pieces of polar liver among pieces of seal meat? Was it his wife? And who could have been driven to shoot the man to conceal the fuss?

I had heard the news through Nunatsiaq News, the official channel. It was one of those gory stories that usually remained secret from the public eye. There had been one that happened the week before, during the blizzard, when a woman was hit by a car in the middle of the street, dying on the spot. She was the mother of one of our students. What were the chances of dying in Iqaluit in a street accident? Was the blizzard to blame, or not? Maybe the constable was busy with this case that some people said was no accident.

I was shocked by the silent way we received the news at school. I'd imagined that this kind of event would strike like a thunderbolt through our small community. Instead, I almost missed hearing the news. The pupil was in Ana's class, yet Ana never spoke of it. During lunchtime, she only nattered on about her ordeal with getting the municipality to fix their water tank. The girl left the school after her mother's death as her close relatives decided to withdraw her from the French school. Ana didn't mention a word about any of this.

Eli's attitude showed no change except for some tardiness in her tasks. And she was yawning all the time, especially during the first class in the morning. Unlike other days, it took her more time to fetch her binders and sharpen her pencils. Sometimes, she asked to stay in with me at the recess. She said she was too tired to put on her winter gear, but I refused, telling her she must go out and get fresh air.

"I get fresh air at home." She tried to convince me in a most unusual soft voice. "Please."

"Fresh air is not something you take here and there. You have to go out every day."

My explanations didn't convince her. All she knew was that I never said yes to her requests.

By the end of the last school week before Christmas, I decided to call Eli's father. Why hadn't I contacted him earlier instead of waiting for Granny's replies and for him to visit? Even if he was not in Iqaluit, I had his phone number and I guessed he could be reached all over the Arctic. He was the person most qualified to know about her needs.

One afternoon, I dialled his number from my classroom, using the phone hanging next to the door. We were in the middle of rehearsing the Christmas show, and the kids were excited about it. Our teaching time had been reduced to make room for their rehearsal, conducted in the Grande Salle by Brigitte and Ana, who accompanied them on piano and guitar.

The phone rang for a while, but nobody answered. I hung up without leaving a message, but a few minutes later, decided to try again. This time a baffled voice asked who I was. Most certainly the man at the other end had awoken from a deep sleep. As I could not see him, I guessed that the voice seemed to be of an older man.

I introduced myself and asked if I was talking to Victor Ivalu. The man took only a second to recompose himself. I imagined him standing up beside the bed.

He was shocked to have me on the phone and didn't try to conceal it.

"Oh, Miss! Hello, Miss! How are you?"

His voice became younger and more alert.

"I am fine," I said in a joyful voice, trying to conceal my embarrassment. "And Eli is fine too."

"That is good, very good. She speaks so highly of you."

I was once again listening to the same adulation, yet this time I hoped it was not just optimistic bunk. Maybe Eli had talked to her father since our meeting and had reassured him as best she could about her relationship with the new teacher. Usually, when a kid says the teacher is fine, parents don't bother visiting the school.

"The reason I'm calling is to invite you to our Christmas show. Eli has a very nice voice, she sings well and she will also do the opening number. She is very excited about it. It would be nice if you could attend."

I was still wondering if I had made the best casting choices for the show. When I first distributed the scripts, I assigned Eli the third one on the list. This way I could avoid putting her under the spotlight too much; she usually spoke way too fast, trying to smooth out her English accent which was the heaviest in class. The next day, though, she was the only one who had memorized the few lines I assigned to her, scribbled on a piece of paper. Her eagerness to play her part successfully convinced me to give her the opening lines. During recess, I allowed her to stay with me in class and helped her rehearse her pronunciation.

"Oh, yes, sure, I'll be happy to attend," the man said in a joyful voice.

"We will be waiting for you, then," I said.

He didn't ask about the date. I imagined he would never come.

However, on December 18 he was there, in the Grande Salle, mingling with the other parents. He seemed a different person now that his bruises had disappeared. He had shaved and his hair was freshly cut, and he wore a white shirt with a black sweater.

The constable was not there. When I asked Eli about him, she said her uncle was in Toronto for some business with the RCMP.

Eli and her father seemed to get along well. The girl kept hold of his hand, sometimes looking up to catch his attention. I was surprised to see her laughing, something she didn't often do. Her father leaned his ear close to her mouth. Then he smiled his approval of what she was saying to him.

Tradition maintained that after the Christmas party, the kids slept over at the school. Parents brought the kids' night outfits and sleeping bags and left them with their teachers till the next morning, when they would come back to join them for breakfast before going on to their jobs. The students got to stay at school in pyjamas all day long.

It was Eli's father who brought her bag with clothing and a small snack for the night. He followed me into the class, where I showed him their places. The girls were settled for the night in the back of the class, near the windows, separated by a row of desks from the boys' location close to the entrance.

The decision about where the groups would sleep caused quite a stir at the beginning as no one was happy with their assigned place. They wanted either a spot next to the window, or to be closer to me. I told them about the medieval tradition that made it mandatory for the men to sleep close to the exit doors. This way, in case of a sudden attack, they could defend the women and children.

They easily accepted this ancient logic from the time of barbarian invasions and settled where they were told to.

Where had I picked up this story, anyway? Was it from some Balkan legend Mother read to me when I was a kid?

Eli put her sleeping bag on the floor and slipped inside to show her father how comfortable she was.

"She is always very excited to sleep over at school," he said to me.

"Yes, I know. They have been talking about it for weeks."

He kept silent for a few seconds before saying: "Tomorrow, I will not be able to help with the breakfast."

"It's okay. We have a lot of parents who can come help out. The eggs are already boiled and the bacon is fried. All we have to do is to toast the bread and pour the juice."

"My wife always used to help in the morning," Victor said in a lower voice.

"I'm sorry for your loss."

I knew that he could hear the sadness in my voice was real. Up to this moment, I had not registered the devastation of such a loss. My struggle with the constable had turned this story into the subject of my own personal quarrel. But this man and his daughter had truly gone through such a tragedy; it was all becoming real to me now.

"Thank you." He kept smiling, though there was no joy in it.

I found it easy to speak with this man. I would have liked to talk more about Eli and her mother, but the kids were running around, and the parents were gathering in the corridor while the teachers were carrying their instruments onto the stage. Everything was noisy and on the move. Only the two of us—Victor and I—occupied this bubble of silence and sadness.

For the last few days of school before the holiday, we followed the usual schedule without much enthusiasm. The kids became unruly, but I didn't care much. I gave them a lot of *temps libre* to draw and play with Lego. With some of them, I played chess at my desk, surrounded by a noisy audience. The only command I gave out from time to time was to speak French.

Eli brought me a present in a paper bag. It was a small carved inuksuk with a little bird on top of it, next to a seal lying on the ground. Eli told me her uncle's explanation of this gift. He said I was the seal and she was the little bird. I smiled at this idealized vision of our relationship. I was no mentor to her, and she was no bird ready to fly.

I was not accustomed to getting presents from my pupils anymore, so that evening I asked my mother if I'd done the right thing by accepting it. She said of course: There was no way I could make that girl return home with the gift bag. How would she feel after such a refusal? The best solution in this case, said my mother, was just to show gratitude to Eli and give her a hug.

CHAPTER FIVE:

Pineapple and Kisses

URING THE TWO weeks I spent in Montreal for Christmas, I got a terrible virus and had to stay in bed with a fever and cough for the rest of the holiday. Mother moved in to take care of me. She brought with her the entire ethnic arsenal against a cold: massages with camphor oil, inhalations, lemon teas, *chaudeaux*, magic bags. Waiting for the effects of her wide-ranging pharmacy, she lay in bed next to me, watching. To her, I remained an unlucky child. I pretended to sleep, the only way to avoid her questioning about my growing old in such a remote place, out of her reach.

On departure day, I forbade her from coming to the airport, saying there was no room in the taxi. She didn't insist, busy as she was stuffing my baggage with preserves, dried fruit and nuts, as well as, more importantly from her perspective, yarn for my students. I told her that I had achieved some success with her knitting methods, and she was delighted to nurture my apprentices' new passion. She had already imagined me running a knitting workshop in the Arctic, carrying on those Balkan patterns she had brought with her over the ocean. I tried to curb her enthusiasm and cautioned her against spending more money on yarn and buttons. Mother always chose the most exquisite wool, sourced from sheep feeding on the Andean or Himalayan pastures. She thought that my students' excitement over beautiful colours and textures would certainly inspire their knitting.

At the airport in Montreal, I took two Tylenols to steel myself for the length of the flight to Iqaluit. During the trip, my body grew heavy and my ears plugged up. I tried to eat that murky, salty inflight breakfast, but I abandoned it after the first bite. The food gave passengers no pleasure, yet everyone else swallowed the greasy sausages, the spongy eggs and the stale muffins to the last crumb. We were heading to a place where waste was a sin, so people swallowed the food without looking at it too closely. In Iqaluit, the temperature was almost forty below. It was like nothing I could have imagined. Scouring winds haunted the treeless hills and shook the houses. There was nowhere to turn against the savage blasts of icy air. The sun in the sky was ferocious, blinding with its merciless light.

The teachers from L'Aurore Boréale School were all gathered at the airport, waiting around the carousel for their luggage. We were not happy to see each other. We were mostly appalled by the idea that we had to spend the next six months together, confined to the same rooms, victims of the same rumours. We didn't love each other anymore, if ever we did.

In September, I had imagined our school as one of those Victorian vessels, carrying among the ice floes a team of people aiming for the same goal. The knowledge those

British crews acquired during the horrific years of the expedition created a rare solidarity among them in the face of the unforgiving Arctic.

Yet, the overall evidence proved that life in the North didn't necessarily bring people together. The solidarity I expected had vanished, eked away by the unspoken competition for power. Our tight-knit society was regularly shaken by ongoing fights over who was the best, or the most suited for various positions. We were no different than the British explorers whose prejudices fractured the crew into many camps. The social hierarchy and the rules set by the British Admiralty were a real plague that came to imperil every voyage. Segregated by class, origin and wealth, the commander, the captain, the cartographers and the seamen rarely conversed. The upper-class officers dismissed many observations made by the captain and his seamen, who had criss-crossed the Arctic as far as the yet uncharted latitude. Nothing was more appalling to the upper-class officers than the idea of exploiting "the fat of the land," as some of those seamen suggested. Instead of wearing caribou-skin boots and fur-lined clothing like the local people, the officers favoured fabrics and tinned meat. It was not until 1857, during the last search for Franklin's lost expedition, that one of the commanders agreed to augment their preserves of salted pork with a generous supply of pemmican, made out of lean meat, pounded and mixed with melted fat. It was a local invention, used on the North American plains from time immemorial. For many years, British officers neglected to use sun goggles, one of the great Inuit inventions, to protect their eyes from snow blindness. Even the scientists onboard neglected local knowledge about the land. Fishermen and whalers had laboured in the region before Frobisher, Davis or Hudson, yet the officers disregarded their experience, as they considered these men simple and uncouth. So the seamen kept their knowledge to themselves and humbly stepped aside to leave the honour of discovering the land to the gentlemen.

As the teachers now eyed one another at the airport, we were as divided as any British party. On one side, there was the commander and his old acolytes; on the other, the crew, people haunted by doubts and suspicions. I identified myself with those neglected seamen.

The friendly faces I met in September were now but an illusion, wholly replaced by grim looks and doubts. We spied each other's bulky luggage that outweighed the amount allowed. What a predictable species we were! Victims of the same lusts and cravings! Each of us relied on stealing a little pleasure from food and fancy clothes.

We exchanged brief greetings only to avoid being accused of rudeness. Then we each hurried to push our baggage cart through the exit door and find a taxi. We were all in haste to get home, close the door and leave the evil spirits outside. Some of our colleagues had friends who came to pick them up at the airport, but no one offered up a spare seat. Friends with cars were a privilege they fought for or paid for, and they were not willing to share.

I didn't want their help and tried to avoid their subtle glances. I was so sick that I disliked them even more deeply.

Despite the cold, the area around my building was quite busy. The post office reigned as the heart of the city. People were still coming to pick up their parcels, trying to keep the Christmas spirit alive.

My apartment was dark and dusty. At the door, a new, unfamiliar smell hit my nose and made me nauseous. The building had crept inside my home, carrying strange odours. I turned on all the lights, then turned them off again, except for the lamp in the living room. By evening, my coughing and fever intensified. I felt thirsty; I drank water like a camel. I stood in the dark in front of the window. A few cars passed on the street, but their noise could not chase away the still ghosts of the city. The houses all seemed to be covered in glittering dew. On the way from the airport, the taxi driver showed me the ruins of four buildings that had burned to ashes the day before.

Exhausted with fever, I tried to have a bite to eat, but I choked and spit the morsels into the toilet. I was fast asleep by midnight.

The next morning, I was unable to leave my bed. I called the principal and told him I was sick. He said okay in a cold voice, clearly more preoccupied with the increased workload my absence would cause than with my well-being. I moved my bedding over to the sofa and tried to read. My headache made it impossible for me to focus on the words, so I abandoned the book.

At noon, I tried to eat again, but nothing would go down. I stayed in front of the window for a while, but the cold breeze creeping from above the windowsill awoke my fever and forced me onto the sofa again.

The day flew by, marked by feverish naps and painful awakenings. My muscles, my bones, my joints all hurt.

The next day, I got out of bed with renewed energy. I went to the washroom, then turned on the coffee machine. Undecided as to what to wear in such weather, I opened the wardrobe; a whiff of perfume and a cloud of dust suddenly came off the hangers. I closed the door, stepped back and tried to regain control. The only way to get relief from the sudden nausea was to vomit. From the kitchen, the smell of coffee amplified my revulsion.

I called the principal again and told him I wasn't well. This time, he told me I should go to the hospital. I agreed but said that for the moment I wasn't able to leave my bed.

The day passed at a slow pace. Since I couldn't read, I just stared at the ceiling, lying on the sofa. By noon, the fever intensified, so I put on a wool sweater and a new pair of socks. One hour later, I brought the duvet to the living room as well.

At two o'clock, I stood up in front of the window and tried to catch the moment when the sun went down beyond the hill. The cross of St. Jude's Cathedral was projected against the sky. The ravens were enjoying the wind, gliding and squawking in their usual slow-motion ballet. I moved to the other window. On the southern side, the shore had already sunk into the bruised colours of sundown.

Late in the afternoon, I heard a knock on the door. Because of the dark, I had completely lost track of time. I looked at the clock. It was half past five. I decided not to answer, figuring it must be a mistake.

The knocking persisted. I went into the bedroom to change my sweater. Passing by the open door of the bathroom, I saw my messy hair in the mirror. I passed my fingers through it and unlocked the door.

It was the constable.

While facing one another, speechless, I inhaled the smell of the snow still clinging to his parka. The frozen air of the day floated around him like an icy aura. He was carrying two plastic bags.

"Eli told me you weren't at school, so I figured you were sick."

I didn't say anything. I just stared at him from within the threshold. The shadow cast by the door protected me from his inquisitive look.

"May I come in?" he said, lifting the bags. "I brought you something to eat. I know how bad a cold can be. I had it through the holidays."

I stepped back and let him inside. I was too weak to stand up any longer.

The constable placed the bags on the floor and took off his boots. He went into the living room and put the groceries on the table. I lay down on the sofa without any explanation or excuse.

"Do you want to go the hospital?" He seemed undecided about what to do next.

"Should I?" I lifted my head from the pillow.

"If it's just a cold I don't think so, unless you feel something's really wrong. Are you coughing a lot? Do you have a fever?"

"Not much, but it's difficult to stand up and I'm very cold."

"Then you just need to rest. And eat. Have you eaten?"

I shook my head.

He took off his parka and put it on the armchair on top of my own. My winter gear had been dumped there since my arrival.

"What d'you feel like? Sweet, sour or salty?"

"I don't know, hard to tell. I am not hungry. I brought some food, but I cannot eat."

"I know, but you've got to start eating. I'll make tea and then we'll see."

He went into the kitchen without asking where the supplies were stored. He found the kettle easily, the tea bags and the honey pot too. Then the cups and the spoons. It wasn't difficult to get oriented in a kitchen that had barely anything in it. The counter was empty except for the toaster and the coffee machine. Next to the sink was a bottle each of oil and vinegar, and the saltshaker.

I grabbed the blanket and covered myself up to my chin. I was slightly embarrassed by my sweaty stench. The day before, I skipped having a bath. Overnight, I had alternated between burning up and cold sweats. While the constable was rumbling around in the kitchen, I covered my hair with the black scarf I had looped around my neck.

Waiting for the water to boil, he came into the living room and sat next to the coffee table.

"How was your holiday?" he asked with a smile.

"It was fine till I got sick."

"How many days now?"

"Five."

"You're in for another two at least. Are you going to stay home?"

"I don't know how many days I am entitled to miss work."

"Three, I think. At four, you need a medical note."

"How do you know this?"

"I just know."

Our old misunderstanding oozed out like putrid slime. I suddenly remembered that he could get any information he wanted about me. He even knew the details of my Nunavut Teachers' Association contract.

He went back into the kitchen and made tea. As the kitchen was down the corridor, I could only imagine him staring at the cupboards, waiting for the infusion to be ready. He filled two cups and brought them to the living room. I stood up and reached for one even though it burned my fingers. I wrapped my blanket around the handle so that I could keep the cup close to my nose and let the hot air soothe my airways.

"My mother made me do a lot of steam inhalations. She almost burned my skin," I said, trying not to choke on the hot air.

"Were you living with her?"

"We live in the same neighbourhood."

He kept quiet for a while. He was sipping his tea but kept watch over me. I switched the hot handle of my mug to the other hand. Did he notice my dirty nails?

"I like to see people feeling close to their mothers. I wasn't to mine, unfortunately. But it wasn't her fault."

"I suppose it's different between mothers and daughters. I didn't always have a very comfortable relationship with mine either. She felt I never did anything properly. I got used to being corrected on everything."

The constable was listening quietly. I was more than surprised by my verbosity. It must be the fever. How else could I have confided in him this thing I had never before admitted to anyone? I had never testified on my mother's authority and my complete obedience to her demands. In many respects, it was like I'd always remained a six-year-old girl.

"Did that make you angry?"

"No, not at all," I said with a faint smile. "*Au contraire!* I was always very comfortable with her because I trusted her."

He remained motionless, waiting for more. I felt how curious he was about such things. Yet I hesitated to tell him how cynical I was about my mother most of the time. I couldn't really criticize her for her ethnic quirks, but was resentful that she was so harsh on me for not being like her. What kept us close was her boundless, infinite love. As ignorant as I was about what a good mother is supposed to be, I could not deny she was a reassuring presence in my life.

I changed my position on the sofa, trying to stand up. But tiredness won over me again, so I remained as I was, lying on my side.

"Do you want to eat something?" he asked after we finished the tea. "I brought a barbecued chicken and some spicy rice. I didn't have time to cook and I wasn't sure what you'd want. So I bought this at NorthMart. And pineapple. When I'm sick, I crave pineapple."

"I would like to have pineapple," I said, "but first I would like to change my pyjamas."

"Sure, sorry." He seemed intimidated by this sudden exposure of intimacy.

He realized now that under the duvet I was only wearing my night clothes.

I pulled the blanket around my shoulders and went to the bedroom. I chose a T-shirt and velour pants from the drawer, then went for a quick wash to freshen up. I let the water run while I washed my neck, prickly after two nights of unwashed sweat. But then I decided to have a bath. I enjoyed it for a long time, oblivious to the man in my apartment.

After I got dressed, I even sprayed a spritz of perfume to get rid of the sickly odour that was still floating in the air. I combed my hair and pulled it back in a bun on the top of the head. My skin was very pale, so I also put on a shade of lipstick.

I came back smiling, even though all this effort exhausted me. I was ready to make an excuse for my long time in the bath, but the constable was in the kitchen, cutting the meat into small pieces. I watched him for a moment, slicing the knife through the white breast of the barbecued chicken. Then he looked at me.

"You're awful beautiful."

He stopped carving. I laughed.

"I feel like sometimes you try to conceal your beauty under your clothes."

I looked at him in surprise but said nothing. I had no energy to argue with him. Was he unaware that he had popped over uninvited to my house where I could wear whatever I liked? Who would put on dressy clothes to lie on the sofa except my mother? She rigorously maintained the habit of changing her outfit every morning as if to go out, even when she hadn't gone anywhere for weeks. I have never had the energy for that. When I asked her whom was she dressing for, she said it was for herself.

"Never lose track of your looks," she always told me. "It's not about physical appearance, but about the inner one."

My mother had too much time on her hands. She could afford to waste energy on her outfits. She was still a very good-looking woman, especially after she'd become a widow.

She completely changed her style, exchanging her long, loose dresses for more fitted shirts. She said that trying to conceal your body made it even more obvious. Best was to show all its attributes at once. An unexpected visitor like the constable would have never found her unkempt with dirty nails.

During my bath, he had set the table. He found all he needed in the cupboard. He'd placed the chicken and the rice in the middle of the table. Even the dessert was there, the pineapple cut in small cubes and put on a plate at the far end of the table.

I helped myself to a few spoonfuls of rice. The smell of curry hit my empty stomach with a pleasant warmth.

"Do you want some chicken?" He pushed the plastic tray in front of me. The meat was floating in a brown, greasy sauce that set off my nausea.

"I will try the rice first," I said pushing it back in the middle.

"You need meat. You have to eat meat more than anything, don't you know? This is the country of meat and fat. In fat you've got all you need to survive."

"I don't like meat."

"Are you a vegetarian?"

"No. It's just that I prefer vegetables."

"That's good, but you might want to adapt a bit."

"Do you eat local food?"

"I do. Granny fed us with seal and char. Eli's not a big eater, though. I'd like her to eat more."

I had observed the same thing during the students' snack time, when she reluctantly crunched her cookies and apple. Sometimes, she brought caribou jerky that she chewed slowly, all by herself. When the school gave them smoked or boiled char as a free breakfast, she would ask permission to get a second helping from the big tray set in front of the secretary's office. I knew she was ashamed to ask for more, so I typically sent someone else to bring her a second help-ing, usually someone who didn't like fish.

The constable put a quarter of the chicken and a good amount of rice on his plate.

"The rest is yours," he said, laughing. "You don't have to finish it tonight, but you should try it tomorrow."

We ate slowly, trying not to spy on each other. This ritual of sharing food should have created a certain intim-acy, but it did not. We remained shy, embarrassed, strug-gling for the next thing to say. We were almost choking on our food.

I finished the rice and stared at the pineapple. He no-ticed and said: "Have it now if you want. Don't wait for me."

I bit into a slice so hastily that the sharp juice caught in my throat. It set off such a coughing fit that I had to take refuge in the bathroom. I coughed for a while then waited even longer to regain my breath. When I came back into the living room, my eyes were wet with tears from the effort.

During my absence, the constable had stopped eating, even though there was still food on his plate.

I put away the pineapple.

"Have some more," he said.

"I think my throat is too irritated. It will make me cough again."

"I also brought grapes, if you want."

I nodded and he went to unpack the box and wash some. As there were no other plates in the kitchen, he put the grapes in a soup bowl and brought it to the table.

I chewed some slowly while he was finishing his chicken. He used his hands to eat, carefully breaking the joints and nibbling the last bits of meat on the bone.

"Sorry, I like crunching the joints," he said. "I have a habit of eating everything, even the skin."

"My mother does that too."

He laughed.

I was feeling the cold again, and he saw me shivering.

"Do you want to lie down?"

"Yes."

I left the table, and he took the liberty to go into the bedroom and bring back the duvet. As he was fixing the duvet around my neck, he touched my chin. He stood above me, watching me as I curled under the blanket. Then he slowly got close to my face. I said nothing, and he kissed me on my upper cheek. I kept my lips tight. He moved back to gauge my reaction.

"I'm sick," I said. "Stay away from me."

"I was sick already, it's no bother."

I smiled. He eased his hand under the duvet and took mine. He held it for a while.

"You're hot but I don't think it's fever. Do you want a Tylenol?"

"I'll try not to. I am sick of it. It doesn't help anyway. It only makes me numb."

"Fight like a soldier then. Never explain, never complain."

I laughed.

"Is that the way a soldier should behave?"

"Some of them. My father was one of that sort. The old British school—although he couldn't stand the British Empire. He was born in South Africa."

I looked at him. Those names placed him on an even stranger map than his Irish origins did. He was part of a larger world and one very different from mine. There was nothing about him that was similar to my mother's upbringing and mine.

"How come?" I asked.

He was so close I felt his breath. His eyes were not green as I thought before, but blue-grey, spotted with black dots. A fan of wrinkles circled his eyes. That close, he looked older.

"His parents ran a chicken farm there. But they were no good at working the land, so they went bankrupt and came back to Canada."

He kissed me again, on the cheek. This time, he held his lips longer against my skin before exploring the corner of my mouth. His breath smelled of chicken and spicy rice.

"I am sick," I said again.

"You're not contagious anymore. And I don't care. Unless you ask me to stop."

He kissed me longer on my mouth. I felt the sharp tang of the pineapple, his last bite at the dinner table. I softened my lips to get more of that sweet fragrance. His breathing came quick as he was kissing me. He grabbed me in his arms, holding me like a little baby.

"I missed you," he said. "You change everything about this place for me."

I kept quiet, shivering under the duvet. My feet were aching.

The constable's mouth was breathing next to my ear.

His lips went back to my cheeks, and once again to my mouth. He felt my numbness and tucked the duvet in around my body. Then, he went to clean the table and put everything away.

He washed the plates and threw the bones in a bag as there was no garbage bin. He put the rest of the food in the fridge.

"I brought you some hummus and cheese. It's easy to eat. And marinated fish. If you need anything else, give me a call. I'm on duty till morning, but I could pass by to check on you if you start feeling worse."

"Thank you," I said with a hoarse voice.

"Are you sure you don't want to go to the hospital?"

"No, I am fine."

"D'you want me to help you get in the bedroom?"

"No, I will stay a little longer on the sofa. It's too soon for bed."

He stood by the edge of the sofa and kissed my lips. He tidied my hair with gentle fingers.

"I'll come by in the morning to make breakfast. You have to start eating. The grapes and pineapple are in the fridge. Try the fruit if you're not able to eat the meat."

"I will, thank you."

I was eager to be alone. But when I heard the front door shut with a soft thump, I jumped off the sofa and went to the window. The police car was on the other side of Queen Elizabeth Way, right in front of the post office. There was no light on in my apartment, so I was sure he couldn't see me in the darkness. I watched him linger, saw him looking up at my window. After a while, he got into his car.

It took me another two days before I felt well enough to go back to school. I started the morning by making coffee and filling my lunch box, but once I was in front of the wardrobe, shivering and nausea seized me again. I returned to bed and covered myself right up to my eyes. For a while, I stayed under the blanket, breathing rapidly, in a desperate attempt to warm up.

When I was finally able to go out, I understood that my body had been trying to protect me over the past few days. The icy air that slammed me when I stepped out of the building was like nothing I had known before. Temperatures had dropped to fifty-four degrees below, and the blistering cold plugged my lungs like concrete. In a minute all my clothes were frozen stiff, with edges as sharp as a razor. The briefest exposure of my skin turned it into a burning white spot.

Since that dinner of chicken and pineapple, Liam and I had grown confident in our new familiarity. The first day, he drove me to the school, but in the evening he was called to Pond Inlet for an emergency. For the rest of the week, I took a taxi twice a day, morning and evening, unable to walk in such weather. The houses looked as if they'd been dipped in creosote, floating in a crystal ball. People were living in a state of siege, haunted by perpetual danger coming from all sides. The air was foamy with ice frost. It was unbreathable, harsh. I had never before experienced that eerie feeling that people could die so easily and so mercilessly. We were living in a ghost city, without a human being in sight for hours on end. Cars went down the streets in a cloud of exhaust fumes.

The temperatures didn't rise above that dangerous threshold for the whole week. We were obligated to keep the kids inside for recess and lunch. By the end of the day, their pent up energy was unbearable. When I took them into the Grande Salle, they started to run, to yell, to climb on the windowsills and roll on the floor. Any attempt to make them stop was useless, so I let them unleash their energy. As long as no one got hurt, they could do what they wanted.

Half of the students were still absent. When their parents went on holiday outside of the community, they usually stayed away as long as possible, sometimes more than a month, to make it worth the high price of the plane tickets. In September, when Ana filled me in on this practice, I smirked because it seemed to me a blatant lack of parental responsibility. By January, I was in full agreement that sun and warmth were as important as education.

Eli had spent New Year's Eve with her grandparents in Grise Fiord. When she came back, I was stunned by how much her French skills had diminished. As she was now less fluent than before, and Isabelle was not back yet, the other girls had become a tight-knit group that did not include Eli, whom they didn't understand. Her withdrawal and lack of interest in the things they were passionate about kept them at a distance. When they did finally mingle, it was never long before someone was doing or saying something that hurt Eli. Afterward, no one would approach her with an apology. Eli would just run away, telling them to leave her alone. Some of the girls came to ask me to make Eli accept their apologies, but she was merciless to those who disappointed her. The more I knew her, the more I dreaded intervening on their behalf. Eli would take no one's advice, not even mine.

The only thing she liked was knitting, to the point that I had to set limits. She was the most persistent of all the students in learning this new art, so I gave her almost all the yarn I had brought from Montreal. She now came even earlier to class and would ask permission to take her needles until the others settled in.

At first, I was happy to see her so passionate about knitting. But when it was time to start the class, she was reluctant to put away the needles. I told her she could knit at the daycare service after school, but she replied in an angry voice that their daycare teacher didn't know anything about knitting and couldn't help her. Eli was now judging her elders according to their manual skills and she was appalled to see how few people around were able to do anything with their hands.

"You can wait till tomorrow to fix your problem," I said, cutting her complaint short. "Try not to tangle the yarn anymore and be more careful with your stitches."

Sometimes, I talked with Liam about Eli over the phone while he was away. Several cases of extreme violence had kept him away from Iqaluit for days. Most recently, he had been called to Arviat to investigate a fatal hit and run. At 3:10 a.m., police received a tip that a woman had been found dead on a roadway. After an initial investigation, they concluded that the victim had not been run over by a vehicle that failed to stop, as they'd originally thought. On examination the body proved to be bruised not by the impact of a vehicle but by a severe beating. The most likely suspect, her husband, had an alibi, as it had been confirmed that he was out of town at the time of her death.

In many of the northern communities where Liam

carried out his investigations, the connection was so bad we could hardly hear each other. A bad phone connection was not the only obstacle between us, though. Our growing familiarity hadn't erased the old issues. He was still the uncle of a difficult pupil, and I remained her demanding teacher.

Liam would quietly listen to my litany of concerns about Eli. Sometimes he was lying down in a dump of a hotel or on a bunk bed in a guest house, but it could just as often be a worn sofa in some hospital or airport. I was astonished at how such an orderly man could be so indifferent to the lack of physical comfort and cleanliness. I imagined the stained carpets, the worn upholstery, the smelly cushions. The worst, he told me, was the mould. The buildings up North were horribly inappropriate for such a climate, but the region was in the iron grip of the housing corporation mafia. Despite the ecological and environmentally friendly projects that were offered to the government by various progressive groups, the construction companies that held most contracts opposed any attempts to improve or change the system. New houses were real wrecks, with bad plumbing and inadequate sewage systems. The insulation was quick to develop mould, which affected people's lungs. No one needed alcohol and drugs to go crazy; the walls of their home did that to them.

When Liam got back to the city, he came directly from the airport to pick me up. He was once again a stranger, with that smell that captured the whole history of the North. His garments were like an anthropological map, charting matter and human evolution through the centuries. His lips were sweet and a little salty. While he was away, he mostly ate caribou jerky and smoked char. Sometimes he drank spirits and smoked a cigarette with his fellow police-men. In their company, he couldn't say no to those trad-itionally manly habits that bound them more than language and origin.

When he entered my apartment, he rushed to kiss me on the lips. This brief contact gave rise to a strong passion in him that I sensed in his quickening breath. He grasped my body and kept me in his arms for a long time. More than physical contact, he was looking for reassurance that I was still there, and that he was allowed to touch me. One of his hands lingered on my back, a good pretext to press me against him and feel my breasts. Then, he stepped back to let me get dressed and took my bag.

When we arrived at his place, he first had to inspect his vacant house and plug in every appliance. Before leaving he always unplugged everything to avoid any fires blazing in his absence. Because of the bad insulation, buildings could be consumed in a blink, before the firefighters could reach the neighbourhood. The houses were poorly designed, such that the electrical wires ran loose along the walls, a few inches away from the fibreglass insulation. Basements were as dangerous as firework warehouses, ready to be set ablaze.

He turned on the heating system before going to take a shower and change his clothes. He locked his gun in a drawer and put the key in a bowl on the wooden shelf of the library. I knew the place and he made no attempt to hide it from me. Then he got undressed and put his clothes in the washing machine. His uniform filled one load and he turned on the heavy cycle.

After his shower, he came to me straight away, with steaming skin and wet hair. He had no patience for a towel or hair dryer. His sex was still soft and hot. I lay next to him on the sofa, both naked, before he penetrated me with hesitancy. We were still shy and sceptical about our relationship.

⟨⟩

Liam's house held only a modest number of Inuit crafts. White people who came up North were typically eager to collect soapstone statuettes, ivory carvings, seal boots and polar bear mittens. They believed such purchases proved their attachment to the charms of the North. All he had was a plate made of mammoth tusk and an inuksuk on the shelf by the entrance. His house was on the Plateau, the richest neighbourhood in the city, with new and elegant buildings.

After his mother died, he had kept their small legacy in a storage locker till he could find a place to showcase her things, like his own personal museum. The first floor was a mixture of furniture and old items: coffee tables, buffets, carved stools, old paintings, rugs, vases, statues, wooden clocks. He also had a lot of potted flowers. On windy days, he had to put them on the floor to prevent them toppling down from their shelves. As with any other house in the North, his own had been built upon iron poles. When the wind hit a hundred kilometres per hour, the house would vibrate like a sailboat. Once while in his bed, I became as dizzy as if I were being tossed about on a raft in middle of the ocean. Sometimes, the howling kept me awake. These trials were periodically overshadowed by the racket of his snoring, blowing in my right ear.

Liam was a good housekeeper. He cleaned and cooked for himself. I was impressed by his tidiness. Once a week, he vacuumed the rugs, mopped the kitchen floor, scrubbed the soap rings in the bathtub. He never left dirty dishes in the sink and he threw out the garbage after each supper.

In the evenings, we'd quietly eat our go-to meal from the NorthMart: grilled chicken, spicy rice and potato salad. He was not a big eater, which I found convenient.

The bedroom was up a flight of stairs, where we often retired late after watching a movie in the living room on the main floor. Sometimes, we'd make love on the couch and stay there, sleeping on till after midnight.

In the morning, he was always the first one to wake up and make coffee and toast that we spread with butter and jam. Breakfast was our favourite meal. Or maybe we were just relieved to soon be parting ways. Our passion was morphing into a routine. The establishment of our relationship was very disturbing to him. While I was there, he was unable to recognize the soul of his home. The walls were mysteriously oppressing us. We remained strangers to each other, longing for the warmth that the frozen shelter could not provide. The ice had caged us and no thaw was in sight. We were like Franklin's boats trapped on the coast of King William Land. Inside *Erebus* and *Terror* there had been life, hunger, fear, but the ice floes imprisoned the crews and forced them to wait. And waiting is a dead end, always.

Once we left the house in the mornings, we regained control of our senses. A lively current nudged us to the open water of the ocean. The biting cold we breathed in after we closed the door behind us was like a rush of endorphins. We were leaving behind a barren land with no known reference points. Our passion came alive under the warmth of the car's fan that mixed together the smells of worn leather from the seats and the coffee from our mugs.

Liam remained faithful to his old routine. Like my oldest acquaintance in Iqaluit, the van driver, he started his days at Tim Hortons. The draw of coffee and a muffin was an opportunity for him to escape his own house, unsettled as he was by my presence. While he was inside the Quick Stop, I looked for the Narwhal van. The driver kept the same tight schedule, now slightly different from mine. When we were arriving, he was generally leaving. The man looked at me and slightly bowed his head.

Coffee cups in hand, we were ready to put forth our public persona. Inside the car, our parkas were untangling juxtaposed stories: Mine was a mix of talcum powder and perfume; his, a mix of cold fumes and fried oil. I was now familiar with those aromas; they placed me somewhere on the map. Here. I finally belonged to a flawless present, untarnished by so many overlapping old stories.

In the parking lot, Liam held me in his arms for quite a while before letting me out of the car. Then he waited as I entered the school, a habit well ingrained in the North where people never left before seeing that others were safely inside. From behind the windowed door, I waved at him and then waited to see his car disappearing down the road to the city.

At that moment, I felt ready to start the day under good auspices. My skin kept Liam's scent and my body still hurt after the tumultuous night. My belly remembered his lips, my vagina was still feeling his presence. He had tormented me with a mute interrogation. I could not escape the sensation of being studied. His lips, his eyes, his broken questions were undeniably proof of some inquiry he held deep within himself. Every penetration became a long voyage of exploration.

When Liam was in town, I spent most nights at his house. I stayed over on the weekends only when Eli was away on hunting parties with her mother's relatives in Grise Fiord. There were also other times when she missed school to travel to some remote community for a family gathering or celebration.

I traced out on the map the small communities where her family had been scattered during the relocation implemented by the Canadian government early in the last century. Many of them had been victims of the policy that attempted to claim the Arctic by inhabiting it. Liam told me the story of Eli's great grandparents, left on the shore of Devon Island with almost nothing. The RCMP had set up tents for the people and told them that game was abundant in this part of the Arctic. It wasn't true at all. There was barely any game that far north, except for a short period in the summer. That meant by early spring they had no supplies to sustain themselves and few tools prepared for the hunting season ahead.

One of Eli's uncles still had a watch, a relic from the early British voyages for the Northwest Passage. No one in the family knew for sure the year when that encounter happened, but it was certainly before the wreck of Franklin's ships. At that time, the British Admiralty organized a voyage to the Arctic almost every year. It was not even a matter of economic potential anymore, but of pride. The empire was at its height after the Napoleonic wars. They had plenty of ships and famous commanders on hand but nothing much for them to do in peace time. The Arctic dream came just in time to give them a new, great purpose. The Admiralty set on the search for the Northwest Passage. Their ships were going farther north and west each year. They were charting the region, naming sites after British benefactors, lords, kings and princes. Very rarely, a commander would even be so generous as to put the name of some brave fellow countryman on the map.

Unlike the Elizabethans, the nineteenth-century explorers learned to rely on the locals. They acknowledged the Inuit awareness of the land and started relying on seal meat instead of corned beef and canned carrots. The also appreciated Inuit women's drafting skills. More so than men, they had an acute visual memory. They knew how to chart coasts, bays, inlets and open sounds for the British captains who were otherwise wandering in the dark. The captains' old maps were not particularly reliable when they ventured farther than the coasts charted by Frobisher, Davis and Baffin.

Who would know those places better than Inuit women, who had so often stared out over their surroundings from dawn to sunset, waiting for the hunters to return with food? The men were acutely aware of the availability and movement of prey, but the women were the ones who knew the terrain around their camp best. A small hill, a heap of ice, a barren land, a cairn, all these inflamed their imagination. In their minds, these peculiarities of the land were monsters capable of rising from the ice, eager to feed on their little ones. Mothers learned to spook their children with stories of terrible creatures in order to keep them safe within the camp. The more I learned from the library books I read in the evenings, the more the Amautalik monster made sense to me.

In exchange for their services, some captains gave presents to the locals when they were heading back home. In such a monochromatic landscape, colourful beads, a wool scarf, or a four-hole button stirred their curiosity. How had people managed to craft such things? The Inuit were drawn to beauty and industriousness more than anything else. Then there were the ticking watches, whose monotonous noise they appreciated during the howling blizzards. Eli's family still retained one of them, made in a British factory in the nineteenth century.

Liam told me he had often listened as Granny sang to Eli when she was a baby; he vaguely recognized Irish tunes. She could not tell him where those songs originated except that her grandmother had often sang them. Her people's love for music was met with enthusiasm by explorers like John Davis who invited the Inuit to take part in their concerts. With so many Irish captains, it's no wonder Irish folklore entered the local music.

When I told my mother I'd met a man, she replied eagerly: "Oh! That's good!"

To her, it was not about love but about protection, despite what I had told her about Iqaluit, a place where women could make a secure, independent living. My mother had her own opinions about a woman's needs.

During our long conversations over the phone, I told

her that up North I'd met more single women than men. They were now taking advantage of their freedom to do the things that were previously forbidden to them. They braved the cold and loneliness with more stamina than the men. They transformed their rented apartments into cozy homes where they entertained themselves by chatting, reading and cooking. On social media, they mapped their voyage to this land where few of their female counterparts had ventured.

At the Frobisher Inn, the women were regulars, and coming for a nice meal was a source of pride and comfort. Nothing was too expensive for their pockets. Women now mingled easily with polar bear hunters, travellers, government men and construction workers. All of Iqaluit dined there: military men, artists, singers, film directors, regular people turned comedians in the local productions that converted the local folklore into fascinating new worlds. Ethnography had become, for the first time, a form of high art.

Men typically came up North to make money. They took on two or even three jobs and cooked the popular local stew to save their earnings. Women came up North for adventure. In Iqaluit, a woman could set aside a lifetime of thrift in exchange for a relatively huge income, placing her within reach of Canadian riches. With all this money, women shopped online for fancy clothing, ate out regularly at restaurants and chose the best and most expensive food in the shops. Women were now the white men in town.

With so many possibilities at hand, who needed a man's protection?

But finding a lover was not the ultimate goal, according to my mother. Aside from being husbands and fathers, men carried history.

"An Irish, *eh*?" she said to me, laughing.

Mother's English wasn't great, but she was good at imitating the accent. So she took up mocking the Irish way of putting "eh" at the end of every phrase, the equivalent of the Quebecer's use of "*là*." As a historian, my mother often talked about the perpetual misunderstanding of British imperialism.

To French Canadians, every English-speaking person was an old-stock imperialist. Yet, the English-speaking community in Montreal had been formed by people who had nothing to do with London. They were mostly Scots and Irish people. The first to get rich in Montreal were largely Scottish merchants. Most of them came from the Boston area of the United States after 1767, when Nouvelle-France passed under British rule as the Province of Quebec. James McGill and Simon McTavish were ruthless fur traders and the new face of Protestant liberalism, a religion that preached that money was a blessing. Money was proof of a job well done and a meaningful life. Many Scots who achieved money and fame in Montreal were people running from murky pasts and debt prosecutors on the other side of the pond. These Protestants mocked their Catholic counterparts for their naive conviction that money was the source of all evil.

Then, there were the Irish indigents whom old-stock English people often loathed. They were poor, fleeing from a country impoverished and exploited by British occupants. They'd crossed the ocean in miserable conditions and eked out impecunious lives. Along with the Italians, they were targeted on one side by the French Canadians, and on the other, by the British rulers. Both communities were suspicious of the Irish migrants, who were said to steal jobs.

These migrants were second-class citizens, living in crowded neighbourhoods surrounding the factories, neighbourhoods designed by the industrial class who wanted to
prevent long commuting hours for the workers.

This was the Irish community my mother knew. I had
to explain to her that Liam had a different upbringing. His
family had lived in Western Canada, and even in South
Africa.

"It could be," Mother said, sceptical. "But if you listened
to his parents, they would tell you no better story than I
have."

"His parents are dead," I said. "The only family he has
now is an adopted Inuk brother."

My mother went silent. She had the decency not to
mock something she didn't understand.

History books rarely mention the North. There is a different Canada here, difficult to map, a state of its own with
its own resentments and apprehensions.

Where do these people belong? Where do their stories
stand?

Mother kept quiet, waiting till she could make up her
mind about what kind of solitude the people up North
represented.

CHAPTER SIX:

Buttons and Old Pictures

L IAM TOOK TO bringing me to school every time he was in town. For almost two weeks, temperatures rarely rose above fifty degrees below zero. Days were blindingly sunny, with no clouds in the sky. The icy wind was blowing from the northwest, bringing a frozen kiss from the Pole. The air was foggy with vapour billowing from heating vents and cars. The streets were deserted. At most we'd see a rare crossing by a pedestrian hidden by layers up to their eyes, body bent against the wind. The only improvement in the season was the light. In the past month, two hours had been gained, so at four o'clock in the afternoon there were still a few shades of blue at the horizon.

I kept up my habit of arriving first at school, even when I had spent the night at Liam's place. We usually made love for a long time before we went to bed. It was good and warm like a long voyage deep into the ocean of our bodies. Yet, in the morning, we were eager to shake off the overall feeling of exhaustion.

When I entered the building, the first thing I did was turn off the alarm system, then I took off my boots and tiptoed down the corridor to my class. The floor was still cold, and I could feel the chill bite through my cotton socks. My attempts at discretion had been useless; everybody had learned about my relationship with Eli's uncle. But nobody asked questions, and I never talked about it

The only person who seemed eager to engage in an open conversation with me was Ana. Her age precluded her from being accused of prying or gossiping. No one could get angry with an old person. Each time we crossed paths in the corridor, she was always trying to catch my eye. Her gaze was an open invitation to confession. I preferred to look after the kids rushing to their classes and get away with a polite smile.

At lunchtime, she persisted in her focus on the Iqaluit murder toll and the spike in the suicide rate. Growing old, people become fearful, the world a perpetual threat. Each time Ana planned her holidays, she started by checking the relevant statistics on casualties lost to street violence. She was planning to travel that summer to Greece, a country where people were living under permanent threat, according to her last readings.

This obsession often grated on the other teachers' nerves during lunchtime.

"Why aren't you staying home then?" one asked.

"Risk won't prevent me from travelling. I'm just taking precautions."

"What precautions?"

"I want to know when I might die."

Travelling abroad was not likely going to be what killed her. We were all aware that her sense of humour was often in short supply these days. She had even changed her colour-ful blouses for drab and severe clothes.

As much as Ana was the most considerate person among my colleagues, there was no friendship between us. I was attracted by the serenity of older women, but I found Ana much too old, stuck in a pessimistic vision of the world. Conversations with her were ordinary and redundant. I became more and more irritated by her heavy accent, which I associated with the small, secluded francophone com-munities of the Great Plains, the vestiges of Louis Riel, fellow Metis scattered along Red River. Most annoying was that particle "*là*," a Quebecois linguistic spasm, a tic she most probably picked up while doing her bachelor's degree at Université Laval in Quebec City. In Quebec, this particle was a living part of the language, a way to imbue conversations with more than just words; in Ana's case it just seemed like misplaced gibberish.

Her presence in the staff room reassured me, though. Teachers often sparred among themselves, in defence of their opposing interests. They tried to make alliances, and tested the loyalty of others while drinking coffee at recess, or while we were all squeezed up around the small table eating lunch. The most insignificant phrase could instantly turn into virulent warfare. Ana's repetitive stories were often handy in defusing the tension. She was waging her own battle, as she secretly felt herself to be the real commander of this ship, principal be damned. The others all thought that she'd conveniently forgotten that the French board had chosen their younger colleague as a leader over her. I didn't. I had a specific flair for detecting old resentments.

Near the end of the month, she underwent a colonoscopy test and had been sick ever since. Cold sores bloomed on her lips and her skin became livid. What might the results of that test reveal? At seventy, she seemed in good health, but at that age things could shift dramatically and at great speed.

By the end of the month, she stopped telling stories during lunchtime. She no longer showed interest in giving lessons or unravelling the past. Her toast often burned while she sliced her tomato. If any soul was interested in my adventure with Liam, they never hinted at it. My only worry was to keep it secret from Eli and her granny. Yet Liam said that Granny knew about it already. Such things were impossible to hide in a place where people were related to each other. I didn't ask for details, and he never spoke about it. There was a part of Liam to which I had no access. Despite the energy he invested in digging out my inner secrets, he remained remote to me, especially when it came to his past.

There was only one person at the school who briefly mentioned my new status. One day, Silvia, our cultural agent, came by my classroom to show me the weekly schedule for my students and, before leaving the room, she said: "You must be the happiest woman."

"Why?" I asked, taken aback by her remark.

"You chose such a good man. I've always liked Liam."

I smiled but said nothing and Silvia left the room in silence.

The next week, we all learned that she'd handed in her resignation and put her house on the market. During lunch breaks, she had often talked about wanting a child. Moving up North had cost her a boyfriend, and now she was contemplating getting back together with him. She even took a week off to fly to Montreal and see him. When she came back, Silvia told us that their relationship was beyond repair. They were too old to wind back time, too old not to acknowledge the passage of all those years during which they had evolved and their lifestyles had diverged. Nonetheless, her decision to leave Iqaluit was stronger than ever. The trip had not only revealed that her young flame had grown old, but that she had too. Silvia had turned forty after six years of celibacy, busy trying to pay off her huge mortgage. Houses were too expensive here to allow people to get lazy or take time off work. She had come up North for adventure, but soon got locked into a three-thousand-dollar-per-month payment. Now she was thinking of going back to her hometown in the Laurentians to run a chicken farm.

Before leaving, she tried to pawn off some of her projects onto us: the compost bin under the Ping-Pong table, the worms stored away for use on fishing outings in the spring, the hydroponic system with all those basil, mesclun and parsley plants for the science classes, the improvisation classes held at noon on Wednesdays. There were no takers. Silvia left disappointed in everybody, and we were disappointed in her too.

⌒

One morning the principal was earlier than usual and he parked his car while Liam was kissing me goodbye. We both looked at him guiltily. Age cannot cure the shame of being caught off guard in an intimate moment. The principal stared down at us from on high. His white Jeep was much bigger than Liam's car, so we looked like teenaged kids caught by an adult in a flagrant, open-air act.

He nodded to us briefly and got out of the car. Liam smiled but then held me even tighter in his arms. The principal's appearance had intruded into our intimacy. Liam understood my reluctance and pulled back his hands.

"He's a good guy," he said in a reassuring voice. "You're not some country teacher in rural Manitoba, y'know?"

I knew they were pals. Before becoming a principal, he had taught the junior classes. Eli used to be his pupil. After doing the calculations, I realized her mother's death occurred when she was a student in his class.

When I entered the school, the principal was in his office, his eyes tightly glued to his computer screen. I said good day through the opened door, and he replied without looking at me. This was nothing new. There had never been any special affinity between me and him. There were times I'd been in his office for various banal requests when I experienced a slight feeling of sexual attraction, but even before I finished talking, his mind had completely moved on to other things, and so had mine.

After this taciturn greeting, I reverted to my adult perspective. His silence made me regain my composure. My private life was nobody's business.

⌒

At school, I saw no change in Eli's attitude. Our relationship had become less stormy since I started allowing her to knit in the afternoons. She now had all sorts of reasons to come to my desk with pressing demands: recovering missing stitches, starting a new row, doing a buttonhole. When the clew rolled onto the floor, the yarn got so tangled that the only solution was to cut out the unravelled mess and make a knot. Sometimes I'd ask her in a reproachful tone if she was doing it on purpose. She'd return to her desk and complete a few more rows. Once as she was counting her stitches on the needle for the umpteenth time, she glanced up at me, horrified. I asked her to come close and, under her mourning eyes, I undid the knitting till I recovered the error. There were times the work of an hour was lost in a blink, and she had to start all over again. This was the best rationale she had to ask my permission to work near my desk. This way, she said, we could avoid undoing her work.

Refusing Eli was exhausting, so I started letting her pull up a chair next to mine. To her despair, the other girls felt entitled to do the same and grabbed their own chairs. Soon I found myself surrounded by half the class, as the boys joined the girls and made the most of this chance to chat.

They were all very impressed with my knitting speed. I shared with them what my mother told me at that age. Knitting was not a leisure activity for women in the past, so they worked fast. They were always under pressure to produce socks, sweaters and hats for their families. They had to work quickly and carefully, without missing the stitches or breaking the thread. Eli knew what I was talking about and tried to do as the women in the past.

Of all my students, Isabelle was most impressed by my skills. During our Wednesday afternoon workshops, she would stare at me for minutes.

"You are so good," she'd exclaim, oblivious to her own needles.

The children around me soon forgot my presence and started chatting on their own. Every now and then, they paused to ask my opinion, seeking confirmation of their ideas. I was surprised by how quickly people got comfortable in this ancestral custom of working and chatting in a small community of their peers. Here we were, in the Canadian Arctic, listening to the howling wind while knitting small purses for our spare change.

Eli began making small bags for buttons. I asked her how many buttons she had, and she replied that her granny had been gathering them for years. Her collection ran in the hundreds, precious pieces in various sizes, colours and shapes. No shirts, sweaters, or pants were thrown away without removing their buttons. I knew this habit well. Mother had done the same since I was a child. Buttons were precious in many cultures, but especially among the Inuit.

Despite their long-time trading with Qallunaat, white people, the Inuit way of making clothes remained unaltered. They never adopted the fashion of fitted parkas with button-holes. Weren't they wise to despise their use when those buttoned-up Qallunaat were freezing to death on the ice? What good were those buttonholes then? The skilful Thule people kept on sewing their garments using fish sinews and softening the skins with saliva. Their kamiks and *kaliktut* made from seal and caribou skins were soft and comfortable. Fashion remained as unchanged as the landscape for a thousand years.

One day, Eli brought Granny's collection of buttons to school to show to me. There were those little white buttons cut off from shirts, then the carved wooden ones, likely from an old-fashioned cardigan, as well as those two-hole metal ones. She knitted three small bags to hold the precious load. On each of them she sewed a little flower, using buttons as samples of what was inside. This way, Granny didn't have to rummage in each of them to identify their contents.

Lately, she had started knitting cellphone bags, first for Granny, who didn't have one, then for some cousins in Grise Fiord. I tried to convince her to start a hat, but she was only interested in projects that could be completed in a couple of hours. She worked hard to reduce the time required, like the women from the past in my stories.

I told my mother about my pupils' admiration for my knitting skills. She giggled over the phone and said: "I hope they will remember you for something other than knitting fast. Will they?"

Yet, the next day she sent more wool by FedEx, so as to make sure that their enthusiasm wasn't impeded.

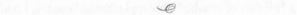

One Saturday afternoon, Liam was called out for an emergency in Resolute Bay. There had been a murderous attack on a mother, carried out by her son. I was there when the phone rang, as Eli was spending the weekend in Pond Inlet for a cousin's baptism and a big-game feast. Eli herself was a good hunter. Despite her frail body, she was able to shoot a seal from afar. Her grandfather would tail her, crawling on the ice, both hidden behind a white screen that allowed them to get closer to the animal.

Liam and I had been lying in bed after we made love, dozing. The radio was on. He was a big fan of this old technology. On the windowsill there were a few old radio sets handed down from his parents. He told me that kids should have mandatory classes on listening to the radio. No pictures to go with the news! Nothing but the imagination to complete the story!

He told me to stay till the next day when he was supposed to be back. There was plenty of food in the fridge and the house was warm. Wouldn't it be a waste in an empty apartment?

Undecided about what to do, I settled on the couch to watch him perform a skilful ballet between his wardrobe and the drawers.

After his departure, a sweet tiredness got hold of me. Maybe it was also the secret comfort of being alone at his place. One day spent on my own in Liam's house might help me get over that feeling of being just a visitor.

I switched on the movie channel and stayed on the couch the whole afternoon. First I watched a movie while eating a full can of crushed pineapple. Since January, I had had a craving for this fruit that I never much appreciated before. Since I was a child, my mother had preached to me that the human body had evolved to digest the food of our ancestors. In the case of my mother and I, why should we set aside those ancestral apples, plums and pears eaten by our forefathers in the Carpathian caves while they hid from the Huns and Goths? I mocked my mother's beliefs, asking her just how far we should go with this gastronomic genealogy. Before or after the Roman Conquest? Before or after the Spanish conquistadores started bringing corn, pepper, beans and tomatoes to Europe?

My mother looked for pedigree in everything, even

fruit. And apples had such a good lineage! It is said that the apple was the most untameable fruit in the history of agriculture. In the Golden Crescent, where the first villages had been established around 10,000 BC, in what is now Turkey, it remained for centuries the impossible crop. No wonder an apple appeared as the image of the forbidden fruit in the Bible. People both loathed the apple and longed for it. Somewhere along the way, the idea of forbidden knowledge became synonymous with this fruit.

In Iqaluit, apples were the cheapest fruit. Perhaps this was the reason why people were quick to minimize the fruit's benefits. Those who had the means were more likely to opt for strawberries, grapes, kiwis. A brief look in Liam's fridge convinced me of this trend's influence. Buying the most expensive and out-of-season produce remained everywhere proof of wealth and good taste. A mere bag of apples would not uphold one's status at the grocery store checkout line.

The other reason my mother cited for preferring apples over other fruit was the story connected to them. We were people of the Bible and took to heart everything the Holy Book had taught us for centuries. Then, there were those local legends flourishing around the apple tree culture that our ancestors carried forward across the years. How much did we know about the history and life story of bananas and pineapples? Things that you do not know do not feed you! It's the same with people, Mother said. You stick with those whose past is familiar to you.

Moving up North was perhaps a form of rebellion against her culinary rules. Despite the constant mockery, my own gastronomic tendencies have always mirrored my mother's. But since January I was now hooked on pineapples in all forms: raw, canned, fried and tossed on top of pizza. This might be the reason why my mother didn't ask too many details about Liam, this man who'd made me betray apples for pineapples.

In the evening, I thought about doing laundry. Then I suddenly changed my mind. Wouldn't it be inappropriate to handle his dirty boxers or socks in his absence? We'd been making love, but we were not that close. We were shy about our bodies' secrets and tried to avoid those embarrassing aspects of our intimacy. We made sure to take a shower if we knew there was a rendezvous ahead. The odour of his sperm was the only physical reminder of our acts.

I also considered making something to eat. I realized that I had never cooked in his house. Liam and I were missing the mealtime communion that emerges from shared traditions. Just as we didn't share the familiar practice of preparing food, we didn't share our memories either. We were not keen to speak about our pasts or genealogies beyond what was politely required in such situations. Our bodies could be naked, but our souls were still cloaked in many mysterious layers. What little we knew about each other, anyone could have learned from a census form.

I had told him about my immigrant parents and my high school friends. I told him about the ethnic culture held dearly by my mother and her obsession with being thrifty, skilful and disciplined. I spoke about her obsession with my well-being and comfort. She had bought me a nice apartment in a good neighbourhood, where she also moved into a rented flat, to be close to me. Property was not necessary to her, but it was to me, she said. I was not to grow old with

that feeling of precariousness. She expected me to stay true
to my ethnic culture by being wealthy yet looking poor. For
a woman, wealth was liberty. I didn't reveal to Liam how
her skilful pulling of invisible strings kept me in her grasp.
The house she gave me was a poisonous gift to draw me
back to her, no matter the circumstances.

He talked about his father's brilliant military career
and his faithful mother who followed him all over the
country. It was late in their lives when they settled down
enough to have kids. They were both Irish, but of different
backgrounds, and they had arrived in Canada at different
times. They had not been the happiest couple, but not unhappy either. His father had died of cancer, his mother of
dementia.

What about the Inuk brother?

Victor's story came up at last.

Liam's parents first took the baby as a foster child, a
few days after he was born in a hospital in Frobisher Bay.
His mother, the nurse, assisted the very young girl who gave
birth to Victor, all alone with no family around to care for
her. The first days of Victor's life, the little boy almost never
cried. He stared at the world outside with big round eyes. In
the picture his mother took of him, Victor's expression
looked like a baby seal's.

Liam's mother fell in love with Victor's stillness. The
couple needed that silent creature to balance the one they
had at home, who created messes from dawn to sunset.
Liam was three years old and not an exceptionally wicked
boy, but when Victor was taken in, the difference between
a good and a bad kid became striking. Yet Liam liked his
baby brother. He needed him more than his parents as his

days were lonely in the company of the old babysitter, a lady whose husband died in a plane crash over the hills of Baffin Island. Aunt Tina, as she was called, decided to pay her respects to the beloved deceased by refusing to leave Iqaluit. She was annoyingly generous and treated caring for Victor as a welcomed change. The little boy accepted any demand, played every game he was asked to, gave up any toy his older brother wanted that very moment, and took it back when his big brother didn't want it anymore.

When Liam was ten and Victor seven, Liam's parents petitioned to adopt Victor. But one of Victor's mother's relatives from a faraway community opposed the adoption and came to take the boy into his original family kinship. This was the rule and still is: The Inuit family has priority in adopting children previously placed in foster care, even after years spent with another family.

So, Victor had to leave. Liam's mother was devastated and so was Liam. His father had not been much involved in the child's upbringing, but he asked for a transfer to Yellowknife to soothe his wife's pain over the loss. Two years later, he died of pancreatic cancer. His mother moved to Calgary where she took up teaching at a school of nursing.

A few more years passed till they got a letter from Victor's family asking if they were still willing to take him in. The relative who initiated contact said they were unable to care for the boy anymore. Victor was twelve years old. Liam's mother decided to move back to the city that had become Iqaluit. She returned to work at the hospital and put both of the kids in the same school.

Liam and Victor still got along, but the time spent apart had put distance between them. Over the years, Victor remained a silent and obedient boy. The most noticeable difference in his behaviour was his passion for sewing skins, a cultural skill that he absorbed from his Inuk grandmother. After doing his homework, he would settle on the couch with his tool basket, tailoring mittens, kamiks, caps in seal and bear skins. He would invent new patterns and embroidery to embellish his crafts. Their mother said Victor was artistically gifted, and she dreamt of a career in fashion design for him.

As for young Liam, he was annoyed by his brother's passion. Liam was already hanging out with youth gangs in bars and dumpy basements. Growing up in Iqaluit sucked, he said. But what choice did they have? Most of his old childhood friends were now dead. All but a few had committed suicide. People blamed the magnetic vortex created by the North Pole, which was said to amplify feelings, especially the dark ones. The first months of the year were the worst. Nature revolted against the human presence occupying it by sending electroshocks through metal items. Every contact with a metallic object pushed you back with a small blast of energy. When the Inuit were stealing iron nails from British ships, they had no idea what a curse these would bring to the North.

First to leave for university was Liam, at the age of eighteen. Victor followed a few years later. He went to Toronto to study art, but came back without completing his degree. He got a job in the new government offices and married a woman from Grise Fiord, a community on the smaller Devon Island, north of Baffin Island. It was his adopted mother who introduced them to each other as she was working with this young lady at the hospital.

That was Victor's story. Liam took only a few minutes to unravel it for me.

That afternoon, I began thinking about how he never showed me family pictures. I looked around the living room, searching in the usual places people might store their albums.

Then I saw the drawer in the middle of the library shelves, the most common place to keep souvenirs. I opened it and there it was, his past, buried in a few boxes full of letters, notary documents about selling and buying properties, insurance subscriptions and birth and death certificates. Everything was neatly lying there, everything that was not yet said, or not voiced enough.

My mother said it was never a good idea to rummage through someone's papers, but I did just that.

Inside were tons of pictures stored in big leather-backed albums fastened with metal clasps. The biggest album was the one with his Irish family. On his father's side were the Irish peasants who came to Canada to escape the potato famine during Queen Victoria's reign. His great-great-grandmother had been a maid in the queen's kitchen, hiding her Catholic upbringing. She was the one who financed their crossing over the ocean with the promise to join them one day. She never did. Then, there was his mother's branch, IRA rebels who ran from the British police after a cousin was involved in a bomb blast in London. She was born in Ireland and retained her heavy Belfast accent, as echoed in Liam's speech. She was the primary parent at home while her husband was often away, and the boys took on the Irish-Gaelic accent from her.

Those were the stories that Liam never talked much about.

In another smaller brown album, there was his childhood in Victor's company: he, a tall fair-haired boy, and Victor, a small dark-skinned smiling boy. Liam was always looking at the camera from a slightly left angle as if he was blinded by the sun. Victor usually positioned himself a pace behind, hanging on to his big brother's sleeve. They were physically close in every image and their mother never seemed far. Their father was the one who took their pictures, so he did not appear in any of them. In the outdoor images, Victor was always wearing oversized parkas, hand-me-downs from his older brother. They were large and loose. Were their parents stingy, saving money by making Victor wear Liam's old clothes? This was the practice in many families, given that new clothes were such a rare commodity, yet when the practice extended to an adopted child, wearing an older child's leftovers seemed sad and unfair.

Scattered throughout the albums were piles of pictures taken at different occasions: garden parties, weddings, Christmas parties, picnics. The names of the figures were written on the back, in blue or black ink. With her dementia his mother must have lost the ability to sort them out and stick them under the plastic.

At the bottom of the drawer, there was another small stack with pictures of Liam in a military uniform. When had he been a soldier? He never mentioned that part to me. I put aside the albums and took a deep breath.

Now would have been the time to stop my indiscretion, but I did not.

The pictures were taken in Afghanistan. He was usually alone in them, rarely in the company of his fellow comrades who smiled with their arms around each other's shoulders, beer bottles in hand. The pictures were mostly taken in the canteen, mess and ceremony hall. At the bottom of the pile, there were a few pictures taken in the desert. They were almost colourless, except for that reddish-brown dust that covered the land, the cars and the uniforms. A younger Liam was wearing his combat uniform. Even the rifle was there, hanging at his side. The only photo in which Liam wasn't wearing combat gear was one with another man, both sitting on top of a Jeep. The photo's verso told me it was taken in Kandahar, in the winter of 2006. They were both smiling at the camera, their helmets carelessly lying at their feet.

The man next to him was Yannis Alexandridis. They were sunbathing on the car that was to be blown up a few months later, in the spring of 2007.

I sat on the couch for a few minutes to calm the racing thunder of my heart. Then I left the picture on the coffee table and got dressed. I cleaned everything I had touched and packed all my belongings. I called a taxi and closed the door behind me. It was a door I never intended to cross again.

When Liam called me Sunday afternoon, I told him I didn't want to see him again. He said nothing but I sensed he had already figured out what happened.

From the airport, he would go straight home to confront the evidence. During this anticipatory moment, I was mentally charting his reaction to the picture I had left lying on the table. Most likely, he would do what I had done the previous day, falling back on the couch to calm down. Before I first agreed to come to his home, he had probably put away everything related to Afghanistan and his former career as a soldier. He hadn't been brave enough to be up front with me on our first night together. He didn't want to spoil what had taken him so long to catch. How could he have forgotten those pictures?

He called me back later to say that he wanted to come talk to me.

One hour later, he was knocking on my door. I was lying on the couch, like a stone, knowing he wouldn't go away. He knocked again. I waited, did nothing. We were only a few metres from each other, both struggling in this prelude to what could only be a dreadful conversation.

"Let me in, will ya? Please."

I remained in the same position. His nervous voice made me feel even weaker, unable to take in his testimony. It was the voice of a man who had cheated me so appallingly, yet there was no penitence in his tone.

"We have to talk," he said.

After a brief moment, he added: "Then I'm leaving, I promise."

I opened the door and turned my back without looking at him, this man whom I did not know. I also didn't want to allow him to see the redness of my eyes. I hated showing how offended I was. Crying was proof I was damaged. I was not! My initial instincts were right, even if for the wrong reasons. He hadn't wanted to sleep with me because I was an easy prey, but because I was a rare one.

He followed me into the living room and sat on the chair. I settled on the sofa, where he'd first taken care of me back in January and where we made love for the first time a few days later. I still remembered his shyness undressing me.

"You knew who I was from the very first day," I said, looking at him.

My anger dissipated, replaced by a gloomy distress. I knew that regardless of his explanation, that sense of betrayal would never fade away. My humiliation had buried itself in my voice, muffling it, rendering it incapable of expressing any feeling at all. I was desperate to get through all this as fast as possible and to resume my life where I left it when I moved to Iqaluit.

"I knew. Of course, I knew who you were."

His voice was more imploring than his empty eyes. I felt he was unapologetic.

"I was at school the first day when the principal introduced the new teachers to the parents. I knew your name and recognized your face. I tried to make myself obvious, sitting in the front row, but you never laid eyes on me. I almost imagined you would recognize me."

"How could I?"

"Of course, it's stupid. How could you?"

I covered my eyes against that vision of his perplexity. I had been next to the principal, facing the small audience of parents and kids. I was intimidated by their inquiring looks. They had all come to see the new teachers. The parents had to endure this excruciating experience every year, fearing the people who arrived to take care of their kids. Had they been reassured when they saw me?

What had I worn? A skirt and a blouse, most probably. As a teacher, I followed my mother's code of manners: never wear pants in class. Kids are sexually aware creatures who constantly scrutinize their female teachers' physical appearance. I was certain that wearing a skirt and a blouse made me look older and trustworthy. I wanted parents to feel confident in my abilities.

But I made a misstep on that very first day. When I was about to leave the Grande Salle and lead my group of students to their classroom, I asked them to line up. They looked at me, puzzled. Line up how? Discipline was loose here as school was like an extension of the home. Teachers were big uncles like the principal, or old grannies like Ana. With little variation, children of the North spent their childhood within the same circle of people.

Liam had also been there, surely seeing how incapable I was trying to make my pupils line up and follow me quietly. The only concession they made was to stop talking and analyze me, my voice, my lips, my hair, my hands. I was a foreign animal in their realm, and before letting their impulses take over, they tested my ability to defend myself.

Liam mulled over his words.

"I was the driver of that Jeep," he said after a long silence. "The day of the accident, they left to supply a garrison with food while I was at the hospital. A spider had bitten my eyelid and I couldn't see for a week. After the explosion, they sent me home with a nervous breakdown. I made a choice to retire from the army and spent a few years as a PTSD veteran. I had almost forgotten I had that picture with Yannis."

I said nothing. I was just trying to silently release the sounds that choked in my throat.

He continued in a soft voice.

"I really wanted to tell you about him. The very first day I came to school to meet you, it was to tell you that I knew you from that magazine cover. But I couldn't say it. I could only think about the last ten years of my life since that picture was taken. Then the time passed so fast, it was late and you looked tired. I couldn't bring myself to tell you about Yannis, sitting in that chair so close to you. I was afraid of your reaction. I couldn't comfort you. I was just shocked you were there, sitting behind the desk. How could so many events come together this way, to see you in Iqaluit, right in front of me? I looked for you at Yannis's funeral. I was disappointed you didn't come. The whole battalion was hoping to see you there and talk to you. You were the last important thing that happened in Yannis's life. But you weren't there, and we all felt like your relationship was an illusion. As if we had just invented that story of you and Yannis. Poor lad! Then, here you were, behind the desk, frightened. I found the whole situation so dazzling, funny even. It took a long time for my soul to heal after that, and I grew awful fearful talking to you might open that wound again. If only I could have been able to start the story! But I couldn't that day. I was hoping it would be easier the next time. I started following you around the city, but it was impossible to talk to you. There was no reason to stop you on the street or anywhere else. You were always on the run, buying things, taking pictures, looking around. I ate at the Legion every Wednesday and Friday, when you were there with your colleagues, but there was no way to come and tell you I had missed dying with Yannis because of a stupid bug bite. After I allowed those first chances to slip by, it was too late. I was using any reason to come and see you at school, but I couldn't say it. We were always stuck on Eli's sweaters."

I started sobbing hard. He let me cry in silence. Again, I covered my eyes.

"I am so happy you came here," he said after a while, then he stood up and headed to the door. In the middle of the hall, he turned once more and said: "I won't bother you anymore, if that's what you want."

Then he closed the door behind him.

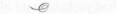

In the evening, I called my mother in Montreal and told her about Liam. We had spoken a few times about him, but she never asked for many details. There was no such intimacy between Mother and me, starting with my first love affair when she disapproved of the guy because he was older than me. My mother trusted me in everything except my choice of partners. In January, when I mentioned Liam's Irish origins, I was expecting her to find some historical rift between our two national heritages. Fortunately, there was no link between her people and the Celts. On the topic of medieval conflicts and resentments, it was all clear. I told my mother his parents where dead and that he had an adopted Inuk brother. But the thing she hung on to was his job.

"A policeman, *eh*?" she said, imitating the Irish accent. "With uniform and all, *eh*?"

To my mother, this was the only hiccup with Liam: He belonged to a cast of lowlife characters, those uniformed guys who show off their guns and testicles, who lower their voices when asking for your driver's licence at the side of the road, who always make you feel guilty. My mother's criteria for crossing someone off her list of suitable partners were so simple and convenient! Why had I refused to hang out with the constable in the first place if not for that reason?

When I called her in the evening, I told her that Liam was in fact one of Yannis's comrades, *le soldat canadien de Kandahar.* She took her time to take in the news. It seemed there was not much sense she could make of my life. I had come all this way only to meet the ghost of my past.

It became obvious to me why Liam had asked about my mother. Yannis had probably told him that it was she who gave him my email address. That was how Yannis started sending me those messages, after the magazine published his first email to them. Women like my mother always made these things easier.

The next day, she sent me an email asking me why I was angry with Liam.

Had I told her I was angry? Why was she always imagining the unspoken? And why was she always right?

Why are you making this into a problem? she wrote in her message. *No secret remains buried for life.*

I did not reply.

I soon became too busy trying, once again, to avoid Liam.

Despite his promise to leave me alone, he continued sending me texts asking for a final discussion. We had to get to the bottom of the story, he said. I didn't feel that way.

I didn't need to know more than what had already been said. The story was dead to me.

⌒

At the end of the week, he showed up at the entrance of the school. I was dressed for my walk back home, with my hood over my fur hat and a scarf over my nose. When I reached the small lobby to put my boots on, I found him there, mingling with the parents who were waiting for their kids. His strategy to deny me any means of retreat angered me even more. How could I make a scene in front of that many people?

I let him open the door for me and lead me to his car.

We drove in silence to his neighbourhood. There was no use in trying to persuade him to drive me home. I only hoped my silence would give him fair warning of my decision not to go back to him.

Liam had bought some food from the NorthMart. He quietly set the table, then invited me to sit down. While he was cutting the meat, he commented that setting the table was a practice originating in the Middle Ages. At that time, seemingly, rooms were not equipped with tables, so when people wanted to eat, they literally had to set up that requisite piece of furniture.

I looked at him anxiously. What he was talking about? Liam looked back, then suddenly he laughed. I did not. Avoiding my gaze, he went to the kitchen to fetch a bottle. Then he came back and busied himself pouring the wine, a smile still on his lips.

He looked at me as though waiting for a question. I felt unable to say a word, very much surprised that he still felt no responsibility for my anger. I knew he was hungry. I was angry but not so cruel to forbid him this meal after a day fuelled on coffee alone.

I took my fork and started moving the food around on my plate. He did the same.

"Were you both friends from back then?" I asked.

Liam's fork had almost reached his lips, but at this he put it back on the plate. He took a deep breath. Then he leaned back in his chair, as though to distance himself from me.

"I don't know," he said with a slow shake of his head. "At war you don't speak much about friendship. Mostly you speak about good comrades who watch your back. We got along well together. Yannis was a little younger than me, but he tried to convince me I was the one in need of protection."

He was obviously looking for more things to add, but finding none, he remained silent for a while. Then a sudden smile bloomed on his face. He looked at me, shy about it. He saw my bleak look and become even more amused. He covered his mouth with his hand to hide his laugh.

"That thing about setting the table in the Middle Ages," he said, trying to hold back his smirk, "actually comes from Yannis. He was very interested in old bits of history. I used to laugh at these kinds of sayings, not because they were funny, but because he found the most unexpected moments to share his wisdom. The things he said were never inappropriate, but never quite appropriate either."

"He didn't strike me as a very funny guy," I said.

Liam looked at me, waiting for more.

I took a sip of wine. Then a mouthful of brown rice. He followed my example. His eyes reflected his relief. Meals

were important moments to him, especially as he usually
only ate once a day.

I took another bite just to allow him to have more.

We ate silently for a while. He filled his glass again.
Was he trying to get drunk?

He looked at me and said: "I was so happy that day playing hooky from the mission. I was planning to sleep all day
long while the team was driving over those rutted streets. It
was a chance to take a break from the mission, but an honest excuse. I knew what trips like that did to you. Even your
eyes hurt by the end. You could almost chew the sand in
your mouth and you'd be in a cold sweat till you got back to
the garrison. We were all worried about Yannis's Afghan
friends. He talked to everyone around; he had an easy way
of making friends. He'd even entertain the little local children. He was the only one to have learned a few words in
Pashto, enough to carry a small conversation. The rest of us
only knew what was related to our drills. Our major believed he died in a trap set by the Taliban, who had inform-
ants everywhere. But I don't know about that. Maybe it was
a set up. Or maybe he just drove over a mine. It didn't
really matter to any of us."

"Did you feel guilty?"

"Guilty that I didn't die?"

I kept silent.

"I don't think so ... or maybe I just try not to think
about it," he said after a while, looking at me. "I mean, do
you blame me for still being alive? Do you think I could
have helped? I couldn't have. Really."

I lowered my eyes.

He spoke fast to clear his accusation from the air.

"I didn't feel guilty, but after the blast I couldn't stay in the army anymore. In a way, it killed me too. They discarded me at my request. Then I took a job in a federal office and moved to Toronto."

I couldn't eat anymore. I pushed my plate away and picked up my glass.

He finished his meal in silence, his eyes on his plate. He ate in slow motion, even though he was usually a fast eater. Now he was taking his time. I was still there and that was the essential thing for him. Sadly, neither of us could find the words to conjure memories of Yannis.

When he finished, he cleared the table and brought out dessert, two bowls with mashed pineapple. He handed me one and I accepted it. We ate quietly and then he made coffee.

He did the dishes while I settled on the couch, and I felt he was intentionally taking more time than usual. He even let the water run, which was not his style. Water was precious and he was usually careful not to waste it. The running tap made me realize he was nervous, despite his outward calm. Suddenly, the house filled with the odour of burnt coffee. He'd forgotten he'd turned on the machine at the beginning of our meal. He poured the coffee into the sink and came to the living room with another bottle of wine, then sat next to me and tried to fill my glass.

"I do not want to get drunk," I said, covering the rim with my palm.

"Why not?" He tried to nudge my hand away. "Let's do like old times! Let's get drunk."

I smiled for the first time that night and pulled back my hand.

"There you go, now."

He filled my glass and leaned back on the couch. As he did so, he tried to touch my leg, but I curled myself up in the opposite corner. He adjusted his position again, edging a little farther away. He turned his body away from me, toward the middle of the room.

He didn't talk for a while. Maybe he stopped thinking at the same time. He was leaning back, his feet on the ottoman next to the coffee table.

"I would like to go back home," I said. "I need to rest."

"You can rest here. I'll sleep on the couch and you take the bed."

"Okay, then I would like to go to bed now. I feel a little dizzy."

"Dizziness is good."

He laughed and kept his focus on me.

"Don't leave me alone, will ya," he said in an unusual voice.

He seemed drunk already. I stood up, but he held my hand.

"Please don't go."

I sat back on the couch. He got close to me and tried to kiss me. I let him. His lips were hungry once again. He held me still a few moments and smelled my hair. He kissed me on the ear, then on the cheek.

He spread my legs before removing the rest of my clothes. His shirt was half unbuttoned, and his socks were still on his feet. We almost glided off the couch, but he pushed me back while still inside me.

Then we lay on the rug. He dragged a small quilt from the couch and covered us. He caressed my neck and held me in his strong grip.

"What really made you come here?" he asked, turning my whole body to face him.

I didn't answer. He maintained his vigil over me by the dim light from the street.

"Yannis said you were a quiet girl," he said, laughing.

"What?"

"Yes, it was a funny thing to say about someone that you've never met. We teased him about it. But I knew you weren't what he expected you to be."

"Is that what he told you?"

"Vaguely. He told me all you did was ask questions. And he took a lot of time to answer you. He would spend hours in front of the computer. I always wondered what he was writing you."

"He spoke about the army."

Liam remained silent.

"I wouldn't know what to tell a woman about the army. There's too much to tell but in fact there is nothing."

He snuggled me closer to him and anchored me across my shoulders with his left hand.

"Did he tell you if he intended to come and look for me when he got back?"

"I don't really remember. Ten years is such a long time. I don't remember much of what he said about you. I imagine he was happy to know you."

"He never said that to me."

"What did you write him?"

"Not much. It was as if everybody was watching us. It was all so serious. We felt we were both on a kind of mission."

"And what was yours?"

"Not to be a frivolous girl."

"As if being in love is frivolous!"

"We didn't have time to fall in love. I feel guilty that I made him waste the last weeks of his life trying to answer my questions. How could I know we didn't have much time ahead? And if I knew it, would I have acted differently? What was the right thing to do? Give him hope?"

Liam put my head on his chest and covered it with both hands. Maybe this was his way of asking me to stop talking. But I could not.

The more I talked about Yannis, the more I understood that Liam was not all that interested in his old comrade in arms. He was interested in me. When my voice choked with sorrow, he took me in his arms and we made love.

CHAPTER SEVEN:

Polar Bears
and Taxi Drivers

A T THE BEGINNING of the month, a polar bear ventured into our community. A colleague, Pauline, was walking her dog around Dead Dog Lake when a police car stopped her and asked what she was doing outside. Hadn't she heard about the polar bear? She hadn't. The police got her and the little dog in the car and brought them home.

It was the second time that winter that a polar bear had come to the city, rummaging for food or just exploring new territory. The first one in October was shot by a police unit, near Lake Geraldine. Once a bear made its way into territory claimed by humans, it would keep coming back. There would always be something available for them to nibble on: greasy pizza boxes, half-empty tubs of margarine, bones, fish skin, caribou hooves, seal tails. They could adapt their diets very quickly. Their presence endangered the kids playing hockey on the lake, people walking their dogs and seal hunters on the nearby lakes. Until the bear was shot, no one was allowed to leave the outskirts of the city.

The bear was put down the next day by a hunter

dispatched to do the job by the municipality. It took him a long day of searching to find the animal, around the garbage boxes on the Road to Nowhere. The meat, except for the poisonous liver, was shared in the community, and the skin was listed for sale on Iqaluit Sell/Swap.

Pauline posted the story on her Facebook wall, along with pictures of the hunter next to the dead polar bear, a picture that she downloaded from the local newspaper. The image was not meant to praise the hunter's deed but to reassure people that it was safe to go out. A wave of heinous comments followed her post, expounding on the consequences of climate change, raging about human cruelty, championing the cuteness of polar bears. How could they kill such a defenceless creature? They should have scared it off back to the tundra where it would passively acquiesce to remain forever.

Pauline tried to explain the matter of public safety up North, but her comments were met with remarks about our role in saving the planet. Pauline responded that the bear would be subtracted from the hunting quota allotted to the community, but this did nothing to satisfy people down South, who thought hunting was always bad. Someone replied with the image of a skinny polar bear dying on an ice floe. It was the image of a sick animal, but sickness was also common in the bear population, which prevented them from hunting and properly feeding. They too could die of starvation, as people so often did on this land.

For many people around the world, the means of survival that had sustained the Inuit for thousands of years had become untenable. Their practice of hitting the seal on the head to give it a fast death was deemed cruel. The

subsistence economy that helped them survive was con-
demned. Everybody around the world seemed to know better about what the Inuit should do in the Arctic than the
Inuit themselves. These strangers were still relying on Isaac
Newton's view of a basic harmony between man and nature. The poorly known North had once again become the
target of illusions and prejudices.

Hunting was a way of life, but it was violent too. Outsiders found the Inuit unsentimental and cruel in their
treatment of animals. Mostly, these critics held naive beliefs
that hunting cultures like the Inuit lived in perfect harmony with the nature, but their idealized image was ludi-
crous. There was murder, warfare and vendettas in Inuit
history. No one from the outside world could understand
what a struggle life in this land was. People learned to be
resilient and practical, facing nature with respect but fear
as well, knowing tragic events were very much a part of
their lives.

Since the time of the whalers and British explorers,
experience has not taught us much. Rumbling among the
ice floes in their search for the Northwest Passage, white
people tried to maintain a semblance of their lives back
home aboard their ships. It's why Franklin's men starved to
death in a region where game was abundant.

Pauline deleted the post. She questioned whether she
had it all wrong and stopped arguing. This was not her
fight and she was in no position to defend anyone. She was
tired and all alone, out of sync with her Facebook friends.
Until that post, they had praised her pictures of spectacular
sunsets and sundogs, the popular name of the parhelion
phenomenon, when two bright spots flank the sun within

a halo. Now it was as though she had become no better than a criminal, sanctioning those violent acts. Pauline preferred to stay in with the crowd and bow to the common illusion about the Arctic and so took to posting uncontroversial images that painted Iqaluit to be a harmonious place rather than the barren, god-shrouded land of Arctic gravel beaches it was. As British explorers once did, Pauline put her faith in a North that never was.

I became quite familiar with some of the taxi drivers during my morning trips to school. When I hopped in their cars, they'd announce on the radio that they were going to the French school. As a requirement to get hired, they had to memorize not only the streets, but the buildings too. They also built up a memory chart of the people they drove. They knew the clients who would not pay the fare pretending they were drunk or forgot the money. Every day, they witnessed violence, suicides and crimes. They often found themselves spending time with police, filling out papers about the side of Iqaluit that was typically hidden. Their clothes smelled of food, smoke and cheap perfume.

In contrast with my previous life in Montreal, I found it convenient to wait for a taxi in the morning, on the back patio of the post office. I would tuck myself into the back seat of the car and begin my day to the musical beat that kept the drivers connected to their other life. Their parkas carried the aroma of the spicy food they cooked in their bachelor apartments. They relied on those ethnic meals to remember home and save money.

Taxi drivers represented the new face of the Iqaluit community, no more a world of igloos, whalers and seal hunting, but of migrant stories.

At six in the morning, they were ready to tell their tales, often embedded with a political moral. They could give anybody a lesson in how to thrive. But despite so many customers hopping in and out of their cabs, they remained nevertheless the loneliest people around.

The secrets of this community's life were revealed to them during the short distances they drove people. The city spanned no more than a few kilometres, long enough to piece together the jigsaw of the human condition in the Arctic Circle.

With few exceptions these drivers were Southeast Asian, Middle Eastern or Black. There were also a lot of women of different origins and ages. The oldest taxi driver I met was seventy-two years old and had been financially ruined by her husband's gambling and drinking habits, which culminated in his premature death in a ditch. She was trying to mend her wrecked life. She didn't speak English. It took the company a long time before they trusted her with a cab, but she'd finally succeeded in getting the job and she was proud of this. She worked hard, both for the money and also to thank the boss who had given her a chance. She hadn't had many of those in her lifetime.

The drivers all knew me and drove me to school via Niaqunngusiariaq Street or through sinuous Happy Valley. When I got inside, the windows of their cabs would still be misty despite the heat being on full blast. On the way up the slope, I'd look at the bay, dyed orange by the sunrise. The ice shone like a huge mirror turned up to the sky. Close to the Aksarniit Middle School, we regularly passed the honey truck and the Narwhal Plumbing & Heating van. We'd often pass one of the young teachers who walked down to Inuksuk High School in any kind of weather. On the porch of one of the houses to our left on the way to school there was a huge LGBT flag.

When the taxi drivers wanted to engage with me in French, they made a point of announcing to the dispatch office that they were going to L'Aurore Boréale School. I could tell by their pronunciation that they were francophone and eager to speak in a language that didn't see much use in Iqaluit. Sometimes we had to make a stop on the way to pick up another client, usually heading to the emergency room.

There was this taxi driver from Calgary I first met in January who took it upon himself to be my financial adviser. He knew the road to the French school blindfolded so he tended to drive almost all the way with his head turned toward me. Born in Bangladesh, he had first moved to Alberta, drawn by the economic boom of the last decade. Now Calgary was dead, he said. That's why he came to Nunavut, mining for gold at Caribou Tuktu Cabs. He insisted I should stay a few more years. The timing was perfect to get rich here. This gold rush was not destined to last. As had happened in Alberta, the river of milk and honey would soon dry out. The hunting of whales, bears and seals was no longer the bonanza of the past. The grip of poverty would once again take hold here.

In the search for his personal fortune, he'd lost his wife and kids, who had refused to follow him to the Klondike of polar bears. Five years had already passed since his arrival, but he still shared a room with two other men from Africa.

He had no time to think about a new family, as he was working eighteen hours a day. Money was the sole reason he was here.

One day, I had to share the cab with an old Inuk woman. It was past ten o'clock in the morning, and the school had to be closed midday because of the coming blizzard. We sent the kids home, then called cabs and waited for them at the entrance. Because of the weather, it was difficult to get a ride and the delay was more than twenty minutes. The cabs were speeding from one part of the city to the other, transporting as many people as they could. As the wind got stronger, everybody was rushing for shelter. Soon, there would be no cars or people on the roads.

The woman was coming from Apex, the village over the hill, rushing to the hospital with a cut on her right hand. The cab stopped to pick me up from the French school and afterward it did another detour to pick up a young man. When we got back to Niaqunngusiariaq Street, the traffic was blocked at the intersection behind the Quick Stop. There had been a two-car crash, and one of them was badly hit on the side. Surprisingly, the tow truck that came to bring it to the garage was not doing the usual manoeuvre of dragging the vehicle by a cable, but was pushing the car from behind with gentle nudges to the bumper. Drivers were sticking their heads out of their vehicles to watch the carnival.

The Inuk woman was uninterested in the fuss on the road, unlike the driver and the front-seat passenger. She was absorbed in her contemplation of a small boy fighting the strong wind. He was carrying a bag of groceries, trying to dodge traffic as he crossed the road.

The woman became worried about the boy's predicament and said to the taxi driver that she wanted to get out of the car. The driver said, without turning his head: "Lady, if you get out, I won't be able to wait for you. I have to follow the traffic."

She sat back in her seat. The boy finally succeeded in crossing the street. Instead of hurrying back home, he remained on the other side to watch the tow truck.

"Whose kid is that?" the woman asked, without addressing anyone in particular.

The taxi driver said nothing. The young man sitting in the front seat tried to have a closer look at the boy's face and said something in Inuktitut.

"This place is becoming too big for us," the old woman said, while settling deeper into the back seat. "How did we come to this? I don't know the kids anymore. And they don't know us."

I looked at her and smiled, embarrassed. She was addressing me, but I didn't know what to say. I grew up in a big city where not knowing your neighbours could often be a good thing.

The flow of traffic picked up speed again, after the tow truck pushed the damaged car onto a secondary road. Despite the wind, people were driving with their windows down to watch the show.

The woman next to me was staring at the young boy, who was now rushing down the road to Happy Valley.

One frosty morning, when the temperature dropped below forty-six degrees again, I was picked up at the post office entrance by a guy who had immigrated from the Congo and spoke French. We were silent, as we left the centre of town and started up the steep slope going to Inuksuk High School and the Frobisher Inn. The car was making an awful racket, as if tortured by the freezing cold, and he drove carefully. He had a gentle touch at every corner and waited a few moments before turning toward the next stretch. Man and car were in a caring relationship; I followed the driver's manoeuvres with much admiration.

The drive took much longer than usual, almost ten minutes. Since there weren't many clients on the road, the man could take his time. He started railing against the taxi companies that had brought solitude and despair to the lives of the local people. Before, they had lived a different life on the land. Now, he said, they were the victims of hidden political interests and a capitalist monopoly that prevented setting up a public transportation system in Iqaluit. The fare of seven dollars per individual was too high for families to visit their relatives regularly. Yet in the past they used to live together, sharing space and knowledge. Within a community as big as Iqaluit, it was much harder to keep connected, and solitude exacerbated the many addiction problems. The fact that some Inuit clients left without paying the fare didn't bother him. This was their land. At one point, they had known everybody in their community from birth. Nurturing a child was the responsibility of the whole community. Now they didn't know their youth anymore. More and more unknown faces were pouring in every day from the outside world. They now feared the future. Who would take care of them in their old age? They could not entrust their lives to strangers! Strangers wouldn't know what was best for them! They would feed them milk and cheese, not food of the land. There'd be no Inuit aunts and uncles to rock and pat the babies. Who would bother to visit them in those government buildings? You raise kids because you need them. You raise your children so the circle of life will continue, each generation doing their part so that no elderly grandmother gets forgotten.

When I went to pay, I discovered that I had forgotten my wallet on the table. The evening before, I had paid my bills online and had taken out my credit card. I told the driver to turn back home and make it a double fare, but he said with a big smile: *"Allez, maîtresse, vous pouvez me payer la prochaine fois."*

Lately, I had stopped spending the night at Liam's. Ever since the day I rummaged in his drawers, our relationship had cooled. Our best days were behind us. Since then, each time he was called out on an emergency, I packed my stuff while he got ready to go. We usually left at the same time, him in his RCMP vehicle, me in a taxi. Our relationship was mending, but painfully. We might have put an end to our short and insignificant affair had it not been for those stories that linked us both to Yannis, whose memory had become a world in itself, one which we revolved around like solitary satellites.

He never asked to see the emails sent by Yannis. I had saved them in a folder under the title *"Lettres."* I never reread them, not even after I learned I was sleeping with one of Yannis's comrades in arms.

Despite this, some of Yannis's words started to pop up in my mind without my even opening the files. After he died, I read and re-read them, searching for something more than the depictions of his comrades' bad habits. In the email titled "Lads," Yannis described his fellow soldiers as good guys, brave even, but that the oppressively long mission had turned them into lazy and impulsive individuals. The ugly routine of life on the Kandahar base annihilated the healthy cooperation between body and spirit, he wrote. Eventually, they all became careless with their physical appearance and hygiene. Beautiful young faces turned into a façade of wrinkles, hair and pimples. They were all masked by a layer of dirt and a constant frown. I was left to wonder whether Liam was one of those good guys who had sunk into bad habits, like scratching his dandruff and rubbing his testicles in sight of everyone.

The worst, Yannis wrote, was the fear. The persistent anxiety they were living with filled them with aggressiveness and scorn. Even their communal life became unbearable as most of the men tried to sidestep their fear by bragging about women and sex. As much as they hated life in the group, loneliness was dangerous in the war zone. Alone, separated from the herd, they were like wounded animals, vulnerable prey.

Was Liam one of these guys who exaggerated his claim to former lovers and dirty sex? How much had he changed in all those years? How different was he then from the person I knew now, tidy and quiet?

How much could I possibly know about a world where men had to put on battle gear and barricade their inner selves behind bulletproof jackets? How could those men return back to society and to the myriad tasks that make up domestic life, become once again fathers and husbands?

How easily would they be able to forget the horrors of war and just mow the lawn, talk to neighbours over the fence, build birdhouses? What would it have taken for Liam to adjust to a normal life after seeing his comrades blown up?

Yannis understood the inevitable failure of the mission in Afghanistan, and this awareness created a gap between him and his comrades. Soldiers were not meant to see the bigger picture of the war. Yannis, though, grew obsessed with their inability to accomplish anything. How had he come to understand that their mission was doomed from the beginning? Was it because he was Greek? His ancestors were the first to learn firsthand the horrors of warfare during their ten-year siege of Troy. And when they finally conquered the city, it was not their swords but a scam that brought them to victory. Ulysses built the wooden horse within which the Hoplites snuck into the fortress. Since then, the Greeks knew best that it is not force but lies that win wars.

Yannis could not stand the public hypocrisy back home in Canada either. In one of his emails, he berated those who opposed the war while still supporting the troops. What were they supporting, Yannis asked me, if not their boys' right to kill? The whole country was praying for them to survive, which implied that the Afghans had to die. He was appalled by public opinion and the Canadians' blindness to the mess overseas. Yannis knew their troops would not be coming back as heroes but as a defeated army.

The Canadian soldier exited the scene with no answers to his questions. He had known how difficult it would be to return to a country that did not need his anxiety. Liam survived because he made peace with his ignorance. He survived because he was able to move on again with this life, whatever the cost.

To Liam, Yannis remained an embodiment of old sayings and odd facts, like the one about setting the table in the Middle Ages. There were other quirks Liam remembered, such as Yannis's predilection for falling asleep anytime and anywhere, even standing up. Some guys mocked him, saying he was a Mediterranean to his core, unable to shake those midday naps.

In response to the friendly teasing, Yannis retorted that he was born in Canada and had visited Greece only a few times in his whole life. Stop bothering him with that Mediterranean crap! Sure, he ate olives, cheese and tomatoes, but that was hardly proof of ethnicity. He also ate hamburgers and drank Coca-Cola, both abundant in the army kitchen. Why was anyone talking about his ethnicity in the first place? What did it matter?

I didn't share my musings about the relevance of ethnicity or my mother's bias against the Greeks with Liam. Once again, I was silent about things that could shame me. I knew my family was bigoted against other ethnicities and races, despite our education and upbringing.

Most difficult to describe to him was my sorrow's metamorphosis. In the last ten years, I had lost all my ease and passion, those two big privileges of youth. How much I had once spoken about things I didn't really grasp! The minor fame I gained because of that *Maclear's* cover photo had given me a voice. In the end, perhaps that was a good thing. But it cost me my happiness.

Liam didn't call while he was away, and I didn't either. I knew how tough his missions were in the communities where he was dispatched to inquire into murders or disappearances in the polar night. Inuit families were not eager to help RCMP officers. There were too many memories of the RCMP forcing them into the Qallunaat houses. Inuit elders told gruesome stories about officers who had killed their dogs as a way to prevent people from going back to the land. RCMP officers, on their side, had never acknowledged any wrongdoing. Some policemen even came out of retirement to deny such allegations. They said that the only animals they killed were stray dogs after they'd attacked passers-by. As no one was feeding them regularly, the packs roved the city in search for food. In the night, they could become quite aggressive. But the truth gets lost amid the bitterness among all parties who haven't yet found a way to heal those old wounds.

Recently Liam and his team were dispatched to find a missing person in Pangnirtung. It was the second case in a month. This community had been hit by a wave of suicides among the youth. As an emergency measure, the government dispatched a few nurses and psychiatrists. But how much support could those outsiders possibly provide to such a distressed community? How little they knew about what was pushing individuals to such extremes!

Even in death, the Inuit were unwilling to be the focus of white people, the ones that were still in charge of their well-being: policemen, nurses, teachers, doctors, shopkeepers, social workers, correctional officers. They preferred to disappear in the whiteout, bringing an end to the intrusion of outsiders. Disappearing in the Arctic is not complicated.

Sometimes their bodies lay just under the snow not far from their houses. They might be found in spring, but often, never. If the ice released the bodies after the melt, bears, foxes and ravens took them. Then the gulls scattered the bones and the waves ensured they sank to the bottom of the ocean.

Though Liam didn't speak of his missions, his garments were an olfactory map of his trips up North. Each time, the scents varied according to where he had spent the night. Sometimes it was smoke and grease, at other times it was only sweat, cold sweat. He smoked on such journeys and even drank spirits, while at home he only drank wine.

Like an old seaman, he followed a disciplined diet. At home, he judiciously measured the size of his portions, the slices of bread, the amount of fruit or the weight of the chocolate square he indulged on. He never broke this routine, whereas I listened more impulsively to my desires. I used to keep track of my diet, noting omissions or excess, and the next day I would adjust my intake, but these days I just trusted that my body would ultimately make good decisions.

One Sunday morning, he insisted over the phone that I join Eli and him at the Aquatic Centre. After a moment's hesitation, I accepted.

When I entered the building, Eli saw me through the glass walls and waved at me. Liam was sitting on a plastic chair next to the pool, checking his phone. He was wearing a bathing suit. When I came out from the change room, he joined us in the water. Eli asked me to compete with her to see who could reach the end of the lane first. I said no! She was a better swimmer than me and I didn't want to race her and risk letting her see that she could beat me.

Afterward, in the locker room, I had to dry Eli's hair, which took me a while. The fans were high up on the wall and the hot air not strong enough. Eli had long hair and had come out of the shower with water running down her skinny back. When we'd come to the pool before with the school, Eli had never allowed me to help her out. She was so autonomous and made a proud point of it. But now she was patiently letting my fingers play in her hair.

Liam was waiting for us downstairs, in front of the cafeteria.

Eli said with joy: "My hair is dry now. Are you buying me an ice cream?"

Liam laughed and took the wallet from his pocket.

"Could you buy one for Miss Irina?"

"Of course." He looked at me with questioning eyes.

This was our ritual when we came with the class to the swimming pool on Thursday mornings: At the end of the session, the kids each rushed to buy something with the money their parents had carefully stashed in a Ziploc bag, tucked next to the swimsuit in their backpack. There was always someone who wanted to offer a treat to all their peers.

My impression had been that Eli was quite stingy. She refused to give or accept any favours. Now she seemed so happy to give me something. That ice-cream cone was her big treat for me. Or maybe it was a strategic move to prove her influence over her uncle. Was this her way of cautioning me that she was in control of that big man?

We stood at the plastic table, licking our small cones. When we finished, Eli proposed to us that her uncle give me a lift home. They drove me to the post office and when the car stopped, Eli asked me to show her my windows. They were the ones just above the red sign with the Canada Post insignia. She looked at them for a while.

I took my bag and opened the door while they were still staring at the building.

Before I got out, Eli said with her usual salut: "*À demain*, Miss Irina!"

<hr/>

That evening, Liam was to be on duty. He called in the afternoon to tell me that Eli had left. Her granny had called her to a family gathering as Eli's grandfather had come from Grise Fiord for a medical check-up at the hospital. He had brought fresh meat and invited over some old acquaintances.

I was wrong to assume that Granny was a solitary woman, lost in the city. Iqaluit, to her, was no bigger than Grise Fiord. Lots of their childhood friends had moved to the capital, following their kids or the government jobs. Liam had told me about her gatherings over tea and cake; those old ladies were the keepers of long-standing traditions and stories. Their resilience helped them face modern life with sanity and humour. They had their favourite TV series and contemporary songs. They read the newspapers and followed the news. In their own way, they understood the traps and pitfalls of the modern world around them better than anyone else, and were able to avoid them. For their visiting grandsons, they fried fish and baked scones.

They mended their friends' clothes and knitted baby-sized hats and socks. Some of them were skilled at sewing quilts they then sold through the elder centre. Everybody helped with cutting and putting together pieces of fabric to create patterns representing solar beams and tundra hills. Despite the long hours and the amount of fabric they used, they never got into negotiations about the price. They asked people what they could afford.

For the last few days, Granny had been busy purchasing things for her old man to take back to Grise Fiord. In the northern part of the Canadian Archipelago, the prices were much higher than in Iqaluit, so people took advantage of trips to the capital to fill their bags with canned vegetables, pickles to eat with the seal meat, clothing and medicine.

Eli was excited to see her grandfather. I imagined him an old fisherman, toothless, with a rough cough from smoking. Liam told me I was mistaken. The old man was one of the best-known photographers of the Arctic region, and his pictures had become a valuable contribution to the Canadian archives. He had travelled with his exhibition to Denmark and Norway. He had also occasionally worked as a translator for adventurers chasing the northern mystery, whatever that was.

The old man had had an adventurous life and a long-time involvement with white developers and tourist agents. He taught them how to build igloos and stalk muskox. He was praised and included in every photograph with all those adventurers, artists, politicians and officials who were pushing different agendas in the Arctic. But he grew disappointed with his role. White people were never eager to listen to the real stories of northern people; they preferred the ones that the South invented on their behalf.

For a while, he was the richest man around by any Inuit standards. He had a house, a boat, a Ski-Doo and modern rifles. Then he lost it all. He grew old and lonely. His daughter's death was the last bitter drop in the glass. He started drinking and became quick to fight after his wife went to help with Eli. He refused to follow her to Iqaluit and for a while he led the life of an outsider in his own community. Bartenders were mindful of the old man's fits of anger. He took in a younger woman as a second spouse. Then one day, he fell asleep on his way back home, resulting in the loss of his toes. He required lengthy treatment at the hospital in Iqaluit.

Granny agreed to forgive him. They both worked hard to mend their broken relationship and the old man struggled to come out of his dark solitude. He stopped drinking and went back to Grise Fiord, determined to remake himself, and he did. He opened up his old trunk with photographic paraphernalia. He resumed his photography. Sometimes he shot owls but his favourite subjects were crows, those unloved, even loathed birds. Unlike those who think of them as black messengers, the old man considered them the most resilient creatures on Earth. He staked out their favourite locations—around garbage boxes—and noted their soliloquies from the tops of the hydro poles. He knew the meaning of their caws and was able to distinguish yells of warning from calls to family. In their obscure way, they too were telling stories no one was listening to.

One of the galleries in Ottawa held an exhibition of his black-feathered accomplices, the distinctive character of each illuminated in the series of photographs. Every item sold quickly. Yet now he was too old to be impressed by the siren song of a successful artistic career. He was just happy to help people appreciate the oldest inhabitants of his land.

After Eli ran to welcome the old man, Liam asked me to come to his place for a few hours before his shift. It had been a week since we last made love. We were both ashamed to confess our lust, but the earlier sight of each other's naked bodies covered only by wet swimsuits had broken down our defences. We had eyed each other's forms, careful not to let Eli see our ardour. Liam had a beautiful body, with bulky muscles and agile calves. The hair on his upper chest was red, more vivid than on his head. The wet swimsuit had outlined his sex. When he came out of the water, he tried to conceal those lumps with discreet movements. Eli too was spying on us with furtive glances, mostly eyeing my breasts. I had shifted from an amorphous teacher to a species she could study.

I accepted his invitation and an hour later we were driving to his place. On the road, we made a detour to buy something to eat. I waited for him in the car. I was still avoiding as much as possible being seen in his company, even though no one seemed to pay attention to him when he was not wearing his uniform. He was more than aware of the mix of fear and hate that the sight of an RCMP officer conjured up in the hearts of the locals.

In the kitchen, I helped him unpack the food and set the table. As usual, it took a while before our conversation flowed.

While we were silently chewing our chicken, I noticed for the first time a slight deformation of Liam's thumbs.

Only once before had I met someone whose opposable fingers could bend backward at such a sharp angle, like there were no bones inside. Eli's thumbs were identical.

The new insight suddenly dawned.

Liam O'Connor was not Eli's uncle. He was her father.

There was no resemblance between them, but for the light shade of Eli's complexion. The girl clearly took her features from her Inuk mother. This was how they had been able to keep the secret in the family. I felt certain that Victor and Granny knew the truth; they had arranged their lives in order to protect Eli.

I said nothing, but I could no longer touch my food. A big lump got stuck in my throat and I coughed for a long time. Liam gave me some water. The coughing was a good excuse to stop eating and go lie down on the coach. I told him I had already eaten.

He carried on at the table alone. From time to time, he looked over at me as I watched TV. He was always on his guard against questions that might pop up about Yannis, but that story no longer threatened our liaison. He now used any reason to be with me. There were only a few months left till my departure. I wondered: Was ours just a convenient relationship that allowed him to hide his secret and spend time with his daughter?

Liam did the dishes while the coffee was brewing. I was waiting for him to settle on the couch, gathering my nerve to ask him the dreadful question: Are you the father?

But then his cellphone rang and he answered. It was someone from outside the city with whom he had a long conversation over some documents missing from a file. He was stern, raising his voice, said he needed those papers the next week. He made reference to a birth certificate. The other person took a lot of time to explain, but ended by finally soothing Liam. The call ended.

Had I witnessed something inappropriate? He laughed, seeing my confusion.

"There's no secret, don't worry." He sat on the couch and kissed me, his breath charged with the aroma of coffee and sexual desire. Food had awakened in him his second most pressing instinct.

At first, I thought I would be able to confront him right away. But it didn't come out. Later, while he was fussing around in the kitchen, I tried to anticipate his reaction. Would he deny it? Make fun of it? Accept it?

⟶

Except for their matching thumbs, there was no physical evidence I could spot to confirm my suspicion. Eli's presence in this house was in such plain sight that no one would think twice about her status. She was simply the daughter of a neglectful father and a deceased mother, taken care of by her uncle. Notebooks and pencils were scattered on the bottom shelf of the coffee table, her slippers were by the entrance, there were some Legos in a wicker basket. As I knew from school, Eli was not an excessive person at all. She had a very economical way of entertaining herself with a few toys, papers and pencils. In the kitchen there were some plastic cups in different shapes and colours, with Disney characters on them.

There was also her room upstairs, adjacent to Liam's. It was only natural that there should be signs of his true feelings for Eli in the choice of wallpaper and bedding, the characters on her pyjamas, the knick-knacks on her shelves, her socks, her combs, her little jewellery.

Now that I knew the truth, I could begin to uncover the evidence, piece by piece. I now considered all those small things that might hint at a fatherly bond. He certainly brought her presents from his voyages, those small things that were very much fatherly: a box of fine chocolate, a new drawing book, a fashionable dress, a pair of socks with little bears.

I thought back to earlier conflicts that everybody just took as the fits of a spoiled niece. One day Eli came to school furious. I noticed it at once but didn't ask. That would have been sure to make her even more secretive. No one could break into Eli's defensive fortress. After recess, we had gone to the Franco-Centre where the school board had prepared a lunch for us with pizza and orange juice. A few parents came to help us, settling the pupils at the tables and serving each a share of two slices and a drink. Liam was among the group of parents. When he entered the room, Eli turned her head the other way. I guessed immediately that Liam was the reason for her bad mood. He nodded at me and went to speak to Eli. I was at the other end of the table, so I didn't hear their conversation. After a few minutes, Eli allowed him to hug her. I took a pizza box and I went to offer Liam a slice, as we were doing for all the parents.

"Is everything okay?"

"Everything's fine," he said, but his expression suggested the opposite. "I ruined her favourite blouse in the washing machine. I put it in warm water and the colours washed out."

Eli gave me one of her looks. She was definitely plead-ing with me to teach her uncle a lesson!

To the other teachers, Liam was the caring uncle who had stepped in to care for a traumatized niece. He had the means to do it; there was nothing there to raise suspicion. It was not unusual for a relative to take care of an orphaned child, to house, nourish and protect them. Family was a selfless institution, without any strict division between households. Neighbours, uncles and aunts often shared the responsibility of raising a child. That taxi driver was right. So was the woman from Apex, right to be stunned by un-known faces on the streets, right to be sad about no longer taking part in the children's upbringing. Kindergartens, schools and daycares were now available. Older relatives and neighbours were not needed like they were in the past.

Once again, I felt abused and betrayed by Liam.

I could not accuse him of having a child, though. As it was, I was free to treat Eli as severely as my authority al-lowed, knowing that she was his niece. How about as the daughter of the man I made love to?

I decided not to bring it up that day.

Liam held me in his arms. I looked at him intensely, hoping for an answer to my unspoken question. He finished his coffee, eager to pull me close and kiss me with all the passion of his mouth. My lips were sucked up between his teeth. There was so much hunger in his kiss, it almost cut off his breath. Both his hands were holding me tight against his body so that I might feel his sex through his pants. His palms were running down my back, to my buttocks, which he squeezed with strength. After a while, he opened my blouse and grabbed one of my breasts. I let him do so while undoing the buckle of his pants. He was in no rush to get into my body. With his fingers, he touched my lips, then my ears. He was exploring the smell of my skin everywhere. My hair was pulled loose; he fingered the few strands that had fallen over my face. He told me a while ago that I had not changed much since he saw me on that magazine cover. My hair had the same length and colour. His was turning grey.

Our clothes piled up next to the couch. I was shy about my naked body and Liam was not very daring either. There were a lot of things we never did and were not tempted by. We didn't explore sexually outside of the conventional way. We were still struggling with the awkwardness that had shot up when I confronted him about being dishonest about Yannis. There was always an eerie feeling between us. We explored each other, not with warmth or joy, but with hesitation. Liam hid his face while nestled in my body, desperately hoping our intimacy would dispel the wariness between us.

That evening I was watchful. I was now preoccupied with reading his intimacy. I stroked his back up and down along his spine, going lower to the small valley that separated his buttocks. I ran even deeper between the softness of his bum. I sensed his pleasure, heard his quiet moans. His teeth were biting into my lips then he suddenly shifted down to my breasts. He took one of my nipples in his mouth and nibbled on it. The shock of that sensation made me shake, with a current that went down my whole body until it took hold in my belly. I held his sex, which was hard. The hair around it was a reddish blond which softened the scarlet of his erection.

In that moment, I knew I was making love to a father,

a careful and cautious one. It had always been like this, from the beginning, but I hadn't understood it till now. He had the tenderness of someone who knew what it meant to have someone dependent on you. The weight of his responsibility made him vulnerable. I could feel the anxiety running through his blood and I wondered why it had taken me so long to understand the flood of feelings that paralyzed him from time to time. He was taking pleasure in something that could blow back on him with great pain. Eli was not an easy load and I felt the pressure of his responsibility flowing through his heavy hands that comforted me in his embrace.

While I lay there next to Liam, my thoughts went back to Eli.

Except for the minor semblance of truce during knitting time, the rest of the day she still annoyed me with her demands to impose justice and her penchant for punching boys. These days much of this went on when the girls' team played against boys' in the Grande Salle. She was waging war particularly against Nicolas, a mischievous boy who had usurped Thomas as her nemesis. Both Eli and Nicolas were tall, slim and agile like panthers. They were the first ones to be chosen by the team leaders for any game. They were careful to soften their throws when aiming at their peers, but they doubled their strength when they targeted each other.

I wondered if this tension between them was a racial or a sexual matter, since Nicolas was a white boy. As the children grew older, they were becoming more aware of their individuality as sexual beings. There was quite a difference since they started school in September. In only a few months, they had grown up. They'd turn their heads away when a kissing scene came on in a movie, but would peer back to see it again before it was over. Such little hypocrites! Justin, the other Inuk boy in my class, took up hugging girls. He'd look at me expecting a reprimand, but I'd feign ignorance. I knew not to get angry with them. I had talked with my mother about whether or not to intervene. Should I be strict around these emerging behaviours? She said I should help them feel comfortable about their feelings. Most importantly, I had to teach them about being gentle and respectful.

I remembered Eli's dance around Nicolas and the boy's attempts to catch her. As she manoeuvred herself around obstacles, Eli would end up sliding on the floor in her rubber shoes, screeching as she shifted her speed. She succeeded, remarkably, in never being tagged by him. Sometimes the game had to stop only because no one succeeded in killing her with a final blow, as required by the rules. She was active even when resting in a corner, her placid eyes always on the lookout. Not belligerent, but always on guard. Nicolas was always around to feed her vigilance.

I was hoping that Eli would never learn about me and Liam. Kids love to entertain strange thoughts about their teachers. They try to escape the tyranny of adults by imagining them in the most inappropriate ways. They spy on our bodies and inhale our perfumes. Little girls grasp at male teachers' bodies and boys eagerly embrace female teachers. It's not sexual; the children attempt to take control of their superiors by reducing the distance between them. Teachers become more than just a bunch of dictatorial rules that way; the children discover we have bodies and appetites.

I felt that way when I was a pupil. It shocked me to see one of my teachers at the grocery store one day. I secretly followed along behind her, peeking out from the shelves to see what she was putting in her cart. My mother seemed to me so provincial in comparison that I took note of everything my teacher was buying. Afterward I realized that her culinary tastes were even more provincial than my mother's.

I have always been cynical about my mother. Not because she was ethnic, but because she was harsh on me for not being like her.

Maybe what Eli longed for was an ethnic mother too.

CHAPTER EIGHT:

Food and Death

I HAD BECOME familiar with the changeable direction of the winds. Before getting ready for my walk home from work, I had a habit of checking its bearing and force online. Despite the persistent cold, the southeast gales promised a pleasant walk. The intermittent gusts pushed me from behind as I went down the hill. Dreadful, though, were the days when the wind blew in from the northwest, racing down from the Pole, slapping my cheeks as I walked face first into its path!

In Iqaluit, March was known for its terrible blizzards with blowing snow and frozen winds. That year, people were elated about it being the most clement March in years. Though they dreaded that the freezing temperatures and endless precipitation would be pushed into April, and they were right to not trust their luck. Our heavy winter gear remained essential right to the end of the month. Temperatures rarely rose beyond thirty degrees below zero and freezing rain forced the school to shut its doors for several days. Afternoons were the worst. By three o'clock, the weather would suddenly deteriorate as if deliberately plotting against those getting ready to leave their offices. Whatever little activity still animated the city happened in that short period after three p.m. A few brave people could be seen on the streets, but mostly, folks took to their cars.

Despite the North Pole's wrath, I kept up my habit of walking home regardless of the weather. Once I reached the centre, I'd make a stop at the NorthMart to hunt for discounts and catch my breath walking among the shelves and analyzing the cans, sacks and jars. The best attractions were the piles of apples, lettuce, carrots, potatoes, mushrooms, bananas and lemons. What a sensation this would have been to the early explorers!

I am someone who likes to pay close attention to my surroundings, observing not only the people and their habits but also details that usually go unnoticed. In my building, these were the smells wafting out of every apartment. Even after countless times crossing the hall to my flat, I was still trying to map the place according to its scents. There was reassurance in the familiarity of that knowledge, of kitchen odours halfway down the corridor suddenly cut short by the fragrance of detergent coming from the laundry room. I was also reassured to know that the number of lights on the ceiling was nine and that the spot on the rug in front of apartment 203 was definitely blood. Here and there, following an odd pattern, there were also stains caused by spilled milk, coffee or juice. On the weekends, Inuit kids ran up and down the hall constantly, leaving behind a crumbly trail of chips. Sometimes, in the middle of the night, the fire alarm sounded. These were the only occasions I got to meet all my neighbours, wearing their parkas and boots, ready to run out in the freezing cold. Some would call their friends to make sure they had shelter in case of fire.

Fraser had left the building without my noticing. One day, I saw that the apartment was rented by a young couple, both working at NorthMart. Every time I came home, I found them smoking on the porch. I sometimes lingered to answer their questions. As any newcomers, they were still genuinely curious about the city and the experiences of others. Stories were better told in person than searched online.

I told them what Ana taught me about the construction of the DEW Line during the Cold War between the United States and Russia, and the mess that white people had created for the Inuit. I also took personal pride in the fact that Iqaluit had the longest taxiway in Canada, you know, for the Hercules military airplanes. They had never heard about them. I asked them if they knew anything at all about the polar nights. Not much, they said. Was it true that it was completely dark for the whole six months? Not completely dark, I said, but almost. The young woman was excited about the chance to experience a night that lasts six months, but her partner looked a little worried. Was it bad for morale? he asked.

"Well, people can do crazy things during the polar night. But you know, the Inuit have been living here for a long time. If you sleep enough but you still feel depressed, there may be something else wrong with you. The polar night cannot be held accountable for everything that goes wrong in our lives."

The first week of April was Spring Break. Liam was in Toronto for training, and I spent the whole time at home, alone. I only went out to buy some fruit and see a movie at the Astro. Because of the blizzards, the city closed twice, on Monday and Friday. The stores were running out of milk and fresh meat. Flights were cancelled for more than three days, causing supply shortages. Shelves were emptied of fresh food within the first hours after the shops opened. People started buying almost everything in sight: canned vegetables, sacks of flour, sugar, oatmeal. Essentials like oil and margarine vanished on the first day.

Hunger didn't scare me. I had enough food in my cupboards and fridge to last till the end of my contract. All I needed were some vegetables, meat and apples. Sometimes I added sweet potatoes, bananas, frozen peas, butter and milk to my shopping list. In the mornings, I typically ate bread and butter, at noon, spaghetti, and in the evening, soup and boiled potatoes. On the weekends, I cooked meat with frozen vegetables and treated myself to cake.

The atmosphere of shortage and parsimony had a morbid appeal for me. So many people had died of starvation in this place! The Arctic held more than a few appalling stories about what famine could drive people to do.

One such story chronicled twin vessels, *Erebus* and *Terror*, part of Franklin's lost expedition in the mid-nineteenth century, trapped in the ice during an especially harsh winter. The fate of any expedition depended on the weather, but at the time, no one could forecast such things. The British Admiralty wrongly believed that a good captain and disciplined crew could out-muscle nature. Some years, when Lancaster Sound was free of ice, ships could easily keep their westward course; other years, they had to wait another twelve months to enter the maze of the Canadian Archipelago. Finding the right route was a matter of chance at the best of times. If only Franklin would have followed the east coast of King William Land and not the west! Instead of being the first to find the passage, he was blocked in a channel packed with old ice pushed in by the currents from the North Pole.

For many years, British, American and Russian explorers wandered the Canadian Arctic searching for remnants of the lost expedition. Yet, ten years after Franklin's glorious departure, a humble clerk of the Hudson's Bay Company reported that these men had resorted to cannibalism in their last attempts to survive.

That clerk was Doctor John Rae, a thirty-two-year-old Scot who had come to Canada at the apex of the fur trade. After years of ruthless hunting, many species were on the verge of extinction on the Great Plains. The Hudson's Bay Company sent the young man to find new fur supplies and complete a survey of the North American coastline.

Doctor Rae travelled along the north shore of the continent by dogsled, accompanied by a small party of Inuit. Unlike the British officers, the HBC employers understood the advantage of "living off the fat of the land." According to some testimonies, Rae was the first Kabloona to adopt their techniques. He preferred to winter in igloos instead of wooden shelters; he refused to carry a big load of supplies and lived like his fellow Inuit companions. As Rae was a non-smoker, his vessels were free of the weight of tobacco, which on Franklin's *Erebus* and *Terror* exceeded the total load of Rae's ships. On land, he wore fur garments and kamiks. This apparel was later carved on his tombstone back in Scotland.

While other rescue teams were wandering across the

Arctic in the wrong direction, Rae reached the west coast of King William Land. One day, Rae met an Inuk who told him about the unfortunate Qallunaat men who died terrible deaths on land that many explorers mistook for ice. The Inuk had heard the story from some Inuit families who had spotted forty white men dragging a loaded boat behind them. They also spoke of cadavers scattered along the coast up to the northern tip of that land. The obvious cause of their death was starvation, but their frozen corpses were said to hold unsettling secrets.

That treacherous land, the west coast of King William Land, was a desolate place where game was rarely seen. The Inuit had few reasons to travel there. This was why they hadn't found the relics of *Erebus* and *Terror* sooner. None of those who spoke to Rae's interpreter had met any survivors. They had only seen the skeletons, carrying telltale marks of missing limbs and scratched bones. Among them, they found a few beheaded corpses, the heads lying some distance away. This part of their stories conjured an unnerving scenario. Had the brave British seamen resorted to the old technique of carrying heads as preserved meat?

Doctor Rae gathered about forty-five relics picked by the Inuit from the cadavers: silver watches, knives, forks and spoons, surgical instruments, coins, a pencil case. Knowing the importance of his finding, he rushed to London to break the news and pocket the sum of ten thousand pounds, which was the award promised to the first one to cast light over the fate of the missing ships.

This award did not help Rae's reputation; his report had already caused quite a stir. Lady Franklin was appalled when the account of her husband's death was published.

How sorrowful this was for her! After years of pressing for rescue missions, it was said she'd started resorting to clairvoyants to solve the mystery. The British Admiralty feared for her good judgment. Instead of bringing renewed acclaim to her husband's ultimate sacrifice, Doctor Rae's testimonies had raised evidence of the British devouring their own. She protested, together with everyone else in the country. No state of hunger or weather conditions could ever turn such fine men into cannibals! With his mighty pen, Charles Dickens became Lady Franklin's fiercest ally in twisting the evidence against the Inuit. They were the ones who attacked the starving crew! A century later, the Inuit still await an apology for those accusations. Rae's theory wasn't new to the Admiralty, though. Franklin's officers had been accused of cannibalism as early as 1819. John Richardson, the surgeon for their field trip to the Arctic Ocean along the Mackenzie River, provided a confidential report on this matter, a document that the Admiralty never released to the public.

Nobody knew at that time that Franklin had probably died of food poisoning, in the summer of 1847. The Inuit laughed heartily at the official drawings of his burial showing the crew lowering his coffin into a tomb. As if those men could dig such a well-cut grave into a frozen coast! As recounted by Rae, wasn't it more credible that the cadaver was probably left aboard the ship by the crew when they decided to abandon it and try their escape by land?

Following Rae's report, the Admiralty refused to finance any more Arctic rescue parties. Only Lady Franklin kept faith, persisting in her crusade. She bought a small ship, the *Fox*, and trusted Francis Leopold McClintock with command. This last attempt was successful in its findings.

Travelling the Arctic, this Irish explorer met Inuks wearing naval buttons—and even gold chains—from a wrecked ship they had located somewhere to the west. None had ever seen those Kabloona alive, yet their relics could be found as far down as the Coppermine River.

Following their directions, McClintock came upon skeletons lying face down in the snow. The bones were bleached, the limbs gnawed away by small animals. The items he found nearby were evidence of dubious behaviour and a deeper problem than hunger. Why had the crew weighed themselves down with so many pairs of boots, slippers, towels, silk handkerchiefs, soap, sponges, toothbrushes, combs, twine, nails and saws? Wasn't it insane to carry so many useless luxuries, when the only food they had with them was tea and some chocolate?

McClintock found no canned preserves among the debris. Yet, when the two ships had left England, they were loaded with enough tinned food for three years or more. Had the crew consumed all that in only two winters? And why did the count of deceased officers outnumber the bodies of seamen? Canned food was considered superior nourishment primarily reserved for officers. What was wrong with the tinned stew? Had the crew eventually understood that the lead used for soldering was fatally toxic? Had they discarded those supplies?

Franklin's choice of a poor manufacturer doomed him. Many other expeditions have survived on canned food. In 1944, the Canadian Henry Larsen found a cairn full of canned meat and vegetables left by John Ross in 1853. The content of these cans was in excellent condition when they were tested by the Canadian Department of Agriculture.

The laboratory rats survived after eating them. Would modern tinned food have lasted so long in such circumstances? Captain Larsen highly doubted it.

The lesson I drew from the Franklin expedition was simple: Not everything considered superior is necessarily good. Sometimes, the more sophisticated the technology, the more it renders food unhealthy. As a general rule, I never bought canned food at the NorthMart except for tomato sauce, and not before checking the expiry date and the manufacturer. My mother taught me two ingredients were essential for survival: tomato sauce and cheese. Such staples could easily be eaten as an appetizer, a main course or a dessert. A solitary explorer on this land, I followed my mother's counsel and stuck with little but fresh foods.

I spent the whole week of Spring Break on the couch, reading, as I could not walk in the bad weather that persisted. The sky changed hourly, turning from cloudy to bright and sunny and back again. The wind blew the shifting snow around. The air was filled with ice crystals.

When school started after Spring Break, the students were reluctant to get back into a routine. Most of them had been on vacation with their families down South. They were tanned and seemed to have forgotten almost all the curriculum. I was in no rush to resume the program. I gave them a few days to settle in and kept them busy with knitting and Lego play. When possible, we made the most of any sunshine in the afternoons. The bay was still a mass of ridges and hummocks created in the autumn by the ice pans that piled atop each other. Every so often, a Ski-Doo skirted across the island.

Eli's knitting was much improved but we soon found ourselves quarrelling over the best technique for handling the needles. Despite what I had taught her, she kept pushing her left thumb too hard and too far while placing the yarn across the needle. In the long run, this technique would make her waste time, but she was trying to convince me it was faster. I looked at her bemused. A few months ago, she didn't even know how to hold a needle and now she was giving me lessons!

"You are to do what I tell you to do! I have made many more sweaters and scarfs than you."

This was not the sort of argument that would convince Eli of anything, I saw that immediately in her eyes.

"If you learn it the wrong way, you will never be able to correct it," I said in a softer voice, hoping that my tone would be more convincing than my argument.

The next day, she gave me yet another reason to argue with her. Recently she had tried to knit a cap in the green alpaca wool that my mom sent in the last shipment. When she figured out how long it was going to take her to finish it, she undid the work and started a scarf.

"It would have taken you less time to finish the cap than to start over on the scarf!"

I sent her back to her place.

⁓

Liam called by the end of the week. He was back, but in a few hours, he would have to fly to Igloolik. A mobile court was to hear some minor cases and he was to assist with the accused.

He tried to inquire about my past week, but the silence of my answer was long and heavy.

He remained silent for a while. I suspect he was wary that another mishap may have happened.

Then, all of a sudden, I said: "When were you going to tell me the truth?"

"About what?" he said after a short hesitation.

"About Eli."

And that was all. He understood what I was talking about.

"We can talk about it when I'm back," he said in a faint voice.

"Does she know?" I asked.

"No! But—"

"Do you really think she doesn't understand something is different about you two?"

He kept quiet.

The fact that I couldn't see him made this void unbearable.

I waited for something more, but he said nothing.

"Okay, let's talk when you are back." And I hung up.

By the time he came back, the school was overwhelmed with the news that Ana's cancer had taken hold in her bones like a shark biting into prey. All the women in her family had died of colorectal cancer and Ana had not escaped her heritage.

When she broke the news to her older sister in Winnipeg, after many years of silence, she was shocked to learn that her sister was now struggling with dementia. There was no way for the two aging sisters to share their pain.

Ana took a medical leave while she made her last preparations to leave for Ottawa, where she would undergo treatment. What would she bring on her last voyage? All the knick-knacks she'd bought over the years cluttered her part of the house. Ana was an avid buyer of Inuit art, mostly polar bears immortalized in soapstone, walrus ivory or caribou bones. She also treasured certain items left by former teachers. They were supposed to be passed on to newcomers, but as a keen collector, Ana had trouble giving up those odd plates, glasses and bottles. She'd let them gather dust in her basement, awaiting worthier generations of teachers. She liked to be generous, but not with just anyone.

At lunchtime, the teachers wondered where Ana would want to die: Iqaluit or Ottawa? That southern red-brick mansion she bought for her old age was empty and mouldy. Even worse, it had no soul and no memories. Where did her memories reside anyway? What difference would it make whether she was buried in Ottawa or on the Baffin Shore?

Brigitte also took a leave to stay home with Ana. The local hospital had no resources to treat her, but she knew that no facility, no matter how sophisticated, could really slow her inevitable decline. Acute pain now gripped her body and kept her awake most of the night. During the day, they watched movies together. Brigitte cooked and Ana grimaced at her plate as usual. How had they survived together for ten years?

After school I often went to visit. Ana had lost her rosy cheeks and stopped dyeing her sparse hair and eyebrows. Now I saw how old she really was. The heat in the house was unbearable, which for Brigitte was a living hell. She had never liked the heat, but Ana loved it. When the rest of the house had been freezing, her bedroom was like a sauna. Now Brigitte had to overheat the whole house so Ana could come downstairs to eat and watch a movie.

One afternoon, I walked over to see them. For a long time, the streets on the Plateau had been like a maze to me. I never dared to cross it on foot. As Liam was not around to drive me, I now discovered that their house was not all that far from his. They must have seen me coming and going in his car, but they never mentioned it to me.

I went upstairs to speak with Ana, who was busy sorting her blouses and clearing out her wardrobe. Most of the items were now too big for her shrinking body and way too colourful even for her taste. The number of items she took out of her wardrobe was amazing. Ana had spared nothing in her life to satisfy her two vices: food and clothes. Piles of dresses, pants and sweaters were lying everywhere, even on the floor.

She asked me if I wanted some. My excuse was that we weren't the same size. Ana was short and chubby, with a round head and short legs. With age, her femininity had been erased. She now seemed genderless, androgynous.

I saw a scarf atop a pile and told her I would like to have it. It was a silk batik bought in Seville during one of their trips. She and Brigitte travelled together every summer and Ana would buy lots of stuff for her return up North. It was her way of keeping a little sunshine through the polar night.

She leaned over to reach for the scarf but suddenly got dizzy and almost fell to the floor.

She laughed and said: *"Tu vois c'est quoi le cancer? T'es*

*soule avant le premier verre. Moi-là, je pouvais boire une bou-
teille-là, toute seule-là."*

Her way of putting *"là"* after almost every word no
longer got on my nerves. She was staying true to that medieval French brought all the way across by the voyageurs,
those fur traders who spoke the language of the first Nouvelle-France settlers, mostly originating from Normandy.
They'd resisted English colonization because they valued
the common roots with their cousins across the channel.

Brigitte too was a francophone from Ontario, but her
French proudly reflected the imperial dominance in that
province. She did not hesitate to use English words when
her French vocabulary failed her. Her outgoing personality
helped her dodge any linguistic mishaps. She could play the
piano, had a beautiful voice and performed in every local
play staged by their amateur team. There was nothing to
apologize for, and no need to add that *"là"* that grated on
her nerves as well. At school she was the biggest defender of
French, but only because it was her job.

I helped Ana lie down on the bed and went downstairs
on tiptoe.

Brigitte invited me to have coffee and cake.

"Imagine, elle parle en roumain tout le temps maintenant"
Brigitte said.

"Roumain?" I asked in shock. *"Comment ça?"*

"Bhen, because she's Romanian."

The veil suddenly lifted from my eyes. It couldn't be
more obvious where Ana's accent and passion for countless
bric-a-brac came from. She was like my mother! That *"là"*
was not proof of her familiarity with the language, but her
fear of speaking it. Even after a whole lifetime in another

country, her mother tongue was barely buried under a thin crust of new linguistic skills. Her original mother tongue and her craving for ethnic food were retaking their hold as she moved toward her last breath.

Brigitte took a sadistic pleasure in my bewilderment, as though it was worth all this fuss just to see my face frozen with disbelief.

Brigitte served herself a piece of cake before launching into her story of Ana's life. She invited me to take a piece as well, while she organized her thoughts and settled her emotions. She cast about for the appropriate words to begin, as she was not a natural storyteller. Her sentences were vague and her ideas, choppy. She hid her lack of education under a dictatorial attitude and theatrical diction. I often saw how annoyed Brigitte was with Ana's stories which she had heard so many times. I suppose it is not easy to live with a storyteller.

⌒

Ana was a political refugee who came to Canada in 1973, before the communist regime drew the curtain over what had been, at that time, the most tyrannical of governments in Europe. Ceauşescu forbade any contact with the outside world until the tragic end of his regime. Passports were seized or never issued to those who wanted to travel abroad, except of course for the apparatchiks, spies and secret police informers. After the regime was toppled in 1989 and the archives of the Securitate opened, the number of prominent personalities who turned informant in exchange for a visa was amazing. Their task was to contact the diaspora abroad and gather information about possible plots against Ceaușescu, who was obsessed with the belief that everyone was scheming against him. He spared no means in his attempts to unveil conspiracies where there were none.

Ana was born in Bucharest. She worked as a nurse after marrying the head administrator of a hospital. Then she became pregnant when she didn't want to have a kid, not yet. Abortion was illegal under Ceaușescu's demographic policy, so Ana underwent an illegal operation that almost killed her, and she had to seek emergency treatment. It was not difficult for the special agents infiltrating the hospital's medical staff to figure out what had caused her bleeding. Her husband was arrested, then released, and they both barely kept their jobs. A few years later, he applied for asylum as a political refugee while abroad at a medical fair. Back home, Ana faced relentless persecution from the secret police. One day, a truck ran into her on the sidewalk, intending to kill her. Luckily, a fire hydrant sustained the bulk of the vehicle's force, saving her life. A few years later, she succeeded in following her husband to Germany, where they applied for residency in Canada. They went to Quebec City where she enrolled in a teaching program at Université Laval. The fear of being followed by the Securitate still haunted her, so she refused to speak her mother tongue. She never stopped concealing her identity and running away from her past. After graduation, she divorced and moved to Manitoba as a French teacher.

Her surname, which was Trop, had misled me. It never crossed my mind that it could be Romanian. On her part, Ana never said a word about my Hungarian last name.

When I called my mother later in the evening, I asked

her if Trop was a Romanian name. She said yes, even though it was uncommon. The only person she knew with that name was a folk singer, an old woman from the Banat, from the southern part of Transylvania.

I told her Ana's saga. What were the chances of finding this Romanian senior teacher here, a woman who'd escaped Ceauşescu's dictatorship? We were both dazzled by the co-incidence, but my mother was not wholly convinced by Ana's story. Many pieces were missing and too much may have been added in over the years. The old members of the Romanian diaspora my mother had met in Montreal told the same compelling stories about their escape. They had all been dissidents, and the regime tried to kill them with a truck.

"You know what?" my mother said. "The Securitate would not have that many trucks to run over all those dissidents. We were not a nation of protesters. But in Canada, no one can check on these stories."

She also said that Ana's escape would not have been all that easy either. If the story about her abortion and her husband's arrest was true, they would have never been able to travel abroad, not under any circumstance, and even less as a guest to an international fair. Once you had a file in the archives of the secret police, you could never get a passport, let alone a visa. And how could you cross the border without papers?

Most political refugees had to make up a web of stories to pass through the Canadian gates. They were not bad people, they were just liars. Ana was no worse than others, but her story certainly wasn't true. Those who could acquire the papers necessary to cross the border at that time were faithful apparatchiks of the regime. Eventually they had had enough of that forgotten land and wanted to move away, even if their life was much better than the rest of the nation's. Seduced by the West, they left the country the first chance they got. Upon arrival in a new city, they all became dissidents.

Mother was younger than Ana, so she had her own version of the communist regime. For her graduate degree, she had studied World War II in the Balkans only to discover how appalling our contribution to the war was. While the Western countries lived in hell for five long years, we were petty opportunists. During her elementary-school years in Romania, my mother was taught about the heroic contribution of our army to the war effort. At the Université de Montréal, however, she had to confront the evidence that until 1944, we were on the wrong side of history, siding with the Axis powers. There was no happy ending to our version of the war. No movie could be made about our soldiers assailing Stalingrad alongside the Germans. After the war, we were played like irrelevant pawns by Churchill, Stalin and Truman, given to the Russians who toppled the reigning king and put in place a puppet communist regime.

Mother told me that Ceauşescu came to power in the sixties with the support of many intellectuals. He was the only leader from all the socialist countries to raise his voice against the Russian invasion of Czechoslovakia. He had also decided to stop paying war debts to the Soviets as decreed by the peace treaties.

The hopes about Ceauşescu's regime ended after he visited Comrade Mao Zedong. The Republic of China was undergoing the terrible purges of the Cultural Revolution, much admired by the petty Ceaușescu. This kind of revolution was something he could understand. The dictatorial model, the cult of personality, the demand for blind obedience and the witch hunt against intellectuals and old stock impressed the illiterate peasant. He could barely read a text and his public speeches were an ongoing joke during his years in power.

Under the influence of the Chinese model, the country became a pit of darkness till its final days. Some people tried to escape the country illegally, swimming across the Danube River to Yugoslavia, or risked crossing the Hungarian border. Fewer and fewer people were able to cross the legal checkpoints as a passport holder. Ana was probably one of them. To the Canadian authorities, the story about her illegal abortion would have qualified her for political asylum.

But what did it matter now?

Mother said that I should cook for Ana. If she had started speaking Romanian again, there was no doubt she was travelling back to her native land. She had finally re-opened the memory vault she had locked away for so long. She was not here anymore. Ana was wandering the places she had left behind and tried to erase from her memory. And yet, we can never escape our origins.

"How should I go about cooking Romanian meals?" I asked my mother.

I had never done much cooking in my life and least of all that mix of Ottoman, Russian and Prussian cuisine that defined the Romanian diet. My mother cooked, and she used to bring me some in Tupperware containers even if I wasn't home. She had her own key, so she could enter any time. Sometimes she even did the laundry and vacuumed the floors. I was always delighted to find the house clean and food on the table. Yet she rarely cooked Romanian meals, as our national cuisine was much too greasy for her sensitive liver. She knew all the recipes, though, and now volunteered to guide me through.

I searched my pantry. There was not much left to last me for the next two months. I counted two cans of red beans, three of peas, three of crushed tomatoes. In the freezer, I had a bag of vegetables and one of pork tenderloin. In another cupboard, there were two bags of prunes, one of raisins, some packs of spaghetti, sacks of semolina, corn flour, sugar, rice and one bottle of olive oil. In the fridge, I still had some feta cheese, olives, sun-dried tomatoes, butter, milk and eggs.

What kind of Romanian meal could I possibly improvise with this?

I called my mother back and gave her the list of my ingredients. She said I could try a stew of rice with prunes. I recognized this dish as one my mother prepared once in a while, but I had no idea how to cook it.

Mother shared everything she knew about the regional cuisine of our old country. The western region was highly influenced by Hungarian and German gastronomy, while the southern diet reflected the four-hundred-year history of Turkish domination in its rich, syrupy meals. I reminded my mother that Ana came from Bucharest, not from Transylvania like her. While we fed on potatoes and sweet soups, we did not know much about what southerners liked.

Mother said then that I should maybe start with *sarmale.*

"Really?" I replied over the phone. "*Sarmale* for her wrecked colon?"

"What does it matter now?"

If that salted sauerkraut was bad for health, it was certainly good for memories. This national dish was present on every table, at Christmas and Easter, for baptisms and marriages. It was finicky, difficult to assemble, comprised of finger-length cabbage rolls stuffed with meat. Mother did not have the patience to craft them, so she resorted to what we called "lazy *sarmale*." She used the same ingredients but instead of rolling the tiny cabbage tubes, she just mixed the ingredients and cooked them in the oven. The taste was the same, only the presentation was different. We served it with a spoonful of sour cream on top.

She proposed sending me a few crocks of sauerkraut. I said that Ana could not wait that long, especially with the potential for spring blizzards and delayed flights. I told her I would try the local stores.

The next day after school, at three-thirty sharp, I walked swiftly down through Happy Valley. I stopped at DJ Specialties, Arctic Ventures and the NorthMart. There was nothing of that sort on the shelves. My last resort was Baffin Island Canners, close to the airport. They were only open till five, so I practically had to run there. My effort was rewarded; I found cabbage marinated in white wine, imported all the way from Poland. It looked watery and murky, but with that much salt the cabbage would still be edible.

The preparation did not take long, since all I had to do was mix the ingredients, season them and put them in the oven. Within an hour, the smell of marinated cabbage permeated the whole building. I opened all the windows, but the cold didn't prevent the awful aroma from infiltrating every corner.

By nine o'clock, it was ready. The meal had become dark brown and lost the fart-like smell. I tasted it and found it delectable. I ate a whole plate. Then I filled a Tupperware container and put the leftovers in the fridge.

The next day after school, I went straight to the Plateau. Brigitte opened the door slowly as Ana was resting. We went into the kitchen. When I handed her the Tupperware she sniffed it suspiciously.

"*C'est quoi ça?*" she asked, reluctant to open the lid.

"It's a kind of cabbage roll. I think Ana would like to eat something traditional. My mother was born in Romania, you know. It's her recipe."

Brigitte stared at me, but her surprise was mild compared to my earlier reaction to the news of Ana's real heritage.

"Ana thought you were Hungarian."

"Well, my father is, but I grew up with my mother."

Brigitte looked inside and smelled it.

"*Mon doux Jésus.* This is cabbage! You want to feed her cabbage?"

Instead of being intimidated, I laughed.

Brigitte stared at me with round, theatrical eyes. Then she suddenly burst into laughter as well. We both laughed for a while.

"Yes, you are right. But I am going to try it first."

She put a few spoons in a small bowl and thrust it in the microwave. The smell of cabbage became strong again.

"*Mon doux*, it smells like a barrel of pickles. Sorry to say, but it's like a fart."

"I know. But just don't think about it."

She started eating.

"Too much salt," she said after the first mouthful.

Then she took another one.

"*Mon doux, ça va la tuer.*"

We laughed again.

She finished the plate and washed it immediately. She brought out coffee and cake, then she sat at the table next to me.

Brigitte was a good housekeeper; everything was tidy and supplies were abundant. She was born on a farm but sent to school by her father who didn't want his girls living like peasants. Her sisters were teachers and she had worked at the hospital. She had had a happy marriage till they moved up North. Then everything ended when her husband traded her housekeeping skills for the virtues of a younger woman. Now she was crying.

"She cannot go all alone to Ottawa," she said between sobs.

I said nothing and didn't dare to touch her hand, though it lay on the table within my reach.

"You know, when I divorced, I had no job here and no house. My husband's company was covering the three grand for our apartment, but on my own I could not afford it. Ana gave up her sponsored flat to buy a house so I could move in with her."

Despite our old resentments and misunderstandings, I now felt close to Brigitte. I had never agreed with her methods or her authoritative manner toward the smallest and weakest. She had always enjoyed such a privileged position: She was a white, fortunate woman and her view of the world had not altered since her birth. There was another side to her, though, eager to disperse care, even affection. As a friend you could always count on her. I was by no means a friend of hers, but Ana had become like a relative to me, as we were tied now by our common origin. I was grateful that Brigitte was there to care for my mother's country-woman.

"What are you going to do now?" I asked.

"I'll put the house up for sale."

"Does Ana agree?"

"You know her! She is not easy when she has to give away something."

"Will you have enough time to sell it?"

"I put it on the market with a realtor. They will sell it for me and I will come back to move things out. I hope to sell most of the stuff by then. Tomorrow we're having an open house for the kitchen items. It you want anything, feel free. There's nothing expensive. I have a room full of stuff at home. I just have to put a price on them."

She wiped her eyes and looked at me.

"Maybe Liam wants some too."

"I will tell him, he is not in Iqaluit right now." I lowered my eyes.

Then she kept quiet. Obviously, there were things she wanted to add. Her silence was a belated accusation of my conduct. I had misbehaved not only as a fellow teacher, but as a woman in love as well. I had denied her the chance to offer advice, small recipes or even cooked meals. Liam was more like her than I was and she could have invited us to her place for a nice supper and a glass of wine. Those kinds of events help forge a relationship more than anything else. She could have invited other people our age and helped us build a circle of friends. Why had I stayed so closed off? The solitude was surely a relationship-killer.

I read all this in her eyes and pretended to be repentant. She was far from understanding the true nature of my relationship with Liam and the fact that Eli was his daughter.

Brigitte went for another piece of cake. I had finished the first one, but I refused another helping. She was a good cook and a big eater. She was sad that Ana never enjoyed her meals.

"I suppose she doesn't like my cooking because it's nothing like your cabbage."

We laughed again. The kitchen still carried that distinctive smell even though she had put the container away in the fridge.

When I said I had to leave, she asked me to stay a little longer. I recognized that it wasn't easy to live with someone who would soon die. It must have been difficult, losing the fellow roommate she knew so well: talkative, rosy-cheeked Ana with the Manitoban accent that was in fact Romanian.

"Maybe you should stay until she wakes up. *Vous pouvez parler dans votre langue.* I don't know if she will want to eat this."

"If she doesn't, just throw it away. I have enough at home."

I left and stopped to see a documentary at the visitor centre. During the film, Brigitte phoned me, but I didn't answer. When I got home, I called her back. She said that Ana wanted to thank me for the cabbage. She ate it with gusto, then she was sick, then she asked for more. Now she was sleeping.

"You should teach me how to cook this stuff. I don't want to torture her anymore with my cuisine."

"Your cuisine is fine. This food is just memory."

Brigitte started to cry again and hung up.

Ana was now openly complaining about her meals. Some magic ingredient had been missing and now she figured out what. Birgitte's meals all tasted the same, every meal, every year.

A few days later, when I went to see Ana, Brigitte led me into the kitchen and took the lid off the pot. She was making a soup of meatballs. This was a very rich meal, served mostly at big parties and celebrations. It was not an everyday dish that a Romanian woman would cook just for her family. Everything seemed fine; the meatballs were holding together, floating among the rounds of carrots and cubes of onions, a few parsley leaves and strands of noodles. Brigitte gave me a spoon to taste and inquired about the damned magic ingredient. One mouthful was enough to detect the flaw: salt and vinegar. This soup had to be a little sour. She could use some sour cream as a final accent, but the best solution was to add a few spoonfuls of vinegar or lemon juice.

"Salt and vinegar! You want me to put vinegar in this soup!"

I knew what was on her mind, and she knew what was on mine. No need to argue. At least I was happy to solve the mystery. If she wanted to spoil Ana a little, she had to add salt and vinegar when needed.

Over the following days, Ana was happy to rediscover the good taste of beans served with a bacon or veal stew. Then Brigitte told me that Ana asked for fried fish with a kind of dip made out of garlic. I knew what she was talking about. This was a recipe from the rural South, where every dish was heavy on raw onion and garlic. My mother suggested some mayonnaise, just to give it a more fashionable look.

To complete the dish, my mother suggested we serve it with polenta instead of bread. The Romanian peasant kitchen relied on polenta even though corn had only been introduced in the late-nineteenth century. From a diet based on wheat, Romanians soon became a people fed on *mamaliga*.

My cooperation with Brigitte produced good results, but the consequences were dreadful. Ana was not able to get any sleep during the night and she ached everywhere. To make matters worse, there was the awful taste of garlic that even brushing with lots of toothpaste couldn't get rid of. Brigitte told Ana that this sort of food would kill her, but the next morning Ana asked for fish, polenta and garlic sauce at breakfast. She was in a hurry to recover all her lost memories.

When she was awake, Ana told me about the years spent in Manitoba. How odd to imagine this young Romanian woman teaching in such remote communities with no family nearby, living all by herself! She did it for twenty-five years before moving to Iqaluit. Where was home for her now?

Brigitte was busy all weekend selling off their stuff. Ana didn't get out of bed to assist her. She had lost all her interest in earthly goods.

Friday was the opening ceremony for Toonik Tyme, the annual celebration of Inuit traditions that brings people from all around the Arctic to compete in games that highlight their skills: hunting seals, building igloos, dogsledding. The school gave us a half-day holiday. My colleague Pauline told me she wanted to attend a burial ceremony at the Frobisher Inn for the stepfather of one of her pupils. The man was thirty-two and had committed suicide. I proposed accompanying her.

We took a taxi and got there by two o'clock. The room was crowded with people. The only empty chairs we found were at the end of the last row. The ceremony began with the lighting of the *qulliq*. One of the performers was Eli, along with her friend Leia, the bereaved stepdaughter. I looked for Liam in the room. He was sitting in the second row.

We had not seen each other since he came back. I had been busy cooking for Ana or supervising Brigitte, who would leave out the magic ingredients if I didn't hold her to it. Liam only called me once, asking me to spend the night at his house, but didn't mention his daughter. Our relationship was once again weighed down by the burden of secrets. I refused his invitation and explained the reason why. He knew about Ana's cancer from Eli. Everybody in the school had learned of it; her pupils were asking when she would get better.

Since he'd been back, Liam hadn't once come to fetch me at school. Eli went home by bus, except during the last week when she stayed at the daycare. By six o'clock, someone would come to pick her up by car. She told me that her granny was back in Grise Fiord because her grandfather broke his arm while driving their Ski-Doo on the ice. Granny had gone there to take care of the house and cook till he recovered. While Liam had been away, Eli stayed with one of Victor's cousins.

Eli and Leia, assisted by an old Inuk woman, took a while to light the *qulliq*. I could see how proud they were of their performance and amused to see so many eyes on them. They went back to their chairs, next to the deceased's family, who came from Resolute Bay, where the man was born. The audience was laughing at all the stories people were telling about Nanauq. His father, a little man with a smiling face and thick glasses, spoke about his son's childhood. He had been an outspoken kid and often argued with his late mother. One day, she told him to stop talking back, and he said: "I'm not talking back, I'm talking front."

There were many funny stories told by cousins, uncles and fellow musicians from his band. The young man had been an aspiring comedian and songwriter. His career had got off to a good start, but shortly afterward depression settled in. He'd left only a few words, with requests for how to dispose of his remains. His ashes were to be scattered in the places he loved the most: Iqaluit, Resolute Bay, Victoria Island and New York.

Pauline left very early. She didn't understand English and the laughter of the mourners was getting on her nerves. As a Catholic, she was not used to this Protestant way of mocking the dead and telling jokes near the coffin. I decided to stay till the end of the ceremony.

People started leaving their seats to greet the parents and hug them. At that moment, Eli saw me, my beige outfit contrasting with the black clothing of the others. I had withdrawn to the back of the room, leaning against the wall. She said something in Liam's ear, pointing in my direction.

They both came to see me.

"My condolences," I said when he was next to me. "I suppose you knew him."

"Aye, I knew him."

"Uncle arrested him a few times" Eli said, her eyes filled with laughter.

He glared at her and smiled.

"Oh," I said, looking around to see if anyone had heard her.

Liam lowered his voice when he said: "Yeah, it was last year, though, do you remember?"

Then, he turned to me: "It was a very unsettled period for him. There was trouble with alcohol. He was singing in bars. It is difficult to avoid drinking around here."

"Too sad," I said.

"Aye," he replied, then he remained quiet for a while looking at Eli. "He seemed to pull himself together over the last months. He moved in with his new girlfriend."

"Leia's mother?"

He nodded.

"But two weeks ago, I heard he was looking for a room to rent."

Eli's impatience was growing and she looked around for Leia, indifferent to our conversation. Liam put his hand on her shoulder.

Leia joined us. Liam told them to go and eat some cookies. The tables with food were set against the wall.

Seeing Liam and Eli together again, I was struck by the lack of resemblance. There was no obvious physical likeness, but I still had no doubt he was the father. He tried to avoid my eyes, but he'd seen me studying them.

All around us people were hugging and crying. There were so many devastated young people in the room. Unlike the older people, they were unable to laugh or make jokes.

They were taking Nanauq's death very seriously. It concerned them more than anybody else.

Liam asked me if I wanted to join him for a coffee. The machine and the cups were near the window and at the end of the big table were plates with hot food now starting to come in.

"Could I talk to you for a moment?" I said in a faint voice.

He turned his head and watched me, waiting.

"It's about Eli."

"I had no doubt about that," he said, smiling, but his voice was heavy.

"Or maybe we should talk on the phone."

"If you don't mind, we can talk later."

"Yes, sorry, you are right."

"Will you call me or should I call?" he asked.

"Well, call me when you are available."

His exhaustion was evident and the black attire only added to his sombre appearance. He bowed his head then walked over to Eli and Leia. The girls had filled their plates with cookies and were eating them, sitting on the window frame. Liam stopped at the coffee machine, filled two glasses with hot water and put a bag of tea in each. Then, he went to join the girls.

I was alone and felt strange. There was no one around I could talk to and some people were staring at me. They were smiling. I guessed most of them knew already I was the French teacher and Liam's mistress. They had been looking at us while we were talking. Now that I was alone, I felt the pity in their eyes. I headed to the door hoping he would follow behind me as usual. He did not.

I went straight to the NorthMart and bought some meat. I wanted to cook it with tomato sauce and garlic, a dish my mother called *ostropel*. She had suggested this recipe during our most recent conversation. I told her that Ana was obsessed with polenta, which Brigitte hated and had banned from the kitchen. She was convinced that corn was a very toxic element in modern food as it was present in every damned list of ingredients. I agreed with her, but I told her that corn flour was not bad. People had consumed it on this continent long before the arrival of the European settlers and the canning industry. Polenta was only corn flour, water and salt; this was a good food. She didn't argue but never agreed to eat it.

Ana now had a craving for polenta, but it could not be eaten with just any meal. So my mother searched for those recipes that married well with it. One was *ostropel*, fried meat with tomato sauce, garlic and basil leaves.

Brigitte approved the recipe and asked me to come and cook at their house. Ready-made meals were well and good, but maybe Ana wanted to experience aromas gradually wafting from the kitchen as well. At the NorthMart, waiting to pay at the cash, I phoned her and told her that I preferred to do the task from home. I was tired and their house was no longer a light-hearted place. Brigitte was surely missing Ana's vivid and pleasant talk, despite her repetitive stories about the Romanian secret services plotting to kill her with a truck.

My mother was not yet convinced she was completely sincere. The problem with Ana was that her memories were frozen in time. She could not grasp that there was no longer a communist regime and she was finally safe to tell the truth. There was no one listening to her conversations and there was no plot to kill her in the North Pole. Despite her smile and easy way of mixing with people, Ana was at her core a gloomy person. This had nothing to do with the regime, but lay within herself.

I went home and slept awhile. The sun was hitting the windows, making the air inside unbearably hot. I opened both windows and left them ajar.

While I was frying the meat, I got the call from Liam. I considered talking with him while I was stirring at the stove, but then I changed my mind and turned off the burner.

The day before, I had discovered that Eli had lice. I was drying her hair after the class swim at the pool when I saw something suspicious in her hair. I tried to shake it out and get rid of it, thinking it was dandruff, but it remained stuck. I squeezed one inconspicuously between my nails and I realized it was not flat like dandruff but round and full. It was a lice egg. I kept on drying her hair, then I said she should gather it up and cover it with her cap. Down the hall, while we were waiting for the taxi in front of the pool complex, I saw that she was scratching her scalp.

"Eli has lice," I said in a timid voice over the phone to Liam.

He remained silent.

"Fortunately, she only has lice eggs. But they will hatch soon, so you should do something about it now. Our protocol is to bring the news to the principal, but I thought you could do something over the weekend. Spare her the humiliation of the whole school knowing."

He remained quiet for even longer. Was he still waiting for the question he dreaded the most?

"Are you sure?"

"I talked to my mother and she said the same thing. And I had some cases at school down in Montreal as well. I assisted with the student check-ups."

"I'll see about it. It happens."

Liam waited for my reply, and when I said nothing, he asked: "Do you think it's bad?"

"I think Eli is too sensitive to get over this easily. I think she would refuse to come to school if her classmates knew about it. That's why I didn't tell the principal. She is a very private person. Kids are very judgmental and they never forget this kind of incident. I know it all too well from my childhood."

"Did you have lice?"

"Not me. Some of my peers, and I remember how mortified they were to return to class after we knew they had lice. Kids were making fun of them, pretending to scratch their scalps. Granny should really do something about it this weekend."

"What should she do?"

"I would assume she knows the drill already."

"In case she doesn't, what should I do? Maybe it's not a good idea to tell her. Maybe we should have washed Eli's hair better."

"It has nothing to do with washing. I'm guessing she picked it up at the daycare. I was told there were a few cases."

"Why didn't the daycare teacher tell Eli to stay away from those kids?"

"How would you like someone telling people to stay away from Eli?"

He grew silent again.

"You cannot tell others to avoid their friends. You have to make it seem like a natural event, even if they know it's not. From now on, you should check her head often."

"Please, just tell me what to do."

"My mother said that vinegar helps. You soak her hair in vinegar then cover it with a scarf for fifteen minutes. You could try this treatment a few times. After you wash it, you have to check every hair. Mother said that lice are very resilient and can survive even several rounds of treatment. You must remove them by hand. They are quite visible; you will see them easily. She has a lot. I think everybody mistook them for dandruff."

I heard his heavy breathing.

"You have nothing to be embarrassed about."

His silence persisted.

When he spoke, it was in a low, distressed voice. "Would you come help me, please? I'm not comfortable with this. And Eli will be even more uncomfortable. I'm her uncle."

"And I'm her teacher. It would be uncomfortable for both of us."

"I think she'd be okay with you checking her. It would make it more like a school thing."

"Why don't you tell Granny about it?"

"She'll think it's her fault. And Eli might blame Granny."

"I told you, this has nothing to do with how often her hair gets washed or what shampoo gets used."

I tuned into Liam's persistent silence, then finally gave in.

"Fine, I will do it! Bring her home first, then come pick me up."

CHAPTER NINE:

Mothers and Wives

THE INUIT SPLIT the year into six seasons. The one starting in May is called *upingaaq*, a kind of early summer, the snow gone from the land but plenty of ice still on the sea. Throughout the month, temperatures remained below zero and heavy clouds intensified the cold. The sun stayed hidden behind a wet and menacing sky. Sparse snowflakes and a stream of ravens danced all day above the city. The strong winds made people edgy.

When Ana and Brigitte submitted their resignations, we suddenly understood how much they supported the balance of our little family. We had lost our elders. Now, we were just a bunch of young, impatient, selfish people. Conflicts and brawls are practically a daily routine in small communities, yet during the time the two old women were among us, they induced in us a sense of forgiveness. Without them, we newcomers played out our ugly impulses, growing lonely and moody, accusing others of their worst traits. We even started to avoid greeting each other in the corridor. When we had no choice, we just slightly nodded our heads.

In the explorers' time, the worst enemy was not the weather, but the risk of mutiny. Humans are a mutinous species and the North amplifies their worst instincts. We were now on the verge of such rebellion while the principal withdrew to his office, waiting for the final days of the school year. He put his hopes in the next, better cohort of teachers.

⌖

One night, Liam and I were lying in bad, exhausted. The room was bathed in a yellow light, anticipating the sunset. It was midnight.

He had kissed me all over for the first time and my skin was still burning with his passion. Our bodies became silent and our voices too. We hadn't said a word since we made love. I was listening to his breath, which was raspier than usual. Like a stalked prey animal, I sensed danger approaching.

"Were you going to tell me about it?" he said all of a sudden.

I gasped for air but remained quiet. His arm resting over my breasts became heavy.

"When are you going to tell me?" he asked again in the same deep, unsettled voice.

"There was no need to," I said, trying to hide my anxiety.

"Why not?"

"Because it's all settled. It's not going to *be*."

A car passed on the road, and its lights brightened the room for a moment. He turned my head with his hand, but I refused to look him in the eyes.

"Are you waiting to go back to Montreal to settle it?" he said.

"Yes."

He got out of bed and put on his clothes that were lying on the chair, next to the side table. Then he looked out through the window. The street was empty. Over the hills, the horizon was orange already. The sun would soon be up in the sky but within a few hours it would hide behind the heavy clouds again.

He looked back at me as I covered my body with the blanket, protecting myself from his inquisitive eyes. He hesitated a few seconds and left the room without a word.

After he closed the door, I remained in bed for a while, staring out the windows. From here, we used to watch the northern lights, while the land was buried in the polar night. We had drawn instinctively closer to one another, two lost specks in the frozen land. Now those indigo maelstroms were invisible in the sky. We had nothing to hang on to and our bodies were drained of passion.

I went into the bathroom, brushed my teeth and took a shower. I felt tired and the hot water made me dizzy. I stared at my naked body, still wet, in the mirror and weighed my breasts. Maybe this was how he found out. I hadn't realized how much I had changed. He could not be fooled by the excuse of just putting on a few extra pounds. People often get fat up North because of the unhealthy diet and lack of exercise. He was a policeman, though, and used to noticing those tiny details that helped him track down culprits and solve mysteries.

I got dressed, pulled my hair back on top of my head, and went downstairs.

He was lying on the couch, his left hand shielding his eyes against the light of the lamp. I said nothing. I put my bag in the hall and dialled the number of the Caribou taxi. I waited by the door for the cab.

From the couch, he said in such a low voice I hardly heard him: "Cancel it, please."

I froze, frightened, waiting for his next reaction.

He came to the entrance and lifted my bag from the floor.

"Cancel the taxi. You're not going anywhere."

The grief in his voice convinced me to do so.

He went back to the living room with the bag and put it on the floor, next to the lamp. Then he settled on the sofa. I followed him and sat in the armchair, facing him.

He looked at me for a while. Under his interrogative stare, I became heavy like a rock.

"Have you spoken to your mom?"

"No."

"Why not?"

I kept silent, eyes on the floor.

He was sitting on the edge of the sofa, hands on his knees. He collapsed back into stillness, his shoulders curled forward. His attitude instilled a new fear in me. My defiance and confidence both fell away.

"Is this the first time?" he asked after a while, with a growing edginess.

"Yes."

"How do you feel?"

"I am doing well."

"No morning sickness?"

"Not really."

"How far along?"

"A month and a half, I think."

"Do you know when it happened?"

"Not really."

"We haven't seen each other much lately. It shouldn't be that difficult to guess."

"I don't want to guess. It doesn't matter."

He passed his hands over his face and leaned against the back of the couch. In this position, he seemed vulnerable again. His gaze flitted all over the room.

I went to the kitchen and filled a glass with water. He watched me while I was crossing the room. On the counter, there was a basket with fruit. I pondered whether or not I wanted some. The last few weeks, I got in the habit of mentally honing in on the taste of what I was going to eat. Did I really want that kind of food? This time, my mouth filled with saliva at the sight of the plums, but I resisted. I went back to the armchair and put the glass on the coffee table. I was trying to release the choking sensation in my throat and compose myself.

The water did me good, easing the bitter acid seeping up from my stomach.

"How did you know?" I heard a new reassurance in my voice.

"I think it was the smell."

I said nothing, pondering. Wasn't it the smell that had first warned me that I was pregnant?

"It's sweet, like a ripe fruit," he added.

Yes, I thought. It was something sweet like fruit, blood and pee. I was urinating so often that the smell had started to obsess me.

"I remember that smell with Eli's mother," he said, and

now I grasped the full meaning of his caution. All this was not about me, but about her.

His words hit my stomach. Dizziness possessed my whole body and bile filled my mouth. I raced to the bathroom and threw up. It was the first time since I became pregnant. Ever since I'd known, I tried to keep my secret hidden away from everyone, but especially from him. My body was now allowed to release its secret.

He followed me into the bathroom and waited on the threshold for my body to settle itself. Then he handed me a wet towel. I wiped my mouth and handed it back.

"Please put it away," I said without looking at him.

He went to the kitchen and washed the towel under the tap water.

"Come sit with me on the couch." His tone was more reassuring than before, yet the mention of Eli's mother was there to stay. There was no point in trying to avoid it anymore.

I sat down, exhausted. He took my legs and stretched them out on the couch. He moved over to the armchair where I had been sitting.

He waited for a while before talking again.

"Eli is my daughter." He waited for my reaction, watching me.

After a while, he decided to resume.

"It wasn't my decision, though. Victor asked me to do it 'cause they couldn't have kids. They tried everything for a few years, then they gave up hope. It was a bad time for them. My mother tried to convince them to adopt. But they felt nothing could substitute if they could not have one on their own. After Afghanistan I came here. I was a total mess at the time and I was in no mood to come up North, but this was the only place I could call home. My mother was acting weird already, but we didn't know yet it was dementia. She talked a lot of nonsense, but we thought she was finally getting rid of all the hate she stored up through her life with my father. His philandering tortured her. He was rarely home and almost never involved in our education. She kept the real meaning of his trips abroad secret from us. As adults, we finally clued in to the meaning of all the whispering and crying behind closed doors. Back then we weren't worried at all. A mother is supposed to take care of her kids and she did it well. We never spoke up for her right to be happy. All her life, she was a faithful wife and mother. To us that was the expectation. Father provided money, but he was harsh on everyone, particularly the kids. I think Mother felt indebted to him for welcoming Victor into our family. And he knew how to exploit it."

He stopped talking as two young men crossed the street, speaking Inuktitut. A small dog was following behind them. Every so often, they stopped to watch the dog and talk.

Liam was indifferent to their presence, but he waited for me to turn my head to him before he spoke again.

"I was very depressed after what happened in Afghanistan, but my mother was no support. I think she disapproved of me for leaving the army. After what she had been through with my father, all she knew was that a soldier was a good provider for the family, even after death. The best part of her marriage with my father was his pension. It allowed her to do whatever she pleased for the first time. She bought a house for Victor and Oona, on the shore of the bay, and she settled in a big apartment. She even set aside a room for me, but I couldn't stand living with her. My drinking didn't help the situation. It became unbearable to listen to her senseless talk. She seemed oblivious to the fact that I had been through something terrible, that it was a miracle I was still alive. Her indifference was killing me. One day, Victor invited me to move into his house in Happy Valley."

After he said Victor's name, he looked at me interrogatively. I knew what this look meant: Was I still calling his brother?

I said nothing. I sipped water from the glass and kept my eyes down.

Yes, Victor and I spoke over the phone when he was in town. I always imagined him lying on a bunk bed in a damp basement, taken in by a generous friend or cousin. In fact, Victor was the owner of one of those luxurious, brightly painted red houses with the best view over the whole bay. He would call to ask about Eli but we would end up talking about his life on the ice. He had asked me if I wanted seal meat or sealskin garments but I refused. How would I explain them to Liam? And after omitting to mention the earlier calls, how could I now confess that I'd been talking with Victor?

Liam looked more closely at me, noticing my sudden apprehension. But he preferred to keep on and let me off the hook.

"I agreed to move in with them, even though I didn't know Oona very well. Victor warned me that she was a bad cook but a kind woman. They fixed up a space for me in the basement where I could drink my mind numb. Which I did, day and night. I went hunting with Victor but not often. I was never keen on the idea of freezing out there on the ice.

Victor was working for Parks Canada at that time, so he was travelling a lot. He made arrangements to take me along with him."

He stopped talking again, awaiting my reaction. He glanced over at me, but I was staring at the ceiling, breathing deeply to fight the churning of my bowels.

Liam changed his position in the armchair, stretching his legs. With his bare foot, he rubbed the rug as if testing its softness.

"One day, Victor told me that they had been thinking of asking me to have a baby with Oona. The fertility tests had identified that it was his fault; Oona didn't deserve to be deprived of having children. They asked me to get her pregnant. We were brothers and so had a special responsibility to take care of each other. This was a way to help them out. People used to do it in the old days, sometimes for pleasure but mostly for fertility. A couple had to have kids. It was essential for their survival to ensure that someone would hunt and bring meat to you when you got old."

I turned my head and watched him for the first time. He seemed grateful. His voice changed as he was now talking directly and intimately to me.

"We decided to do it but not when Victor was in the house. And I think that was our biggest mistake. He told everybody he would be away for a month of training in Ottawa. In fact, he went to his in-laws in Grise Fiord. I remained with Oona and we tried to have that baby."

I don't know when I started crying. I was trying to silence myself, but he caught my sobs. He didn't try to soothe me. He kept on talking, but now with his gaze directed at the windowpanes.

"We thought it would be easy. We told ourselves this was an old solution to this problem. Victor and Oona didn't need someone to hunt for them, but they needed a kid to sustain their relationship. One month later when Victor came back, we knew there was no old way to rescue us. The old way does not work for anything. I stopped sleeping with Oona, but the first night back Victor could not join her in their own bed. He got drunk and spent the night in the living room. The next morning, he was still sleeping while Oona prepared breakfast for us. I came up from the base-ment and helped her set the table. Victor woke up and showered. We heard him vomiting behind the closed door. When he came back, he was smiling. We sat at the table and ate. Victor asked me if I wanted to come ice fishing with him. I said I wanted to go see our mother. He understood that while he was away, I'd never gone to visit her. His smile sud-denly froze. All that time, I was with Oona, living like hus-band and wife. Oona said nothing. Even now I struggle to understand how she felt about this whole period. She never spoke about it. That day she went around silently doing her chores without looking at us. During Victor's absence, we had made love every minute we were together, except when I was drunk. I was drinking heavily whenever she was out, waiting for her to come back so I could drag her off to bed, no words needed. I held her in my arms and went up to their bedroom. She was a small and frail woman, almost a child. We did it a few times a night and she never went to wash. She was keeping it all inside. The most intense was over the weekends when she was home. We stayed naked in the house all day long just to be ready. I was exhausted and my willy was burning, but I took no breaks. Sometimes, she helped me with her hand. Sometimes I'd be lying somewhere in the house while she was cooking. When I was ready again, I'd go after her in the kitchen and take her."

I stopped sobbing. He too remained quiet for a while. How often did he think back to those days?

"After Victor came home, I couldn't stay with them anymore. I couldn't look my brother in the eyes. I couldn't eat in that kitchen. Oona never said a word. By the end of the month, I felt that sweet smell of ripe plums coming from her body, and I was sure my mission was completed. I moved in with my mother. Suddenly, she regained a strange period of lucidity. She asked me if everything was fine with Victor and Oona. She said she hoped I had not done something bad. I said no, but she kept on asking. They were both her children, more than I was. I had known it for a long time, but I didn't care. I was never high in her affection, but it didn't bother me. Victor deserved her love more than I did. He was the better son."

I wiped my nose with the back of my palm, trying to be quiet. He didn't seem disturbed by my runny nose.

"Victor and Oona paid us a visit after a while and told Mother they would have a child. The test was positive. Victor kissed my mother on both cheeks and said she was finally to be a grandmother. Oona smiled and looked at me straight on for the first time. Victor caught her gaze and said I should move back into their house. I said no. At that moment, Oona stood up and went over to the kitchen. The smell of her body hit me once again. This was her only way to call me back. She was warning me about something heavy that was floating in the air. I thought it was her pregnancy but in fact it was her misery."

Liam went to the kitchen to bring me a fresh glass of water and a wet towel. I drank it all and then I sponged my face. I lay down again.

The wind rose up outside. The forecast had been warning of a blizzard for the last few days and it was finally upon us. A strange pink covered the horizon. I was staring in awe at that light through the window and he caught my eye. He too turned to the window. It was about two in the morning according to the big wooden clock on the wall.

He sat in the armchair and looked at me, waiting for a question. His story was to be told that night, and it was clear he would not be side-tracked.

"A month after, I decided to leave Iqaluit and moved down to Toronto. For a while, I was stuck in a cycle of drinking and throwing up almost day and night. My body was fighting my alcohol intake, but I refused to stop. I lost over forty pounds. My pension was enough to support this lifestyle for a while and I didn't let myself worry about anything. The only favour I did for myself was stay alive. Then I met someone, a woman living next door with her young boy. Her husband had been in prison for two years, accused of having killed a man. She could hear the noise coming every day from my bathroom, adjacent to her kitchen. One day, she knocked at the door. I didn't hear her, but the door was unlocked and she bravely entered my apartment to check on me. The living room was a mess. I was lying on the couch and I thought I was dreaming when I saw her next to me. She said she would clean things up and bring me something to eat. I told her not to bother. But she did just that. The next day, after her boy went to school, she came to my apartment with soup and rice. She did the laundry. I was in such bad shape that I could not care less about the fact that a stranger was handling my dirty shirts lying around everywhere. I didn't care about anything. She came every day with food and made sure I ate. Sometimes, she drank a glass with me. She never said I should stop, but I did, slowly. I would send her to buy me a bottle and she would come back with beer instead of spirits. She brought white wine and kept me company. My whole system revolted against that vinegary wine she always chose, maybe on purpose or maybe by lack of experience. Then, I finally reached the point where I had enough of being miserable. I told her about Victor and Oona and she said I had done a good thing for them. I did what my brother asked me to. And then, there was the child. A child could never be bad, could it?"

He looked at me again, intensely, waiting for an answer or a slight confirmation, but I said nothing. He gazed out the window.

The gusty wind from the Atlantic had picked up. In a few minutes, we heard the rain spattering against the windowpane. We let that soothing noise wash over us for a while.

The tone of his voice became softer when he resumed his story.

"One day, I got a letter from Iqaluit. It was from Victor telling me they had a daughter who was much like her mother. A subtle way to inform me that no one would guess she was not his own. They sent me pictures. Our mother was in many of them. Her eyes showed that her mind was not completely there anymore. Victor wrote that recently he had to place her at the elder centre. He needed all his influence to register her since she was white and normally had no access to those kinds of services. But Victor did everything possible, fighting with them, telling them she was his real mother, who had cared for him since he was an infant. He had to visit her almost every day to help with her meals, which at the centre were mostly country food, familiar to the Inuit. Mother was not used to it and could not stand the smell. She would become aggressive when the nurses attempted to bring her to the table. Oona cooked Kabloona food and sent it over in portion-sized containers. The staff agreed to heat it in the microwave and serve her in her room. Victor told me that our mother was playing with dolls."

He shifted around in the armchair to change his position. He stretched his legs and massaged his knees. I looked at him, how he was growing old. He passed both hands through his hair, as if to lift a weight. He looked back at me, waiting for something, but I said nothing.

"When I first went to see them, they looked like a blissful couple even if Victor was drinking more than usual. He was away most of the time and the life of a hunter was not easy, out there on the ice. When he came back home, he continued to live as if he were still at the camp, meeting the same people and fighting over the same things. Oona was happy to show me the baby. She frequently asked me to hold her in my arms. I was afraid at first but then I grew comfortable with her little body. Eli was very energetic. She started walking at nine months. If I didn't know the truth, I would have said she was like Victor, the same round eyes and small face, like a baby seal. I stayed with them my whole vacation. Afterward, I'd buy a ticket to Iqaluit to visit them from time to time. Things were not going well for any of them, though. My mother became increasingly wretched, sullying her underwear on purpose and pestering people around her. Victor and Oona were growing apart and Eli was caught in the middle. Three years ago, I decided to move up North. Mother didn't have much time left to live and I was ashamed at how little I had spent with her lately. I was ashamed that Victor had to endure such an ordeal with her reputation in the elder centre. It was my duty to take care of her. I did the training to become an investigative officer and moved to Iqaluit.

Victor and Oona seemed happy to have me back. To them, this was proof I wasn't ashamed about what we'd done. Or maybe they were just worried about Eli. Oona had to undergo a surgical operation to remove her ovaries. For a while we felt happy to see each other, even if we didn't live together. I rented an apartment and I went to see Eli every day after visiting my mother at the elder centre. Sometimes Oona was alone, but we never made love again. Victor was often away when I came to visit. I think he did this on purpose to leave me alone with Oona. He thought we needed to settle something between us, but I was blind to this arrangement. The only proof we had done what we did was Eli. To me it was all we needed."

I was looking at him, how he struggled to find his words. He was obviously trying to get through his story faster. His voice was getting more emotional than before. Perhaps this was his first time putting everything together, piece by piece.

"After a few months, I met my wife and we got married. She came from Halifax and was teaching math at Inuksuk High School. It was her first year in Iqaluit. We settled temporarily in my apartment while we looked to buy a house."

He suddenly seemed very exhausted. He went to the

kitchen for a glass of juice. Water could not wash the bitterness out of his mouth. When he came back, I saw his brief hesitation whether to sit in the same place. He chose to do so. This time, he crossed his legs.

The name of the school brought back the memory of Tanya Kagaq's concert and Liam's pursuit of me. This was the place where he would wait for his wife and drive her over for a drink at Steakhouse. The armchairs where we sat near the fireplace were maybe the ones they also sat in, for a drink with friends and colleagues. Those two men who left their places after seeing Liam, had they known his wife? Were they wondering who I was? People bore their secrets on their skin around here. Your whereabouts followed you like a shadow as you walked the streets.

Liam sensed that my thoughts somehow related to us. It was easy to guess that his wife caught my imagination. More than Oona, she was a threatening phantom to me.

"My mother died shortly after I married. I think I was right in my decision to move to Iqaluit. She was waiting for something or somebody before she could say goodbye and that was me. Her body was still healthy and doctors said she could have lasted another year or two. But then she just stopped breathing. We held the ceremony and then went to Yellowknife, to bury her next to my father."

I stood up, feeling sick again. The nausea was invading me with renewed vigour. The taste in my throat was so deep and bitter that I had to run to the bathroom to get rid of it. The odour of vomit floating in the toilet bowl provoked another wave of spasms. He was standing behind me, without touching me. He helped me stand up and clean my face with the wet towel.

We went back to the living room and this time he settled on the couch next to me. I pulled back to the opposite
corner to watch him from a good distance. He was slowly
sipping his juice. The orange pulp had by now dried on the
sides of the glass, and the acidic smell unsettled me again.
He looked at me and saw my revulsion. He went to wash it in
the kitchen. Then he came back and sat a little closer to me.

"I tried to convince my wife to visit Victor and Oona
more often. I wanted to take care of Eli. My wife knew Victor was my adopted brother, but she believed it was not our
business to tell them how to raise a child. For her, after my
mother's death, they were not even my real kin. She was
very involved with school activities and making new friends.
We went out often. For the first time, I felt like a tourist in
my own town, dogsledding and picnicking in the tundra at
forty degrees below. My wife brought new sense to a life I
knew as dull and monotonous. But I couldn't enjoy it like
she did. She was on Facebook all day long sharing her experience with her friends back home, who were congratu-
lating her on her courage. She felt brave being here, dressing
up like an Inuk woman. She ordered a tailored parka with
seal fur, mittens, kamiks. She even wore an amautik without a child to put in it. But the longer she stayed here, the
more disappointed she was to see local people living in
houses instead of igloos, buying food at the NorthMart. She
wore folkloric garments, very much surprised that most
Inuit women preferred The North Face parkas and rubber
boots. Kamiks and seal mittens were for people like her who
wanted to escape consumerism and search for a simpler
life. There was no such thing as a simple life in the real
world, and least of all in Iqaluit. She rarely invited Victor

and Oona for supper. When they did visit, they came without Eli. Oona's mother had already settled in to take care of the baby."

He remained quiet for a while, rummaging through the bulky stores of memory. There was a lot of stuff in there and he seemed to be wondering what else to share with me.

"Once, I tried to talk to Victor. We both knew that things were unsettled between us. But he only smiled to me and said: 'I'm very grateful, brother. You did it for us.' But there was no gratitude in his voice. We had no idea what we were going to stir up when we decided to do this. The worst was the change in Oona after I got married. The way she watched me and my wife while we were together made me guess that she had never been a woman just longing for a baby. She was a mother looking for a love child. I realized that she had loved me all along and she still loved me. Seeing us together, she knew there was no place for her in my life. There never had been, but she lived with that hope. She was now rethinking the meaning of all this and she knew in her heart it was only a dirty business between brothers. She could not tolerate that there was no love for her in this. One night, in December, she took some sleeping pills and went out to lie down in the snow."

I had to throw up again. There was nothing left in my stomach, but the burst of green gall came again and filled my mouth with horror. He followed me to the bathroom and, this time, he held my forehead. He was scared about how exhausted I was becoming. I asked him to leave me alone. I needed to pee and the red-orange splash of urine filled the room with a terrible smell.

I stayed sitting on the toilet to recover. When I felt

better, I came out. He was waiting for me on the couch. Now that I knew I gave off that smell, I tried to put even greater distance between us. While I was fixing the pillows at my back, I suddenly had the feeling that I was not the only one listening to this story. The growing thing inside me was also peering at this upsetting outer reality. Without thinking, I looked down at my belly.

He followed my eyes then turned his gaze away, ashamed of his indiscretion. He remained quiet for so long I was afraid he would stop his story.

"What happened to your wife?"

"I decided to tell her the truth after Oona's death. Eli needed my support. I thought it was a good idea to tell my wife I was the father. Well, it was not. We split and she left Iqaluit before the end of the school year. She wasn't happy with her teaching position either. That's the problem with people like her who get too enthusiastic about their voyage north. They're easily disappointed once reality settles in."

A sudden peace fell upon me. I was hungry and thirsty, but I was ashamed to ask for food at this hour. I tried to remain calm and avoid thinking of those plums on the counter.

He came closer and tried to hold me in his arms, but I refused to let him encircle my body. I felt sickly and I was afraid of a new wave of nausea.

"Let's go to bed," he said. "Let's try to have some sleep. Let's take a day off tomorrow!"

When I stood up, he seized me in his arms. I had no power to oppose his will. I headed to the stairs, and he followed me.

I went to bed with my clothes on. He got undressed and

lay close to me. I kept my back turned to him, and he covered me with the duvet.

For a while, we stayed motionless. I was tired but I could not fall asleep. Neither could he.

He put his hand on my thigh, rubbing it through my clothes. Then he slipped his hand under my arm and around my waist. His palm settled on my round belly, in the middle. I felt his warmth pass through my skin like a heat wave. I almost shivered with passion. He turned me to him. I felt sick again but held it in. My desire for him had never been so intense. He pulled away my dress while kissing me. He spread my legs and penetrated me. His moaning intensified. His breath was burning and every bit of my skin was shivering under his touch. Our bodies were sweltering, starting from the epicentre of our sexes. We were both held together by a new presence. Liam was now spread all inside my body.

❧

May was a wintery month till the end. The temperature remained steady under minus fifteen, with blowing snow and glacial winds. Depression carved deeply into our small society's core.

At school, the atmosphere was charged with a heavy vibe of despair. As a francophone community, we did not interact much with others. We lived by our own rules, language and standards. On weekend evenings, we gathered at each other's places to share food and chat about the daily hardships. Country food was never on our table. We tasted raw meat only as a courtesy to the local people, preferring instead to feed on canned food and frozen cake. We took refuge at the Franco-Centre for concerts and shows that could give us a taste of our own culture. We rarely spoke about the world outside of our small circle unless it was about suicides in the city, which killed at the rate of a plague. Francophones still associated this northern region with imperial dominance, the British explorers looking for the Northern Passage. The barrier that kept us away from the others even here was not built like the ice that broke up yearly in late June; it was a solid berg grown of century-old ice, the type that never melted. We were locked within our own world.

I rarely joined the communal tables in the staff room at lunchtime. My belly might still seem flat under the loose sweaters I had taken to wearing, but my ferocious appetite risked betraying my secret. I was always hungry and afraid that other people would see my Tupperware full of rice, potatoes and greasy sausages. I now ate almost double my usual portion. I'd go to the teachers' room early and finish by the time the others arrived. When they were ready to sit around the table, I'd nibble at my dessert to keep them company for a while. Then, I'd go to my classroom, lock the door and lay down on the rug for a short nap.

Liam asked me to come live with him till the end of my contract, but I refused. I limited my visits with him to the evenings, or the weekends when Eli was away. When she was in town, he had started looked for excuses not to bring her over to his place. I told him this embarrassed me, and he said: "You're leaving in a month and I might never see you again."

I kissed him on the mouth and hooked my arms around his neck. He seemed unaware of my new passion. I was

burning from inside, longing for his caresses, fighting to
keep him inside my body as long as possible. But I only
enjoyed my new condition in his presence. Outside of his
house, I was worried about what was growing inside me. He
knew a doctor who gave me a prescription for food poisoning as a cover so I could take three days off work. During this
time, I lay, stunned, on the couch, unable to read or think. I
just stared at the sunbeams playing on the ceiling. By noon,
the room was becoming unbearably hot, so I had to pull
the curtains and dozed in the semi-darkness.

The smells in my apartment were upsetting me. There
was a new acuity to my senses. I felt every breath permeate
me deeply, down to the tiniest of cells. All this time, the
little ball in my stomach was growing. When I reached
down to touch my belly, it felt like a fireball upset by my
inquiry.

Liam came to have lunch with me. I was cooking more
often, meals that I could give to Ana. She was growing
amorphous, paralyzed with pills. Her taste for her country-
men's food was fading away. Ana would take a few spoonfuls then push aside the dish. These old foods had been like
a faithful companion to her lately, but at some point, she
understood what awaited her. This knowledge curbed her
enthusiasm. Brigitte, however, kept on exploring ethnic cuisine. She had learned a lot about the multiple uses of vinegar, dill, garlic, pickles, polenta, spicy sausages, eggplants
and stuffed peppers. She would encourage Ana to look on
the Internet for meals she knew from her childhood. Ana
had to translate the ingredients and the cooking process.
Exhausted, unable to give many details, Ana took to calling me during the lunch period to help Brigitte with the

translation. It was easier for me to just call my mother who had bought a cellphone so as to be available wherever she was. I was too busy with my own life to wonder about this latest marvel: my mother with a cellphone. Yet, surprisingly, despite being newly plugged in to the technological world, she was still missing my calls. I put her in contact with Brigitte so they could speak at length about culinary mysteries. Mother taught Brigitte all her tricks about how much spice, fried onions or garlic should be added to turn those meals into a true success. I didn't doubt Brigitte was warping those recipes, adapting them to her taste and style. Maybe that was why Ana was showing a renewed lack of appetite. But it was too late for her to complain.

Brigitte began pressing me to come over and have supper with them, but I was afraid they would discover my secret. I think she knew already, but I didn't want to confirm any suspicion she might have. So far, Liam's presence shielded me. We went to see a few movies together. We had dinner at Steakhouse. We drove on the bay on his Ski-Doo. We were a couple to everybody except ourselves.

Once he asked me: "If I came to Montreal, would you keep the baby?"

I was so taken aback that I remained silent for long time.

"I understand," he said.

We never talked about it again.

One evening, he brought me a pair of gloves made out of sealskin, trimmed with white fox fur. They were a perfect fit for my hands. Eli's grandmother had sewn them for me.

I looked at him and asked in shock: "Does she know?"

"I didn't tell her. Why should I?"

"Why did she give me these gloves?"

"Maybe because you're a good teacher for Eli."

"I'm not. I'm not a good teacher at all. I don't understand kids."

"You're the best teacher they ever had. You're weird and sometimes you have no empathy. You're harsh and then very sweet and kind. You're like them."

I started to cry, shattered.

"You treat them like adults. Maybe this helps them feel more responsible and grown-up. Eli tells me much of what you say in class. If I didn't know you, I'd be worried about your methods. You don't realize that you are talking to kids who have no context for what you're saying. One day, you told them that kids understand complicated things but not the easy stuff. You're kind of a weird experience for them, but they feel good about it. You make them feel smart."

I was crying so hard, he had to hold me in his arms. I hid my face in his shirt. I breathed him deeply into my heart and kept on sobbing.

⁓

That Sunday, we sat in Liam's living room and watched the wedding of Prince Harry and Meghan. Eli had spent Friday night at Liam's, but the next day he told her he had to fly to Ottawa. He drove her home, then came to pick me up. Her toys were still lying in a corner of the living room since she'd refused to tidy her things. She didn't believe him.

I had told him of my insomnia caused by all the light during the night hours, so he fixed up thick blinds for the bedroom windows. It had been such a long time since I'd slept in a dark room. The next morning, I woke up completely restored. He was surprised to see me in such a good mood. He didn't know this side of me.

I was pulling my nightgown over my head when I felt his hands grabbing me. In the darkness he seized the outline of my body and guessed at my movements. He laid me back on the bed and penetrated me in haste. I was rarely as naked as at that moment, and not the least afraid to spread my legs. I was enjoying his quest, his tenderness, his kisses. I was no longer ashamed of my pleasure.

That day, the sun was finally shining in the sky, injecting a hint of daytime around the edges of the blinds. Still, it was dark enough to spare me the usual shame over my new plumpness. I deliberately stretched my hands and legs and let him explore me. The final act left him more exhausted than usual. It seemed almost painful for him. But then he got close to my face and kissed me on the lips. He said he would sleep for a while.

I came downstairs and turned on the TV to watch the live ceremony in London. I even dozed on the couch waiting for the royal couple's arrival at the cathedral of Westminster.

Half an hour later, he came down to make breakfast. He knew I was hungry, and my grateful look when I saw him entering the kitchen confirmed his intuition.

From the kitchen counter, he'd stop chopping from time to time to peer at the screen. He was preparing an omelette. He knew my craving for comfort foods: bacon, toast, eggs, maple syrup. The little seed inside was growing in a frozen land and it was gathering strength.

The smell of fried oil made me turn my head often to check on his progress. I didn't dare tell him to hurry up.

"Did you have a marriage in a church?" I asked him.

"We didn't. Just a civil service."

"Was it because of Oona?"

"I don't know exactly if I understood that my marriage would make her unhappy. She always looked unhappy, even before that. But yes, maybe it was because of them that I didn't push too hard for a church ceremony."

I turned my head to watch Meghan walking into the venue, led by Prince Charles. Liam was watching too, while stirring the tomatoes and the peppers in the frying pan. The smell of fried vegetables made me salivate. The coffee aroma added a notch to my hunger. I wanted to keep on watching the screen, but my eyes were drawn like a magnet to the kitchen.

"How about you? Did you have a church ceremony?"

"No." I turned my head back to the screen.

The spatula stopped moving and the increased sizzle in the pan called for an urgent stir.

"Why not?"

I pretended to be absorbed by the images on the screen. Prince Harry made his vows in his soft voice, a little smile in the corner of his mouth. Most of the time, the camera was turned toward Meghan's mother, showing her face in close-up. She was just listening, taking in every word. I liked her calm and dignified attitude.

Liam was looking at me, the spatula suspended again in the air.

"We didn't have time for all that," I said. I stared at the pan, a clear suggestion he should speed up his chores.

"Why not?"

He knew how to chide me for my vague reply.

"It was too tiresome to look for a dress, make a guest list, send invitations, look for a restaurant. We were not in the mood for it."

"How about your mother? Didn't she want a church marriage for you?"

"Not really." I smiled. "She is not like that, believe me."

Liam had certainly pictured her like any immigrant mother, eager to check that exhausting ceremony off her list and prove to her community she had raised good kids.

He stopped his questioning until he had finished up cooking, letting me listen to the speech of that American bishop. I was embarrassed by the smirks in the audience caused by the man's theatrical excitement. I was sure he would create a stir.

Liam took his time setting the table. He understood what my keen eye on the kitchen was all about and he gently teased me by extending the torture. I tracked his every movement as he was putting the omelette on two plates, waiting for the moment when he would invite me to the table. He looked at me oddly, as though to scold me for my impatience, but I didn't care. I only wanted to eat. I knew he was holding back difficult questions for me and that getting too close to him would give me no chance to avoid them. Yet, I was too hungry to care.

I stood at the table and started eating before he did. He put a mountain of fried eggs on my plate, surrounded by pieces of chorizo. My mug was already half-full of milk when he poured the coffee and added a spoonful of honey. Then he stood motionless, watching me eating with such appetite. The food on his plate was getting cold.

"Why did you divorce?" he asked, sipping from his mug.

I caught the slight hint of derision in his voice, but I kept on chewing, undisturbed.

"Could I finish eating first?"

He laughed and started to dig into his breakfast. The little bugger inside was evolving into a person. And Liam was assisting in this process one day after another, doing every task required by the one inside me.

After a few mouthfuls, he put the fork aside and held his mug with both hands. He was drinking and watching the TV over my shoulder.

I had lost all interest in the proceedings. I had finished my eggs but kept my eyes down on table, wondering about my next options. There were croissants with butter and two pots of jam. One was quince and the other plum. He'd bought them for me during his last trip to Ottawa. When he unpacked his haul of food items on the table in his living room, my reaction disappointed him. In my new condition, my body didn't crave that food anymore. All I wanted was fat and meat. He put it all back in the bag, except for the plum marmalade made in Poland and the quince jam from Portugal, the same ones that my mom had bought for me since I was little.

I eyed the marmalade jar and considered whether I wanted any on my croissant. Yes, I did, but I should have asked him to microwave it first so the butter would melt into it. I looked at him as he sipped his coffee, his eyes on the screen. His attitude was obviously suggesting that for an adult I was not very responsible. His fingers began to fidget, and I sensed his growing impatience. It was time to set aside my appetite and answer him.

"I didn't get divorced. I'm a widow. My husband died."

I was right to think he would get that same astonished look on his face at hearing the news. Everybody did. I knew all too well this sympathetic look when I told people I was a widow. They'd offer me condolences and try hard to look devastated. Widowhood implied something unsavoury in the life of a woman. More than tragic, it was a bad omen. Did this come from the Middle Ages, the belief that a widow was a wicked creature? Was widowhood a kind of punishment cast upon unworthy women?

Liam regained his composure quite rapidly.

"You said you were divorced," he said, trying to contain the ire in his voice.

"Yes, I know. I didn't think we would get involved enough to tell you the truth."

"You've never really thought of this as your real life, have you? I bet you won't bother mentioning me to anyone when you go back home. I'm supposed to vanish into thin air when you take the plane to Montreal."

"You don't feel the same? You only wanted me because of Yannis. I think we should call our relationship what it is."

"Right. What was that stupid Arctic joke you had for it? A one-night stand? That's it? You're carrying my baby and you still consider this just an affair. I've got news for you. The polar night's been over for a while."

I ran into the bathroom and knelt next to the toilet bowl, but nothing happened. My hungry body was still enjoying the food and would not let it go. It was developing a selfishness of its own, fighting me with all its means.

I went back to the living room and lay on the couch. Liam cleaned the table and did the dishes. Then he hovered behind the counter, contemplating his next move. He decided to settle in the armchair, pretending to look at the TV. Prince Harry and Meghan were now touring the city in their open carriage, waving at the crowd gathered on the sidewalks.

It was a long procession and the commentators were so annoying. Yet, staring at the screen allowed us to stall the discussion. We both needed to buy some time. I knew that talking would give me nausea again.

"How did your husband die?"

I was troubled by what he said before, but I chose to answer his questions.

"He was born with purpura, a rare blood disease. He survived childhood without much medication, but later on it caught up with him again and turned into cancer."

"Did you know he was sick when you married him?"

"Yes, of course. He was the vice principal at the school where I was teaching. He was a year younger than me."

On the screen, the cameras were now focused on the guests, mostly the women with their hats, whom I watched with interest. The most spectacular dresses were the yellow and pale green ones.

"Why did you marry him?"

I looked at him, trying to overcome the flood that was drowning my voice.

"Because I loved him. And I wanted to be with him as long as possible."

I turned my head back to the TV, but tears now blurred my vision. I swallowed quickly to keep my breathing normal. I tried not to let my voice quiver.

"We had no idea how long we would last, maybe one year, maybe ten or twenty. But the cancer developed shortly after we married. First they removed his spleen. Then there were terrible nose bleeds and spots caused by clots underneath the skin. He had frequent seizures once the metastases started taking hold in his body. Then he went blind. Then he could not go to the toilet and we had to help him with our fingers. His mother wanted to take him home, but I didn't allow it. We had been so happy together all that time despite everything. We were bidding farewell every minute. I was hanging on to him, to keep him with me as long as possible. One night he had a brain haemorrhage. I didn't call the ambulance. He would not have wanted it."

Liam turned off the TV and sat on the couch. He held me in his arms, which set loose my sobs. In the silence that now settled in the room, my moans seemed so loud, I tried to muffle them in his chest. He lifted my head and kissed me, all over my wet face. Then he just let me sob, cuddled up against his chest.

CHAPTER TEN:

Dreams and Hopes

I<small>N</small> J<small>UNE</small>, <small>EVERYTHING</small> turned brown again, just like the day of my arrival. That smell of ocean that surrounded me at the airport in September had not yet returned though, as the ice still covered the bay. The hunters' Ski-Doos and *kamutiq* were still criss-crossing it from one shore to the other. In the evening, they returned with sealskins wrapped up in plastic bags and meat packed in iceboxes. Dogs paced frantically around while the men divided the day's haul into shares, completing their task at the back of the house. The dogs begged for a treat, without daring to approach their masters.

Despite the cold temperature typical of the season, the sun's strength penetrated the thick clouds to the city below. During the unending polar day, the ice over the small ponds, pools and streams softened in plain sight. The crust became gradually thinner and translucent until it broke. Streets everywhere were now soaked by rivulets running across, fed by the dark patches of melting snow.

The Atlantic winds blew the dust into every corner. Even the ice rafts and hummocks on the bay were dirty, that mid-winter purity now lost. The hills around were a quilt of black and white patches. In some places, the snow-drifts were as thick as ever between hillocks. On close in-spection, what seemed like barren land was a soft tapestry of berry bushes. In some places, there was still frozen fruit hanging on the tiny branches from last fall.

For the past few days, I was feeling exhausted because of sleepless nights. At school, we had a lot to do; instead of enjoying my remaining days with the kids, I was trapped in report writing and planning.

By the middle of the month, I had grown even more restless and impatient. From sunset to dawn, I was in a perpetual state of waiting, without knowing what for.

Liam checked on me every day. He even made a com-plaint about the state of my building to the housing cor-poration. One day, he took the back exit from my apartment and was appalled by the mess. The corridor had not been swept for months. A layer of dust coated whatever people had dropped on their way. On the stairs, someone had vomited. Eggs had been thrown at the windows. On the first floor, someone had dropped a few pieces of fried chicken from a delivery order. The day after Liam complained, the mess was meticulously cleaned up.

Ana and Brigitte left the city without a big farewell. They got rid of most of their old things except the furniture from Brigitte's bedroom. She said the set was carved by her own father, an old-stock farmer who could do anything with his hands. It was the only physical link between Bri-gitte and her long-deceased dad. She paid for a container and loaded the pieces into it for storage until the ice would break up enough to allow ships access to the bay. By then, she would be in Ontario, ready to receive the shipment loaded with her precious memories. Ana gave no sign of attachment to the belongings she had accumulated, not even to her polar bear carvings. Brigitte was free to sell them, but she did not. Not yet.

I was surprised to see how fast they sold their knick-knacks. I recognized their kitchen items and living room decorations on Iqaluit Sell/Swap. Rummage sales were one of the most popular activities up North. Buying used household items was a way to dig into people's secrets. It was also a way of developing new tastes and habits through the newly purchased objects. As soon as someone posted a rummage sale, people rushed to that address with great excitement. Owners had not only to put a price on their goods, but to describe them and educate a potential buyer of their utility.

Electronics were the most appreciated items. At Arctic Ventures and the NorthMart, they were ten times more expensive than in the South, so people usually bought second-hand every time they had the opportunity, even when they did not really need the items. The market for odd tools perpetuated an old practice of learning about people and faraway places through personal effects. When the Inuit saw the first white men coming ashore, they questioned whether they were from the moon. Before long, they started collecting their buttons and watches.

Brigitte's clay vases, dishes, spoons, pots and pans were a reminder of her ordeal in the vessel that was Iqaluit, into which people from all over flowed. The Northwest Passage to this destination was still open and people continued to search for the shortest way to a better shore. Someone once said it was the desire for fame, money and knowledge that brought people up North. Brigitte was here for none of that, hence her sour attitude and bitter tongue.

I didn't go to see them before their departure. None of us did. Brigitte had told us about Ana's fatigue. She didn't want to be seen in her new condition. She had lost weight and, under continuous sedation, her skin had become transparent. Her mouth was dry and she could barely speak. The linguistic ordeal had stopped bothering her. Memories were not raw wounds anymore and food no long evoked recollections of the past. What was the past good for anyway? She did not belong anywhere. The plane to Ottawa was just the last stop before her terminal point.

The principal bade farewell in the most disrespectful manner to the women who had been his colleagues for ten years. He offered them a card. No departure gift, no party, no tears shed over the generation of kids they helped raise. He was happy to get rid of them and renew his staff with people who would never question his authority.

⌒

After Ana left, I stopped cooking. Liam took charge of our meals, attentive to my cravings. He gave me no lectures about the unhealthy food I was consuming. There was no point in arguing about anything. He didn't seem to notice that I had stopped smoking.

My mother told me over the phone that she had bought some flowers and planted them on my balcony. For her too, the early-summer weather was difficult, as any stretch of high temperatures was often interrupted by heavy rains.

She had to push the pots against the wall to avoid drowning the plants in the runoff. But the next day, if the sun showed up, she would run back to my flat to push them into the reach of its beams.

It was such a pleasant image to me, those blooming flowers next to the two tiny armchairs and a cast-iron table. Every year my mother switched the upholstery of the cushions on my garden furniture. This year she said it was brown velvet. Why brown? I asked

"It was on sale at Fabricville," she said. "I bought five metres for only ten dollars. I could cover everything in velvet. Maybe we can change your cushions in your living room. Aren't you tired of the old ones?"

"No, but you can change them regardless."

All the fuss about my balcony was only small, insignificant chit-chat, meant to offset Mother's big news. With some hesitation, she apologized for not being able to welcome me at the airport. She was to be away on vacation.

"Vacation?" I practically choked on the word.

Mother never took vacation. Her five-star hotel was her own dwelling; her three-Michelin-star restaurant, her own kitchen. She could never stay away from her empire.

Where was she going now?

She said it was a business trip.

Mother had found someone. It had been a few months since I had become aware that her schedule had changed and other new behaviours had emerged, including that cellphone she had supposedly bought for talking to me about Ana's meals. Brigitte's attitude toward me had changed, much to my surprise, ever since my mother became her living cookbook. They got along so well that Brigitte finally forgave me for questioning her competency. Someone who had such a good cook for a mother could not be that bad!

My mother's new man was the grandfather of a little girl attending one of her painting classes. They had met at my mother's workshops. She was now mingling with the ethnic parents obsessed with perpetuating their traditions overseas. The community school was providing classes in math, science, languages, singing and dance. Mother was in charge of instruction in drawing, knitting and sewing.

Among those who brought and picked up their offspring every Sunday morning, there was a well-off widowed grandfather, living in the suburbs.

I imagined my mother lounging around, cooking and watering the garden in that man's grey-stone, two-storey house. He certainly had a pool as well. I pictured expensive leather couches in front of the fireplace, bone china and Bohemian crystal glasses. Maybe some Venetian chandeliers too, or other luxuries that moneyed people buy during their trips abroad as an expression of their wealth and good taste. Did that man have a big garage with electrical tools hanging on the walls? Did he have the latest brand of appliances in the kitchen and the indispensable ice machine?

I imagined him putting on his best suit, buying flowers, chocolates and perfumes for my mother. Was she mocking him for using his ethnic ways to impress her? I guess not!

It had been a while since I started feeling a resurgence of my mother's ethnicity, which showed up in her knitting workshops and Ana's recipes. Now that she had a good excuse to make use of her heritage, she understood how much her identity was woven into the fabric of those customs. She too had started the long voyage back to her motherland.

The man fell in love with her on the spot, apparently, but she hesitated to respond to his advances for several weeks.

"And why was that?" I asked in surprise.

"Well, you said it yourself. I could not have a relationship with my pupil's relative."

I started laughing so hard that my mother got nervous.

"It's not funny at all. You did the same. We don't mess with these things."

"Mother, it is not at all the same."

"What are you trying to say? Am I a second-class teacher?"

I remained quiet.

This time, something was very different in my mother's voice. Her silly questions and candour were a sign that Mother was not only on the way back to her motherland, but going back in age as well. She was not the master anymore. She was becoming a child again. It was time for me to grow up and take her under my wing.

The man she met was a project manager working for a Swedish company. He travelled a lot, to various places around the world. He had had enough of sleeping alone in five-star hotels and eating solitary dinners in expensive restaurants. Mother was now like luxurious baggage for him. He paid her plane tickets, her hotel and meals. Mother was finally travelling as she always wanted, not only in deluxe conditions but better still, gratis. Like any baby boomer, Mother thought that being young and broke had its attractions, while being old and poor was appalling.

Last month she had been in Mississippi. Because of her cellphone, she was able to conceal the fact she was not home when we spoke. Now they were going to Mexico, where the man was supervising a two-week project. They would be back some time after my return.

"He is a southerner," she said after a while. "From Craiova. But he is so funny!"

All that funny stuff! Why do women care so much about laughing? After a marriage with someone who considered her to be beneath him, and then with another who thought she was too snobby, my mother was now finally laughing in her mother tongue.

It was only one week left before my departure. I did not have many things to do except to set an appointment for my apartment inspection by the housing corporation. Preparing for the inspection would be easy; the space didn't carry much evidence of my presence. I had already given my notice to the Qulliq Energy Corporation to turn off my meter, and I remembered to cancel my house insurance.

Liam asked me to bring all my things to his place until my departure. I agreed, and he took care of my move.

He packed everything himself, cleaned the apartment, scrubbed the fridge, the stove and the bathtub. He wiped the floor and emptied the cupboards. He listed my microwave, the TV set and my toaster and sold them all for a hundred dollars. As a bonus for the buyer, an elderly woman moving to Iqaluit from Pangnirtung, he left behind the rest of the food from the fridge, the towels, the detergent and the kitchen utensils. As for the unsold items, he put them in a box and donated them to the elder centre.

That Friday evening, he meandered around the apartment doing various tasks while I watched a movie on TV. I had not noticed his preoccupied mood till the last commercial break. I looked up and saw him staring at me. I turned my head back to the screen.

He hesitated a few seconds, then he came to sit next to me.

I knew immediately he was going to tell me something terrible. Once again, I sensed his laboured breathing, caution in his movements.

"Tomorrow evening you are invited to supper at Granny's," he said. "She wanted to prepare something for you."

His words hit me like a blow!

"That's impossible," I said, almost crying. "I can't go there. I see no point in meeting Granny."

I tried to stand up and flee to the bathroom. But he caught me and forced me to sit down. His gesture was rough but nothing he did could scare me more. He forced me into his arms and held my head against his chest.

"Listen, listen to me. Eli's very sad you're leaving. And Granny said this would make her happy. Eli has a present for you. And she's baking you cookies. This is the right thing to do. Don't worry about anything else. Victor will be there too. He came from Grise Fiord for this occasion."

I stopped trying to free myself and get away. I remained in his arms for a while till his hold loosened and became more of an embrace. I straightened back on the couch and looked at him. He was quietly stroking my hand, which remained tightly clenched in a fist. Tears were running down his cheeks.

Involuntarily, I swept them aside.

"Have you told Granny I'm pregnant? Have you told Victor?" I said.

"I did. I told them both."

"And Eli?"

"Not her. She's too young to understand."

I stopped rubbing his cheeks.

"But why? Why should they be involved? This is over, Liam," I said, whispering close to his face.

He kissed me on the lips.

"They have to know you better. Granny and Victor and Eli. They have to know where I am once I leave this place. Victor will have to take care of Eli now. I think he's ready to be her father for good. We will both take care of Eli. And one day we both we'll take care of your baby."

I pulled back on the couch to be able to look at him properly.

"What are you talking about?"

All the candour in his eyes dissipated. Now it was his turn to stare at me reproachfully.

"It is your child I'm talking about."

"My child? There is no child here to talk about. I told you that from the beginning."

"You told me what you wanted me to believe. But you never planned to have an abortion. I know pretty precisely when it happened. The baby has to be more than four months. It's too late for an abortion. I'm sure he's already quickening."

My lips went cold.

"I know you went to the hospital. It's a boy, isn't it?" He tried to grab my hand.

I avoided his touch.

"Please don't meddle in this. This is not your business."

He kept quiet for a while. His hand reached for mine, but I didn't allow it.

Then the anger surged through me, stronger than before.

"I don't want anybody to be involved in this. Not Granny and not Victor."

"Maybe not," he said, "but Eli will grow up and she'll need a father around while I'm away. And one day she'll find out where I am and why."

"Please stop talking about Eli. She is not my daughter. That is not my business."

"She is mine, and I need to know she has a father around when I'm not here."

"But where are you going to be?"

"With you and the baby in Montreal, you crazy woman," he said, holding me in his arms.

It was my last Saturday in Iqaluit when Liam drove us far away to the tundra to soak up some sun and pick berries. Eli was our guide. Liam was right: She knew this was about more than barren hills. She also had a special knack for finding the best frozen berries. He drove his car as far as the road safely allowed, then we walked across the valleys.

Eli led us to the places where she went berry picking

with her granny in the summers. Then we went over the hilltops to search out spots of white moss. They looked so fragile, like pieces of lace dropped on the barren land. She said that this moss was the best food for caribou. After the caribou had thoroughly grazed the area, though, it took the moss many years to grow back. This was why the herd changed their paths so often. An ancient instinct brought them back after as many years as was necessary to find the pasture regenerated. The migration of the Inuit, in their pursuit of the game, was strongly connected with the life cycles of this frozen prairie.

Back in the valley, Eli tried to spot some dwarf fireweed and mountain sorrel, both good for tea. There was none around at this time, but we chanced upon a large patch of blueberries. Our lips and fingertips soon turned purple. She said that in Inuktitut they were called something like "that which causes the teeth to be removed" because of the blue specks of berry that stick to the teeth. Then she showed me a patch of bearberry that she called *kallait*. She identified it by its jagged-edged leaves, whereas blueberry leaves have smooth edges. There was also a difference in taste. Bearberries are the only fruit that taste better before they are ripe.

For a while, Eli explored the rocks on her own while we lay in the sun. Then she called us to eat some crowberries that she had found on a little slope. They were the most common berries in the region. Her granny's term for them was *paurngait,* and she used them to poach char. The bushes were easy to spot because of the needle-like leaves that stick out of the branches. They looked like tiny Christmas trees, reaching along the rocky tundra. The fruit in summer had a tangy, sweet taste. Despite their abundance,

Granny did not allow Eli to eat too much at once, to avoid a stomach upset. Now Eli took advantage of her absence to stuff herself with the frozen fruit.

Farther away she spotted another big patch in between two big rocks. Crowberries liked the sun but they also needed protection against the wind. Hunters looked for these plants, knowing that such ground would give shelter against the gales in bad weather. We ate as much as we could while Liam was still lying on a rock. Eli was also picking crowberries for her granny, dropping them into a little plastic jar. I told her to eat them and promised we would buy a frozen bag from Baffin Island Canners. She obeyed but handed me half of them. Liam said he deserved some too since he was the driver of our expedition. He threatened to abandon us in the wilderness if we didn't pay him his fair share.

Our rubber boots were slippery on the wet rocks. In the valleys, the snow had become watery and crystalline. In some places, we sank down to our knees, and the snow filled our boots. We rushed to take them off and clear away the melting snow from our socks.

Eli was wearing a woollen sweater.

I asked Liam about her outfit on such a hot day.

"I told her you chose it," he said.

One evening, Liam had been looking online for new clothes for Eli. Her birthday was coming up and he worried about getting her a present. As usual, he was lingering over the blouses and leggings. I told him that young girls could be very fashionable in wool and cotton, so he let me shop for him. I chose a black velvet skirt and a multi-coloured alpaca wool sweater from Simons.

I nodded, intimidated. Had I told him to keep it secret? I did not remember.

"Did you notice she didn't bring her parka?" he asked.

It was true. She was only wearing the small bandeau she knitted in class. It was the same size and colour as the one she made for me.

Eli was picking berries a few metres away. She glanced at us and must have guessed we were talking about her. She lowered the eyes and moved away.

What would my life look like in ten years? Would Eli knock on my door in Montreal, a young woman, bags in tow, and ask me to kick some ass on her behalf? I really hoped so, but life is unpredictable. The only thing I could count on was that, one day, my son would start his own search for the Northern Passage.

Acknowledgements

A FEW YEARS ago, I responded to an invitation made by Professor Carmen Cristea from Dawson College in Montreal to meet her students who were reading my novel *The Darling of Kandahar* as part of their curriculum. Young people were appreciative of my book, except for the ending that left them puzzled. After the Canadian soldier died, what happened to Irina? As a class exercise, I proposed to them that they feel free to imagine a sequel to my novel, which they did. This is how I got so many brilliant ideas about Irina's possible life afterward. I really thank Professor Cristea for the chance to meet my young readers and listen to them.

There are also a few people I would like to mention here. First, there's Claire Sullivan, my first reader, my first editor and my first admirer. There is also Connie Guzzo-McParland and Michael Mirolla from Guernica Editions who gave this book a chance. Last but not least, there is Margo LaPierre, the young and brilliant editor who gave this book the chance to become better and avoid some faux pas. She was the ideal editor to meet the many demands imposed by so many characters with different backgrounds and mother tongues.

About the Author

FELICIA MIHALI is a journalist, a novelist and a teacher who lives in Montreal. After studies in French, Mandarin and Dutch, she specialized in Postcolonial literature at the University of Montreal, where she also studied History and English Literature. Her career was launched in 2002 with the highly-praised novel *Le Pays du fromage*, followed by six others books in French. In 2012, she published her first book in English, *The Darling of Kandahar*, which was inspired by a news item reported in *Maclean's* magazine. Today, she writes in French and in English. Since 2018, she has served as the founder and president of Éditions Hashtag.